MW01236076

The Continuous
History of
Hermie Brambleweed
s e r i e s

Presents

Book 1: Hermie and the Origin of Dreamer

By

Rene Lopez, Jr.

ISBN: 1466406526
ISBN-13: 9781466406520

Dedication

I would like to dedicate this book to my mother, Fela, and my late father, Rene Lopez, Sr. It was them that got me started in bowling and encouraged me to improve my skills. I was too small for football, too short for basketball, I didn't know what a 9-iron was, and I needed something to do. But I was able to pick up a bowling ball and knock down some pins. I remember my parents used to accompany me on many tournaments and supported me, despite my scores. My father and I bowled together only one time and he outscored me 147-145. He never knew about my ambition on being a writer, but he would have encouraged me nonetheless. None of the experiences, tournaments or stories would have been possible without him. God bless him.

Acknowledgements

I would like to thank my wife, Sharon, for enduring all those nights I was up late writing, re-writing, editing and proofreading my book and for trying to write and record music to accompany this book. I would like to thank my family and friends for putting up with my unending ranting and raving about my book ever since I began writing it. I would also like to thank all the readers who took the time to pick up this book and read a page or two. Finally, I would like to acknowledge the "big man" upstairs that gave me good health and endurance so that I could complete this effort.

This project was not an easy one nor was it fast. This project represents several years of gathering, recalling and documenting many experiences, events and stories from the past. This book also represents a snapshot from a point in time that has been captured forever in the upcoming pages. I hope you enjoy reading this book as much as I enjoyed writing it.

— Rene Lopez, Jr.

Introduction

It is December, and Hermie Brambleweed is a 16-year-old sophomore at Pibb High School, in Central Texas. He met a girl named Jane Leuistan in his Home Economics class at the start of the school year, in August. She was struggling with some class work and he came to her aid. She was very thankful and very impressed with his knowledge in the kitchen. Hermie credited his grandparents for showing him around.

Coincidentally enough, the two became partners in their Home Economics class and their academic relationship turned into a good friendship. Hermie and Jane began talking about things other than school. They talked about dating and parties and doing things. They both really liked each other's company.

Hermie also likes Jane but has not told her. He likes being around her and likes the light powdery smell of her perfume. Once, he asked Jane out on a date but she declined, telling him that her parents won't let her date until she turned 16.

One day at school, Jane was in a very good mood and decided to give Hermie a hug in the hallway. This caught him by surprise, but both of them liked the feeling of holding each other. Jane was really excited by this and wanted to do it again later, but was afraid of getting caught by her older sister, who also attends the same school.

But Jane wanted more. She really enjoyed Hermie's company and wanted to see more of him but was limited because she could not date yet. She was also starting to like Hermie a lot, but didn't want to tell him that.

One day she asked him to come over to her house late on a Friday night and tap on her window so they could talk. At first, Hermie rejected the idea, because he was afraid of being caught by her parents. But after she explained it to him, it made more sense, so though it was risky, he decided to pursue this activity. They had a "window visit," which allowed them to talk and be together outside of school. It was so exciting and different that they decided to try and have these things once a month.

Hermie loves bowling, and bowls whenever he can. He also practices very diligently and is always trying to improve. He has bowled some tournaments in the last year with average scores and very little success, but has never made it to the winner's circle. He hopes to stop that jinx one day and break on through to the other side because he loves the thrill of competition. He also watches lots of bowling on TV and that inspires him. He thinks it makes him better. He also watches the faces and emotions of the winners on TV and wants to experience that same feeling.

Hermie currently bowls on Saturday mornings to work on his game, get a feel for competition, and give him something to do. Last year he got teamed up with a guy named Scott. Scott is a year younger than Hermie and also a good bowler. Both boys became friends really fast. Hermie likes Scott's intensity but thinks Scott's attitude needs some work. It seems that sometimes Scott gets upset and angry pretty easily.

This year Hermie and Scott got two new teammates on their Saturday morning league. Last year, Scott pointed out Hank and Charlie as good bowlers and wanted them on the team for this year. Scott asked Hank and Charlie to join the team and they joined. Initially, all four boys were apprehensive on the lanes, not knowing what to expect, and they didn't score very well. But after a couple of weeks, they became good friends and started to hang out together and do things together. Sometimes they act like brothers.

Hank is Hermie's age but is very large; he plays football for the school team. He is not a great bowler but bowls because it gives him a chance to be with Charlie, who has been his best friend since their elementary school days. Hank tends to muscle the ball most of the time, not realizing what he is doing. Many times he throws the ball so hard that the ball does not have a chance to go into a full roll.

Charlie is a year older than Hank and Hermie, but is only a freshman due to missing two years of school when he was working. Charlie has lived a tough childhood and it has not subsided yet. He exercises in his garage and bowls with Hank to forget about reality for a while. Charlie is a good bowler but misses some weeks due to "things coming up." Charlie is short and stout, but has a good style and form. He just needs to work on his confidence.

Since Hermie was not big enough to play basketball or football, or fast enough to run track or isn't interested in golf, he felt that being on the school's bowling team was his only way to achieve something in high school. He has no interest in the band or science clubs, and he is at that age where he feels he needs to belong in some social group and be accepted, even if it's a sport that many people do not consider to be a serious one.

In September, which was three months ago, Hermie and his three close friends tried out for the school's bowling team. Hermie was surprised by the number of entries for such a small school. Initially, he was under the impression that there were going to be fourteen open spots, seven for each team. Then the coach changed his mind and opened up only twelve spots, leaving two spots reserved for his nephews who are mediocre bowlers at best.

This irritated Hermie but he still bowled the tournament. In the end, Hermie finished in eighth place out of 20 entries. Just as he was about to celebrate his spot on the team, the coach made another announcement. He decided to keep his nephew's team intact, even though they had another bad season. This meant that only seven spots were available, and Hermie finished in eighth place. Hermie was really enraged and called the coach's team "a bunch of losers." Hermie thinks about this disappointment all the time. He knows he is not the best in the world, but he is getting better and wants to prove it. A spot on the bowling team really meant a lot to him, but now he has to wait another year.

Hermie and his grandparents are still involved in a lawsuit with Acme Chemical that has been dragging on for more than a year. Hermie's family is accusing Acme Chemical Company for the wrongful death of Hermie's father, John. They claim that Acme knew the dangers of John's last project but chose to cover up the facts. Acme denies the charges and is trying to find ways to stall and delay the case. Acme thinks that by delaying the case, the Brambleweed family will go bankrupt and drop the case.

Hermie's grandparents, who are John's parents, know that somewhere in John's basement are documents that point out all the guilty parties in the case and proof that the project was very dangerous. John kept very accurate notes and kept all of his interoffice memos while employed at Acme, and these documents are currently locked up in the basement. Even Hermie is not allowed in this secret room.

Hermie is living in his parent's house five or six days out of the week, all by himself. On the other days, he stays in his grandparents' house. He still gets a little scared at night and thinks he hears strange noises in the late hours. His goal was to be living in his parent's house on a full-time basis by the end of the summer, but he got a little bit behind schedule. He thinks he can be on his own in another month.

He still works at the local grocery store as a bagboy. He bags the customer's groceries from the conveyor belt and then takes the groceries to the car for a tip. Most days he would rather not work, but overall he likes the job. He works just about every day after school for a couple of hours and most Saturdays after his bowling league. On some days he does not even show up; he practically shows up when he pleases.

At the store, he does not make a lot of money, but he doesn't need a lot of money right now. He buys a few small things and he is happy with that. In addition, the trust fund his parents left him will make him wealthy and he probably won't have to work, but he has to pass over a few obstacles before the money is his. The main obstacles are being 21 years old and earning 66 hours of college credit. He works at the store to keep that secret safe and because his grandfather taught him the value of a dollar.

His mother mysteriously disappeared about four years ago on a routine trip to the shopping mall. She never came to the meeting site they agreed upon, and he had to take the bus home that night. And because he forgot his house key, he tried to break into his own house and that led to being arrested by the police for breaking in. The arrest then led to an 18-month stay in a local orphanage from which he broke out. This is a darker side of his past that he would rather forget about. To the best of his knowledge, only he and his grandparents know about this terrible ordeal. He still thinks about the special friends he made during his "life in captivity."

He misses his parents a lot and he is always thinking about them, especially after seeing his buddies talk about theirs and growing up with them and all the things they do together. Most of the time, his grandparents act like his parents, watching and looking over him, and that's fine with him. To the best of his knowledge, he, his grandparents, and their lawyer are the only ones that know about both of his parents. For now, he has to keep living a secret life until the time is right. Hopefully, nobody will spill the beans before he does.

Chapter Listing

Chapter 1

A Night in the Point of Time

It's a cool Saturday night in the middle of December, and Hermie Brambleweed just went to bed. Tonight he had the most incredible experience ever and he is sitting on top of the world. He kissed a girl and she kissed him back! It was a little scary at first, because he was not sure what to do or what was going to happen next, but it all fell together just right and it felt great. Her lips and skin were soft, she had a light trace of a powdery scent she was wearing, and it was dark and they were alone in her bedroom. They planned this night for over a month and it finally happened. Wow.

Hermie is a sophomore at Pibb High School and the girl he kissed is Jane Leuistan; she is a freshman at the same school. Hermie has known Jane for about four months; they met in their Home Economics class when they became lab partners.

Jane had some difficulty in the kitchen, such as identifying and using certain utensils and knowing how to sew, and that's where Hermie stepped in and helped her out. He showed her the basics in the kitchen and initially she was a little embarrassed, but she was impressed in the end. It didn't bother Hermie at all and he eventually started to like her. He just was not sure how she felt about him.

When Jane asked about his skills, he told her his grandparents helped him out in that area. They taught him how to cook, read a recipe, wash dishes, do laundry, sew, repair his car, vacuum, and mop. All these skills really got Jane's attention and she quickly began learning from him. Soon, they were the best team in the class.

At home, Hermie lies on his bed thinking about this girl. He remembers what started out as infatuation from her side turned into friendship on his side. Before too long, they were talking in the hallways between classes. They would begin by talking about school related items, but they would later change the subject.

Hermie has a good feeling as he slowly drifts off to sleep thinking about this momentous night. He has a big smile on his face and doesn't even realize that he left the lights on in his bedroom. He also wonders what she is thinking about and if she enjoyed the kiss as much as he did.

The next morning, Hermie wakes up and begins his morning of weekend chores. He has one more week of school before he is off for three weeks for the Christmas break. The same is true for his bowling league. He keeps busy around the house and makes plans to visit his grandparents later in the day. He thinks about Jane all day long.

Their first kiss has come and gone, but every time Hermie thinks about it, his heart and mind begin to race. He is not sure what's going to happen tomorrow when he sees her at school. He begins to think that their friendship just changed. He is not sure where they are headed because he has never been down this path before. All he knows is that it felt great and he wants to touch her lips again. He wonders if she feels the same way too. He will find out soon enough.

On Sunday night, Hermie has a brisket dinner with his grandparents; one of his favorite meals. Grandpa tells him, "Well, we got letter from our lawyer. He said that Acme got our paperwork about the case and is planning to prepare a defense. Geez, it took them that long to say that?"

Hermie is not very familiar with the legal system so his knowledge is limited, but his perception is that Acme is trying to slow down the process for whatever reason. He says, "Maybe they are being slow so maybe we can forget about the case."

Grandpa tells him, "Who knows what Acme is trying to do. They are a big company and have lots of money to buy lots of fancy lawyers. They might be slowing things down, but we can't make them hurry up. All I know is there is a mountain of documents in the basement of your dad's house that is under lock and key. One day, these documents will prove that Acme is guilty. But it's not today."

Grandpa tells Hermie that Acme is probably scared because they know they are at fault and are probably trying to find loopholes to help get them off the hook. Hermie has no idea what his grandfather is saying.

Hermie vaguely remembers the accident that his father endured at his job about four years ago. He was only 12 when it happened. All he knows is that has father fell down while at the office and had to be taken away in an ambulance. The doctors at the hospital could not revive him and Hermie never saw his father again. He was too young to know what death was all about. He was also too young to know about revenge, deceit, sabotage, and greed. He just sat and waited for his father to come home, and he never did.

Hermie asks his grandfather, "The basement? I didn't know the house had a basement. It must be hidden real good."

Grandpa replies, "Yes, it is. I'm not sure why your father built the house with a basement, because this part of the country has lots of clay in the soil and could make underground structures very unstable. But the basement came in real handy when he had to hide documents. Your father was very diligent on keeping paper trails for every task he performed, every request he sent, and every response and memo he received."

Grandpa adds to the story, "Your father also kept copies of every purchase requisition he sent and received documenting the equipment and supplies that were purchased. Sometimes he spent hours behind a photocopier machine copying documents, taking them home and putting them in boxes in his basement. He learned to cover himself well."

Hermie is speechless and wants to hear more. He asks, "Is the basement in the closet under the stairs? I found a small secret door one day and then I saw some stairs going down. Maybe that was it. The door had wires on it."

Grandpa says, "That's the one. Don't play with the wires because the alarm might go off."

Hermie asks, "So those papers sound pretty important. What's on them?"

Grandpa answers, "Most of the papers documented the whole process for his project. But there are papers that contained names, phone numbers, and addresses of vendors, customers, associates, and other peers. Your father even kept personal notes about suspicions he had on people or how he felt the project was progressing."

Hermie is in awe at how meticulous his father was. He says, "Wow, there must be a lot of papers down there. I bet he saved everything."

Grandpa says, "You bet he did. Before your dad passed away, there were probably 20 boxes of papers in the basement. After he passed, you mom was asked to go to his desk and pick up the rest of his items. He had some good friends there that helped pack up his things and helped bring them to the house. There were probably another 20 boxes of papers and stuff from his desk and lab."

Hermie is excited and says, "Wow, 40 boxes? That's a lot of stuff!"

Grandpa replies, "A few days later your mom started noticing cars driving by the house in a slow manner. Some cars would park at the end of the block and sit there for hours. It was almost as if somebody was watching the house."

Hermie asks, "Who were they? What did they want?"

Grandpa concludes his short story saying, "We're not sure who it was, but I think it was somebody from Acme looking to see where your dad lived. This was right around the time we filed the lawsuit against Acme. So I think somebody wanted to find your dad's house and steal all of his documents so there would not be any evidence if our case went to court. Your mom got pretty spooked with all the cars driving around so I installed some timers to turn lights on and off when she was out of the house. I also installed that alarm on the basement door. I didn't want to take any chances. After a few weeks, the cars went away, but we still wanted to be safe."

For the rest of the weekend, Hermie thinks about what his grandfather told him. He visits the basement and just sits and stares at the locked door that holds the evidence in his father's case. Hermie cannot believe how mean some people can be. He is also very curious about that locked room and wants to ask for the key to get in. But he knows the answer will be a strong and resounding "no."

His grandfather already explained to him that he is too young to understand everything that has transpired. However, grandpa did promise to show Hermie that room and all of its contents when Hermie is at the right age. Nobody is exactly sure when that will be. In addition, with the possibility of going to court, grandpa doesn't want to take a chance on damaging the evidence; then he reminds Hermie to get a haircut.

On Monday, Hermie goes to school for the last week of classes for the year. He notices the teachers are being nice this week and not assigning a ton of homework for the holidays. That's a relief. He goes to each class expecting a skate day and he is pretty correct in his prediction. He has a couple of pop quizzes but knows he passed them all.

He sees Jane in the hallway and she stops him just before lunch. She says, "Hermie, I need to tell you something," as she leads him to his locker.

Hermie is surprised to hear that those are the first words to come out of her mouth, considering what happened Saturday night. He follows her down the hall.

They arrive at his locker and she waits until the hallway is nearly empty, constantly looking to the left and right, to see if the coast is clear. She pushes him against his locker and gives him a huge kiss, then another. She is breathing heavily and breathes a sigh of relief, just as if a marathon runner finished a race and was drinking some much-needed water. Hermie is so rattled by this action that he drops all of his books and stands in a trance. He doesn't know what to do or say.

Jane looks up at him with a huge satisfied smile on her face as if a junkie had just been given another fix. Her cheeks are a little flushed.

She tells him, "Oh my gosh. That felt sooo good. I was thinking about our first kiss all weekend and I couldn't wait for another one. It felt so good I can't describe it." She gives him a quick peck before going to her next class.

Now Hermie cannot think straight. He tells himself, "Yup, I guess she felt the same way I did," as he walks to his next class.

For the rest of the day, every time they see each other in the hallway, they wave and smile. Hermie is starting to wonder if he will get another surprise kiss from her. Jane wants to kiss him again but does not want to make a scene by kissing between each class. She wants to try to ease into it.

For the rest of the week, it's pretty low key. Hermie and Jane see each other in the hallways and say hello. Sometimes they sneak in a quick kiss. On Friday they have a semi-private kiss in the hallway and they ask each other about their plans for the holidays while holding each other.

They do not date right now because Jane's parents are very strict and because Jane is only 15 years old. Her parents had to get strict because of her two older sisters, Sheryl and Kelly, who abused the "date at 15" policy. These girls practically did what they wanted when they were 15 despite their parents' views of teenage dating and what it can lead to. The girls found themselves in trouble a few times and it forced the parents to raise the dating age in the household to 16. So Jane has to wait until next June until she can officially date Hermie and consider him a "boyfriend."

Right now, the only way these two kids meet outside of school is through their "window visits." This is where they agree on a date and time, and Hermie comes to her house, usually around 9 or 10 at night and knocks on her window. Jane opens the window and talks to Hermie while he stays outside. At the end of the night, she closes the window and Hermie goes home. Last week was their second such visit.

Both cannot wait until their next window visit. Right now they have not discussed a date, but they try to have one about every month just to keep it a low-profile rendezvous. Both can sense that these visits are about to get more intense. Hermie has no idea what's going to happen on the next one.

At the end of the day, all of the kids say goodbye to the other kids until January. Hermie finds Jane in the hallway and gives her a Christmas present. He got her a cassette tape of a band called The Talking Heads. He knows she doesn't listen to music very much, but hopes she may start. She is very excited and gives him a big bear hug and pops his back a couple of times.

She also got him a present. It is a cassette tape from a band called Pink Floyd. She knows Hermie listens to music all the time and knows he has a healthy collection. She hopes he doesn't already have this recording. Hermie hugs her back and sneaks in a kiss. They say goodbye at the end of the school day and maybe they will see each other before January, but it's doubtful. Hermie thinks about a surprise window visit, but later decides against it. He hopes to see her during the holidays.

Hermie spent most of the Christmas holidays with his grandparents. On Christmas morning, Hermie and his grandparents sat around the tree and opened the gifts brought in by Santa Claus. Hermie received some new pants, shirts, and a pair of shoes. He also got a new computer with a few new games for it. Hermie was excited and couldn't believe he actually got the same computer he has been eyeballing at the store for several months.

Hermie was so excited that before grandma served their traditional Christmas feast, Hermie had already opened up the computer, connected it, and powered it on. He was playing some games on it and was showing his confused grandfather how to play.

For New Years Eve, Hermie invites Scott over to his grandparents' house and they play some board games while drinking apple cider. They turn on the TV and watch a celebration in New York City.

At the stroke of midnight, they bring in the New Year with a toast of champagne. Hermie and Scott are hesitant to take a drink, but since his grandparents gave it to them, it's alright. Hermie and Scott take a few sips and begin to enjoy this bubbly liquid. After a couple of glasses, they get lightheaded, silly, and giggly while Hermie's grandparents get a laugh from watching the boys get goofy.

Hermie tells Scott, "My New Year's resolution is to get better at bowling and to bowl more tournaments. I bowled a few this year and I sucked real bad. I wanna do a lot better and maybe win one. What about you?"

Scott replies slowly, "Well, there's this girl at our school that I really want to start talking to, but I'm scared. Her name is Suzi and she's pretty cool. Sometimes I see her hanging out with Jane and her friends. That's what I wanna do; I wanna start talking to her once I get enough nerve."

Hermie and his friends continue to talk about girls and bowling and other things they want to accomplish over the next year. They both look forward to the new calendar year because it will be a year of new opportunities and that gets them excited. At the end of the night, Hermie spends the night there while grandpa takes Scott home.

During the rest of the holiday break, Hermie continues to go to his job at the grocery store bagging groceries. Because there are many people out of town during the holiday season, the store is pretty slow overall. Some of the bagboys are also out of town, which makes some days a real hustle. Now that Hermie is out of school, he can show up for a full day instead of the usual 4-8 evening shift.

A couple of times over the Christmas break, he sees Jane and her mother at the grocery store while he is working. They greet each other, have a small conversation. She hints at another window visit, but they never schedule one.

Some days Hermie doesn't feel like working but goes through the motions. He tells himself that he has enough money to quit his job, but he knows that people would get suspicious if he was buying things and didn't have a job to pay for it. Working is also part of the discipline that his grandfather taught him about the value of money. In the beginning, Hermie didn't like it and didn't understand it; now he just doesn't like it.

On some nights after working at the grocery store, Hermie rides his bicycle home and purposely rides through Jane's neighborhood. He hopes to see her outside so they can talk and be together. And on some nights when he sees her bedroom light on, he wonders what she is doing. Maybe she is thinking about another night in the future, just like he is.

Chapter 2

Saturday Night Scoring

It's a Monday morning in the middle of January and school is back in session. Hermie didn't visit Jane at all during the holiday break. He wonders if she thought about him. He thought about her many times and can't wait to see her.

He has Home Economics for his third period class, finally sees Jane, and asks her, "Hey. What's up? How was your Christmas break?"

Jane is very happy to see him, hugs him, and replies, "It was about the same as last year. You know, we had a small Christmas with just our family. Then for New Year's, my two older sisters went out while I stayed home with my parents and watched the countdown on TV. What about you?"

Hermie tells her, "We had a small Christmas too. And for New Year's, I went to my grandparents' house and watched TV. Scott came along because his parents let him. We got to try some champagne at midnight and started getting dizzy. We were both laughing and acting silly and my grandparents thought it was funny."

Hermie waits to see if Jane talks about them, but she doesn't. Then he adds, "Maybe next year I'll get invited to a party and I'll check it out. I heard some of them parties can get pretty crazy, and wild things happen. I just don't know enough people right now, but that could change this year!"

Jane responds with, "Yeah, they might be fun. My sisters have gone to some of those parties and they said they were really fun. There were lots of people celebrating and loud music and champagne. I was hoping you would come by during the break and visit me. On some nights, I waited for you, hoping you would stop by after work or something and tap on my window. I left my light on, just in case."

Hermie is surprised to hear that and tells her, "Oh, no, I didn't know that. There were some nights that I was coming home from work and I passed by your house. Sometimes your light was on. Most of the time I passed by too early, like 7 or 8 o'clock, but a few times, I got stuck cleaning the place and I left the store at 9. I didn't know you were waiting. Rats."

Jane asks, "Why didn't you come by?"

Hermie says, "I don't know. Maybe I'm afraid of us getting caught. I really wanted to see you and surprise you, but I didn't know if you would get in trouble if your parents saw us together."

Jane tells him, "Well, maybe you can give me a surprise visit during spring break or something."

They continue to play catch-up while they are doing their team assignments. At the end of class, Jane leads him to a private corner in the classroom and gives him a kiss followed by a big hug. Hermie notices how her face glows after kissing him.

Over the next couple of weeks, Hermie and Jane's relationship begins to blossom into a nice friendship. Besides being kissing buddies in the hallway, Jane uses Hermie as a sounding board for questions or problems she has and trusts his judgment. Hermie does the same thing when he has a general question about girls. Both kids trust each other, and sometimes they talk about things that are bothering them.

They work well together in their Home Economics class, and they find private places at school to sneak in a few kisses and hold each other. They do not consider themselves steadies because they are not dating, but they really enjoy each other's company. Jane thinks she is physically addicted to Hermie because she loves the way he makes her feel, not just his company, but also his touch. Hermie likes how nice she smells and how soft her skin is.

Both are trying to find ways to see more of each other after school and on weekends, but with little success. Hermie has invited her several times to the local arcade/pizza parlor, but she cannot go unless one of her female friends goes with her. The issue is compounded because Jane's female friends do not like going to the arcade very much. They do not like the food or play video games, though they do like watching the boys with tight pants play their video games and see them squirm while playing.

Hermie has invited Jane to watch him bowl on Saturday mornings. But Jane cannot attend unless accompanied by a girl. Jane is so honest that she can't even make up a story that a female friend is going to the lanes. She is afraid that her parents will call her bluff and try to verify her story. Right now, the only way the two kids meet during off-hours is through the window visits that both have become quite fond of.

Scott turns 15 during the first week of February. He has a very small party and invites a few friends. His parents have the party over at the arcade. They have pizza, hot dogs, and soda. Scott's parents give each boy a roll of quarters to play in the arcade machines. All of the guys get their money and scamper like bugs. Beforehand, Hermie told Jane about the party to see if she could show up with a friend and hang out. She never made it, but that's not a problem because Hermie was busy beating Scott in some video games.

Charlie, who also attends the party, looks as if he were bored. He tells the gang that his birthday is next month and he is inviting everybody he can to his party. He is not sure where or when the party will be, but he expects it to be a great event. He will be turning 17 and the boys indicate they will attend this party.

On Friday, during the third week in February, Jane invites Hermie over for a window visit Saturday night and Hermie is not as hesitant as he was last time; in fact, he is eager to attend. They decide to meet at 10 o'clock. Hermie is excited that he gets to see Jane again. Even though it is not the perfect scenario for either of them and there is some risk involved, this is all they have and both enjoy their moments together. Besides, he got a kiss from the last visit; who knows what he will get this time?

That Saturday, Hermie wakes up to a very cold morning. The temperature is currently 40 degrees, will climb to 60 by afternoon, and then drop back into the 40s in the evening. Cold weather makes many people lazy and Hermie is no exception. He tells himself, "Gee, it would be so easy to unplug the phone and stay in bed all day and just watch TV."

He is supposed to bowl this morning, followed by working a few hours at the grocery store. He doesn't even feel like going to the lanes, much less going to work in the afternoon. Then he changes his mind after thinking about seeing Jane later that evening. That will be his reward for enduring the harsh weather all day.

He decides to drive his car because he is feeling lazy and cold. He arrives at the lanes and sees his friends. He is not in the mood to bowl because he would rather be at home doing nothing. Sometimes, doing nothing means a lot to him. He ends the day with a 570 series and his team wins 3 out of 5 points against their opposition, thanks to Hank rolling a 650. The guys plan on going somewhere to eat, but Hermie politely bows out because he has to go to work and expects a busy and hectic day because of the cold weather.

From the lanes he drives to the store. All the way there, he motivates himself by saying, "This is going to suck … this is going to suck…." When he arrives at the grocery store, he looks around and sees lots of cars but few bagboys and says, "I was right, this is going to suck." He slowly exits the car and gets ready for a day of being pounded by the high volume of customers, combined with cold weather and wind.

After a profitable but cold day bagging groceries and being outside and the store being short handed again, Hermie leaves work and sits in his car with the heater running. He can already feel the temperatures starting to sink. He is very tired and it is only 6 o'clock. He begins to wonder if he will be awake long enough to see Jane tonight. He knows it will be worth it.

Hermie goes home and takes a hot bath. He brings his portable TV into the bathroom so he can watch the U.S. Open Bowling Championships. Just as the show starts and he jumps into the tub, the phone rings. Hermie is debating whether to answer it or not. He chooses not to answer it since he has an answering machine. The caller does not leave a message. He ignores the phone and enjoys his soak.

After his bath, he gets dressed and has a quiet meal of fried rice; his other favorite meal. He is still a little scared being in this big house all by himself, but he only stays in this house five or six days out of the week. The other days he stays with his grandparents. Hermie hopes to be living in this house on a full-time basis by the summer. He figures one way to get tough is to live alone a few days at a time.

After dinner, he goes upstairs to his room and plays some video games on his computer. This keeps him busy until 9:30. He is not sure whether to ride his bike or drive his car. After remembering the current weather conditions, he decides to drive his car, since his bike doesn't have a heater.

He leaves his house about 9:50 and arrives in 5 minutes. He parks his car five houses down the street and walks to Jane's house just to keep a low profile. He is starting to feel how cold it really is outside. As he gets closer, he notices that the light in her room is on and her window is open halfway. He keeps on walking until he slowly enters the front porch. He hears silence from her room and lightly knocks on the window.

The bedroom light is suddenly turned off and two hands open the window further. The curtains are partially pulled back and Jane's happy face appears in the window. Hermie is relieved and glad to see her as he sits down next to her window. No sooner does he sit down, when she reaches out of the window to give him a small kiss. She invites him inside but he refuses. She looks warm and comfortable.

She tells him, "Hi. I'm so glad you could make it tonight. I was thinking about tonight ever since I invited you."

Hermie is quite cold and replies, "This morning it was so cold, I didn't wanna go bowling or go to work. But thinking about tonight made me forget the cold weather. I thought about this all day and it made me work harder."

They begin talking about minor stuff such as school and teachers and classes. Hermie notices that when he is talking, she is looking directly at him, giving him 100 percent attention. She will also not take her eyes off him, even when he looks away from her. He thinks that is odd behavior, but it doesn't bother him.

Soon, Jane notices that Hermie is starting to shiver. She invites him inside but he refuses, saying he is fine. She keeps on asking him until he finally gives in. She tells him it will be only for a few minutes, since he is uncomfortable being inside her room. He slowly and cautiously climbs through the window and into her room.

Once he is inside, she closes the window halfway and closes the curtains. Hermie looks around her bedroom and it's pretty dark but very warm and toasty. That's why Jane isn't cold while wearing her stretchy shorts and tank top. He sees a small nightlight between her bed and the window. The rest of the room's illumination comes from the streetlights. He is starting to feel warm too.

He sees Jane approaching him and she takes off his jacket. She puts her arms around him and gives him a big hug as if she hadn't seen him in years. He hugs her back but she does not let go of him. She can feel that he is still cold. She tells him to sit on her bed and she will get him a mug of hot chocolate. Hermie likes that idea and waits as she walks out of her room. He sits there smelling the light powdery scent of her perfume in the air. He is a little excited and a little scared, hoping that nobody finds out about this window visit or about him being inside the house this late at night.

She comes back less than five minutes later with a mug and gives it to him. He sees the steam rising and knows it is very hot. He blows on it then takes a sip. He quickly pulls it back saying, "hot, hot." She sits next to him and takes a sip. She gives the mug back to him and they continue their conversation.

Hermie says, "Starting this year, I wanna bowl more tournaments, even if I have to go out of town, like San Antonio, Dallas, or Houston. I'm getting better and I really like the competition side. The Saturday league is okay, but I get excited when I am competing."

Jane asks, "Are there any tournaments during this time of year? I thought it would be slow because of Christmas and New Year's?"

Hermie replies, "There were no tournaments around here, but I'm sure there were some in the big cities; and they're not very far away. I didn't try real hard over the holidays because I didn't think about it too much. I was kinda lazy."

Hermie continues to talk about his bowling and how he wants to win, even though he has been bowling for only two years. Jane is not a bowler, but she listens to him with unmistakable enthusiasm and total eye contact. She has never seen him bowl but figures that he is pretty good since he always talks about it and is really excited about it.

As Hermie continues his discussion on his off-season regimen, she leans over and kisses him. Then she kisses him again, but this time a bit longer. He finally responds and she pushes him backward onto her bed. She is on top of him. They kiss a few more times and soon there are hands moving all over the place touching many things. Hermie finally gets a chance to put his mug of chocolate on her nightstand before it spills. She stops and hugs him again. Eventually, she gets off him and lies next to him.

The two kids are in a nearly dark bedroom lying next to each other in her bed. Once again they are breathing heavily and their faces are red and flushed from the exciting action and all the movement.

In between breaths Jane tells Hermie, "I don't know what it is, but you make me feel sooo good. It's like I don't want to stop and I want to keep going. Whatever it is."

Hermie replies, "I feel pretty good too. And you smell really nice."

Both kids continue to lie on their backs while experiencing another intimate evening alone. Neither is remotely worried about the possibility of her parents coming in through the door. They start talking about school and other extra-curricular activities for another half hour.

Around midnight, Hermie leaves with a big smile and says he will see her at school on Monday. As he drives home he knows their relationship has gotten that much stronger; so have his feelings for her. It also feels great kissing her and she smells wonderful. He also can't turn down her big blue-green eyes and her innocent look. He knows they can't do very much due to her dating rules, but he still likes what he has.

The following week is Charlie's birthday. He is turning 17. That's pretty old for a 9th grader, considering most freshmen are about 14 or 15, but many people know that he dropped out of 8th grade, took about two years off from school to get a job, and helped his father pay bills after his parents got a divorce. Then when he returned to school, he flunked miserably and had to repeat 8th grade.

Charlie invites the boys and other friends to the theater for his birthday party on Saturday night. Charlie likes the theater compared to the arcade because he can sneak in a flask and sip his drink without being too obvious. Although the arcade is pretty dark too, Charlie knows it is easier to sneak in a drink when you are sitting down with chairs in front of you.

The gang consists of Hermie, Hank, and three other guys that are not in high school anymore. They decide to watch a science fiction movie that takes place in outer space. Charlie also likes action and horror movies. Charlie really doesn't care what kind of movie it is, as long as it isn't a "chick flick." Charlie just wants a place to drink his booze and share it with some good friends.

As the movie starts Charlie pulls out a flask, takes a swig, and passes it to Hermie, telling him, "Bottoms up, bro."

Hermie asks, "Bottom who?" and takes the flask. He just looks at it.

Charlie tells him, "Bottoms up. Put the flask to your mouth and take a swig; you know, take a drink."

Hermie is not used to drinking liquor, but since Charlie is a pal, he will take a drink. Hermie says, "Happy Birthday, dude" and tilts the flask into his mouth and takes a swig. The initial taste is a bit harsh and burns his throat. Hermie blurts out, "Whoa, what is this stuff? It kinda burns at first, but has a good taste later on."

Charlie tells him, "That's rum. It's from South America and made out of sugar cane. That's why it has a good flavor." Hermie decides to remember that flavor for future reference. Now he can't wait for that flask to come around again.

Later on during the movie, one of Charlie's friends passes around a flask he brought. It finally reaches Hermie and he decides to take a whiff. For some strange reason he cannot smell it and almost thinks it's water. He takes a swig and the liquid burns his throat worse than the rum. He is told that it is vodka, and Hermie is amazed by the lack of smell and taste. However, he can certainly do without his throat stinging.

By this time, Hermie is getting lightheaded again and is feeling pretty good. He does not say much but just sits back and waits for the rum flask to make another round. It seems the rest of the group is feeling pretty mellow.

Charlie asks Hermie, "So man, how you feelin?"

Hermie replies, "I'm feeling pretty good. After a couple of drinks I started getting a warm feeling around my body. Then my bones felt funny; you know, like my shoulders and knees. They felt loose. Then my brain felt funny. I don't know what's in that stuff but it's pretty good."

Charlie tells him, "Don't sweat it. You're buzzin. That means you're drunk."

Hermie says, "I'm buzzin? Wow, it feels kinda neat."

The movie is almost over and he totally forgot what it was about. He notices that Charlie and his friends look a little bit drunk and are laughing loudly at the funny parts of the movie. Soon he gets the munchies and makes a trip to the snack bar and gets a hot dog and a soda. He is so hungry that he chokes down the hot dog before returning to his seat.

After the movies, Charlie wants to go out cruising. Hermie is feeling pretty good but knows he cannot party like Charlie. Hermie says he has to help his grandfather do some things in the garage early in the morning and gracefully bows out. Hermie forgot that he rode his bike to the theater because the distance didn't seem that far during the day. Now he has a challenge. He has to ride home in the dark and under the influence. He takes a final gulp of his soda before riding home.

He tries to find his way home in the dark and makes several wrong turns before finding some familiar street names. A few blocks later he arrives in his neighborhood and finds his house. He is so tired that he does not even feel like parking the bike in the garage and brings it into the living room. He also doesn't feel like going upstairs to change clothes and go to bed, so he just falls asleep on the couch.

Chapter 3

The Origin of Dreamer

It's now the middle of March. It has been three weeks since Hermie's last window visit. Jane approaches Hermie in the hallway for her usual kiss between classes. They average one or two kisses per day, and sometimes as many as four or five, whenever she sees him in the halls. This is usually dependent on her and how she is feeling.

Hermie loves the attention, but sometimes Jane acts like a junkie needing a fix. They both figure it's pretty harmless anyway, but it sure feels good. When there is a large crowd in the halls, the kids just stand close and wait for the crowds to dissipate, then they kiss. It's also pretty hard to tell Jane 'no' when she flashes her eyes at him.

One day, Jane asks him, "What are you doing this Friday night? Me and my friends are going to the movies. Maybe you can meet me there and we can be together."

Hermie likes the idea but tells her, "That's cool, but what about your friends? Are you going to just leave them there or are we gonna sit with them?"

Jane says, "No silly. We're going to get our own seat so we can be alone, away from everybody else. The movie is about some babysitter that gets in trouble. It's supposed to be real funny. I hope you can make it. I'll be waiting for you."

Hermie says, "That's cool. I'll see you out there. What time does it start?"

Jane tells him, "Around 8:30. Bye."

Hermie looks forward to seeing her and knows that's the only way Jane can get out of the house without her parents tagging along; she has to travel with her friends. Hermie also remembers what happened the last time he went to the theater, but he is pretty sure her friends won't be packing a flask, or at least he hopes they're not packing one.

Both kids can't wait to see each other. Hermie is excited because this will be the first time they are together outside of school. He knows this is just the theater, but it's better than nothing. He is already counting down the days.

On Friday, Hermie wakes up and goes to school thinking about seeing Jane away from the school surroundings. After school, Hermie goes to work for three hours. He goes through the motions of work, even though his mind is not on work, it's on the theater. At 7:15 he leaves the store and goes home.

Once inside the house, he suddenly gets lazy and makes the mistake of lying on the couch. As luck would have it, the Women's U.S. Open Bowling Championships is being televised and he suddenly wants to watch it. Eventually he takes a shower and gets dressed. For dinner, he has a leftover Brisket sandwich in case he does not eat at the theater. He remembers the nasty taste of the rubber hot dog he ate at the theater last time, even after he drank from the flask. He leaves the house at 8 o'clock, and drives his car.

He arrives at the theater in less than ten minutes and looks up at the schedule to see what movie starts at 8:30 that is about babysitting. He finds the movie and buys his ticket. He goes to the snack bar and gets his customary large bag of popcorn and a large cup of lemonade. He starts munching and slurping immediately.

He walks into the semi-dark theater and slowly walks down the aisles looking for Jane. He can't see a thing. Just as he is a third of the way down the aisle, he hears his name called. He looks back and it's Jane with three other girls sitting in the back row of the middle section. He says hi to Jane's friends and the girls giggle. Jane gets up and leaves the group. Both kids find a seat in a semi-private area and away from any crowd.

They sit down and begin to talk. Hermie can tell she is excited to see him by the way she is facing him, the gleam in her bright blue-green eyes, and her warm smile. His heart is starting to pound and his mind is starting to race. He does not know what to expect and has no idea what she will do. He will just try to keep his cool.

The movie begins and they both stop talking to enjoy the show. During the movie, they occasionally hold hands. Sometimes Jane puts her head on his shoulder and sneaks in a kiss or two. They enjoy the movie while having popcorn and lemonade.

It's about 10:30 and the movie just finished. They both walk out and Jane tells her friends "goodnight." Hermie also tells the girls "goodnight" and they giggle again. Hermie leaves his car in the parking lot and decides to walk Jane home, since the weather is nice. Jane thinks this is very generous of him and thinks it's kind of romantic too.

Her house is about eight blocks away; they hold hands all the way home as they talk about the movie. Every block or so they stop in a secluded area behind a tree and kiss, then they continue walking. Hermie is feeling pretty good, and Jane acts like the trees are too far apart. She keeps holding his hand. They are not talking very much.

They arrive at her house and stop at her doorstep. Hermie is anticipating a goodnight kiss. Both stand there and look at each other. Nobody is speaking. Jane looks at Hermie, smiles at him, and just stands there.

Hermie asks, "What's up? It looks like you were about to ask me something."

Jane hesitates again and finally asks Hermie, "Well … I'm not sure how to say it, but how would you feel about … um … spending the night tonight?"

"What? Here in your house? Are you kidding? How do I feel about getting lynched by your parents? Sure, sign me up for that!" Hermie quickly replies.

Jane explains, "Well, my parents are out of town and I'm all alone in the house. I'm also a little scared at night. If you can't stay, can you just come in for a little while until I fall asleep? That's all. Then you can leave whenever."

Hermie thinks about it for a minute, hesitates, and says, "Okay, I'll come in for a minute, but just for a minute or two, then I gotta go. I can't believe I'm doing this and I hope we don't get in trouble."

As she opens the front door, Jane tells him, "You won't get in trouble, I promise. As soon as I get sleepy, you can leave. I won't tell anybody about this."

Both kids walk into a dark and quiet house. Jane turns on the living room lights and walks toward the kitchen. Hermie finds the couch and plops himself down. He turns on the TV and flips through the channels and finds an old black and white horror movie. He is not sure what movie this is or why he is suddenly watching it. Jane sits next to him, trying to share the excitement of the movie. She sits closer to him and puts her arms around him.

Jane asks Hermie again, "Are you sure you can't spend the night? You can sleep on the couch," as she kisses his neck and cheeks.

Hermie enjoys her advances and replies, "I just don't feel right about it. I'll just stay here until you fall asleep. Then I'll leave."

Jane gets the hint and asks, "I'm thirsty, do you want a soda?"

Hermie says, "Sure, need some help?" as he tries to stand up.

Jane pushes him back down, telling him, "No; I got it. You are the guest in this house and I will be right back."

In the kitchen, she gets two glasses from the cupboard, goes to the icebox, and puts ice in them. She opens a can of soda and fills the glasses near the top. Then slowly, she opens a drawer and pulls out a small, dark, glass vial that looks like a medicine dropper. She leans over to see if Hermie is still sitting down and he is.

She opens the vial and squeezes about four drops of a clear liquid into one of the glasses. She smells the glass with this mystery liquid and it smells like mint. She pours a little more soda in that glass to cover the smell.

She takes the two glasses back to the living room and gives Hermie the drink that has more in it, which he thirstily slams down. She tells him to slow down so that he does not choke or get a stomach ache, but he is too busy gulping to listen to her. She cannot believe how thirsty he is. She wonders what will happen next.

A few minutes later, after the TV show is over, Hermie begins to feel lightheaded and starts to sink deep into the couch looking very comfortable.

He says, "Wow, my head feels funny and this couch feels good. It must be working in the cold weather that has me feeling like this. I can't get too sleepy cause I have to leave pretty soon."

Jane watches him slowly flip through the channels using the remote control. He is moving slower and moving less. He finally decides to watch an old King Kong movie.

He tells Jane, "I'm more tired than I thought cause I'm all mellow and this TV remote won't stay in my hand. Crazy stuff. And that's a big monkey on TV."

Jane watches him fumble with the TV remote control and begins to study all his movements. She knows those drops in his drink are starting to take effect. He compliments her on a very soft and comfortable couch. She tells him to relax and watch the show. He watches the TV for another 15 minutes, then he blacks out.

The next morning Hermie wakes up in a bedroom that's not his. His head has a very slight buzzing feel and he is still a little dizzy. He also feels some ringing in his ears. All he remembers from last night is the soda, the couch, and some movie. He tries really hard to remember anything after that, but he just draws a blank.

He sits up and looks around the room. He is in Jane's bed! Next to him is Jane and she is still asleep under the covers. His heart and his mind begin to race, and he begins to breathe very fast. All he can think of is getting in some serious trouble. Right now, he is envisioning her parents hanging him off a tall tree with a short rope.

He looks under the covers and he has only his pants on. He looks at her and she only has her panties on. He gets a good long look and likes what he sees. Then he puts the covers back on her and quickly jumps out of bed, scared.

He says, "Oh my God, I am in so much trouble. I'm gonna get killed."

Jane wakes up from hearing his rant and tells him, "You're not in trouble, and you're not going to get killed. Nobody is home."

Hermie asks her, "What happened last night? How did I get here?"

Jane replies, "You were really tired and fell asleep on the couch. I felt sorry for you sleeping on the couch so I helped you move to my bed. I was really cold in my bed and you felt really warm, so I let you stay there with me. I hope you're not mad at me."

Hermie responds, "No, no, I'm not mad, I'm just freaking out right now. I wasn't planning on spending the night and I still ended up here. Did we do anything?"

Jane has a guilty grin and tells him, "Uh, nothing happened."

He looks at his watch and it is 9:30. His bowling league starts in 30 minutes! Now he is starting to panic. He tells Jane to get up so she can join him at the lanes. Both quickly get dressed, not even worrying that they are standing half-naked in front of each other. He looks at her partially clothed body one more time before it gets covered up, but he is too busy panicking to stare at her. They get dressed in three minutes.

They run out of the front door and Hermie does not see his car. Being excited, he says, "Hey!! Where's my car? I don't see it here. I gotta get to my car!"

Jane tells Hermie, "You big silly. You drove your car to the theater last night and left it over there when you walked me home."

Hermie thinks for a moment and slowly says, "Oh, oh yeah, that's right."

Now Hermie is worried that something may have happened to his car and that he would never forgive himself. They jog for four of the eight blocks and walk the rest of the way. He examines his car and there are no signs of damage. The panic is mostly over. They hop in his car and Hermie drives to the lanes.

They arrive at the lanes and both walk in to see the large crowd getting ready to bowl. Jane has never been to a bowling league and cannot believe how many kids are there. She sees some kids from her school. Hermie finds his starting lane, greets his friends, and introduces Jane to his teammates. He puts on his shoes and gets ready for his ten minutes of practice. Jane is excited by all the action going on.

The lanes are turned on for practice and, as usual, Hermie does lousy. He throws splits, throws gutters for his spares, and is bowling like a complete idiot. This does not surprise him because he usually does this poorly in practice. Jane is not sure if this is normal behavior for him, but later he tells her that his practice time is usually ugly.

Finally, practice is over and it is time to begin the competition for the day. Hermie's team is in 1st place and will be challenging the 2nd place team. Today's games are very critical because each win will put them further ahead of the other team. Jane gives him a hug for good luck then sneaks in a kiss. Hermie and the boys act surprised.

Hermie throws his first shot and it looks real good. He leaves a single pin. He puts on a show like he is pretty angry and yells out "Whatever!!" to the pins and throws his hands in the air, as if he was already giving up.

He keeps his cool and converts the spare. To everybody's surprise, he gets the next six strikes in a row and ends up with a score of 246. Jane is clapping and very happy. Hermie's teammates congratulate him as they win the first game. Hermie cannot believe how good he just bowled. It seemed so easy and effortless.

Hermie starts the next game with the first four strikes and is getting excited. He is already thinking of beating his first game since he is having really good pin carry. But during the middle of the game, he leaves the dreaded "big four" split and cannot believe his luck. Now he thinks his whole game is doomed and almost gets upset again.

He picks up a ball designed to go very straight and shoots at the spare, throwing the ball very hard. The ball hits the pins on the right side, one pin slides across to the left side, and he converts the spare! He gets excited, as do Jane and the team. He gets a few more spares and ends up with a 211 game. Jane thinks he is awesome as she claps and cheers. Hermie's teammates are excited and are bowling better as a result. They win the second game too. Hermie is shaking his head, not believing his good fortune.

The third game begins and Hermie starts off with three strikes. He is not too excited right now, but does make a comment that the ball feels real good as he lets go of it. Even the guys on his team are making comments that he is acting differently and throwing the ball really well.

After eight strikes in a row, a small crowd gathers and the bowling center is getting quieter with each frame. This makes Hermie a little bit nervous. The boys are at the edge of their seats. Jane has no idea what is going on until Scott tells her what this means. Now she is at the edge of her seat too, almost biting off her nails. Hermie gets up in the 9ᵗʰ frame and throws a good shot. He leaves a single pin and everybody sighs as Hermie drops his head, looking down as if the wind was taken out of him. He was already thinking of rolling a perfect 300 game. He makes the spare in the 9ᵗʰ frame and gets another spare in the 10ᵗʰ frame for a great 268 game and a 725 series, his highest ever as his team won all five points today.

Hermie walks back with a huge smile on his face, shaking his head. Jane and his team await him with "high-fives" and pats on the back. Hermie cannot believe this. The front desk makes the announcement and several people clap for him. Nobody has ever seen Hermie bowl this good before, including Hermie.

Jane is so excited and caught up in the mania that she runs up to him and tells him, "Wow, you're the best! You threw so many strikes today; just like the guys on TV!" and gives him a kiss right in front of everybody.

Hermie is too excited to realize what happened and tells her, "I think I drank some strongman soda last night to make me bowl this good."

Hermie is on cloud nine thinking about his scores today and realizing he was only two shots away from a perfect 300 game. That would have been something huge. He probably would have wet his pants. Either way, a 268 game is a super achievement and he will not complain about it. Now he knows he is capable of shooting big scores.

Hermie and Jane are invited by the gang to grab some lunch and they agree to join in. They find a local burger joint and enjoy their lunch after a successful day on the lanes. They cannot stop talking about Hermie and his scores. Hermie tells them that he never thought about a big score or a big series. He just thought about how comfortable the ball felt in his hand and how the pins were falling down so easy.

Scott also bowled a great series of 670 and nobody noticed. Hank talked a bit about his 650. Charlie even felt good with his 625. More importantly, Hermie's team swept the second place team and are on their way for a huge lead in the league standings.

Jane tells Hermie, "You were great!! You were bowling like the pros you watch on TV. Are you going to be a pro someday?"

Hermie tells her, "I don't know; I've always dreamed of being one ever since I saw those guys on TV. But I still need lots of work on my game, and a better haircut."

She tells him, "I know … I'll call you Dreamer, since you have always dreamed of being a pro."

Hermie scratches his head and says, "Dreamer? Hmm … I like that. That's a cool name, Dreamer. Thanks."

The rest of the guys agree it's a good name and that it fits him. Jane tells Hermie, "Don't ever stop dreaming about being a pro. You might be the best ever someday".

After lunch, Hermie and Jane say goodbye to the crowd and both get in his car and drive to her house. She compliments him on his performance and both cannot believe what happened today. She sneaks in a quick kiss on his cheek while he drives and it puts a smile on his face.

They arrive at her house about ten minutes later and exit the car. Hermie is scheduled to work today, but he decides that he will take the day off due to a major accomplishment.

They enter her dark and quiet house, and Hermie finds a comfortable spot on the couch where he quickly falls asleep. Jane lies on the other couch and watches him sleep, even without the TV on. She replays today's events in her head. Within 20 minutes she falls asleep too.

Chapter 4

A Weekend with a Girl

About an hour later, the telephone rings and it wakes up the two kids. Hermie opens his eyes and notices that Jane is snuggled in his arms. He likes that feeling and apparently she does too. As Jane gets up to answer the phone, Hermie looks at his watch and notices that it's only 4 o'clock. He stretches and lies back down, trying to sleep some more. Right now, sleeping sure feels good.

Jane answers the phone and her older sister, Kelly, is on the line. She tells Jane she will be spending the night again at her friend's house and not to worry about her. The sisters say goodbye and Jane hangs up the phone with a surprised grin on her face.

Jane sits close to Hermie, puts her arms around him and tells him, "Guess what? My sister is not coming home tonight, so we have the whole house to ourselves again. Isn't that great? What do you wanna do first?"

Hermie is pretty excited and starts to think. He knows he doesn't want to stay at her house all day and do nothing, even though taking another nap sounds very tempting right now. Jane has a puzzled look on her face as she waits for his response.

"I know! Let's go to the mall and hang out. I wanna visit the computer store to see if there are any new computer games. Come on," says an excited Hermie.

The two kids exit Jane's house and get into Hermie's car. Before they leave town and drive to Austin, Hermie stops at a gas station and fills up his car. He enters the store, gets a large soda for himself, and a bag of pork rinds for Jane. On the way, Hermie turns up the music and enjoys the sounds while Jane continuously looks at him and occasionally holds his hand. They keep driving.

They arrive at the mall in an hour and almost immediately, Hermie gets out of his car and bolts toward the mall entrance. He completely forgot about Jane. He looks like a zombie in a trance.

She gets his attention with a sharp and sudden, "HEY!! Wait for me," and Hermie stops to wait for her.

She catches up to him and both enter the mall together. She has not been to this mall in almost a year and is curious to see how it has changed.

Once inside, Hermie makes a beeline to the computer store. Jane watches his mood change from cool and sullen to excited and energized. They arrive at the store and walk in. Hermie marches straight to the Atari section and examines the available titles. After a quick scan of the goods, Hermie travels to the "New Items" section and begins to lick his chops. To Jane, all these games look the same.

She decides to play a trick on him and says, "Just pick a box and let's get out of here, they're all the same anyway. I can pick one for you if you want."

She just hit a nerve. Hermie stops what he was doing, puts the box down, and turns around. He has a serious look on his face as he approaches her.

"Playing games is a fine art. You can't just pick up a game and master it the first time around. It takes time and discipline. You're not a gamer so you have no idea what you are talking about. Each game is different and requires a different set of skills. Not everybody has these skills," rebuts a very stern Hermie.

Jane just stands there listening to his speech. With each sentence that Hermie speaks, she is that much closer to bursting out in laughter. She has never seen him that serious about anything; especially video games.

She can't take it anymore and begins to laugh and hugs him telling him, "You are so cute when you are trying to be serious." Hermie smiles back knowing she just duped him. He just shakes his head.

Eventually Hermie selects two games and takes them to the register for checkout. The total comes out to $45 and he pulls out a small wad of cash, completely forgetting that Jane is right next to him. She notices the stack of cash and her eyes pop out.

"Wow, I didn't know you were rich. That's a lot of money just for computer games," says Jane.

Hermie quickly replies in a humble manner, "I'm not rich. My parents give me an allowance and I have a job." She quickly remembers.

They leave the computer store and walk around for a while. She holds his hand and smiles at him. When she is not holding his hand, Hermie opens the bag from the computer store, pulls out the game, and re-reads the box.

They arrive at a women's clothing store and Jane enters with excitement. Hermie is at a safe distance behind her. She goes to the section of long-sleeve Oxford knit shirts. She looks at all the colors and tells Hermie that light blue and pink are her favorite colors in these tops. She eyeballs a light blue shirt and puts it to the side. She looks at the price, her jaw drops, then she puts it back on the rack. She continues her shopping.

Hermie noticed the look on her face when she put the shirt back. He takes the shirt off the rack, looks it over, and carries it to the back of the store where Jane is. Jane is currently looking at accessories.

Jane follows him and asks, "Why are you carrying that shirt around? I'm not going to get it. You can put it back."

"What's wrong with the shirt? It's nice and it looks good," says Hermie.

Jane replies, "Did you see the price tag on that thing? I need some more allowance from my parents before I can get it. Maybe I'll buy it next month or something."

Hermie, who can be pretty stubborn when he wants to be, walks toward the front of the store as if he were going to put the shirt back. Suddenly, he makes a sharp right turn and walks to the cash register. He puts the shirt on the counter. Jane watches the whole thing and rushes up there to stop the purchase.

She tells him, "It's okay, you don't have to do this."

Hermie replies, "I want to get you something nice. It's a gift."

The cashier tells Hermie that his total comes to $35. Hermie pulls out that stack of money and removes two $20 bills. Jane is trying not to stare at the wad of money but cannot help herself. She knows it's a small fortune as he quickly puts it back into his pocket. She also noticed there were several $20 bills in that stack.

They leave the store and she hugs and kisses him on the cheek, telling him, "Thanks so much for the shirt. I will take great care of it." She is very happy and her face is glowing. They continue walking and end up at the Food Court.

They stop at a sandwich shop and look at the menu. She orders a ham and cheese, which is her favorite, while Hermie gets the club, which is his favorite. They get their food, sit down, and eat. They talk about what their next activity will be.

Neither of them is sure what they will do next until Hermie says, "I bet I can beat you at putt putt golf. You look weak today."

It's a strange way to describe miniature golf, but Jane knows what he is talking about and accepts the challenge. They finish their meal and leave the mall around 6:30.

Hermie begins to drive around as if he were lost and tells Jane, "I know there's an arcade near the mall that has putt putt. I've been to it before. It won't be long before I smash you on the course."

Jane defends herself by saying, "Don't get too brave, I've played this before."

Hermie makes a few turns and a few circles before he finds the arcade. He is wearing a huge grin and is already celebrating the victory. They exit the car and enter the building.

Since it is getting dark outside, they decide to play only nine holes. Hermie jokes, "This will be quick work kicking your butt today," and Jane's face lights up with surprise.

"Keep talking. You're just digging your own grave," Jane retaliates.

They play the first hole and Hermie wins that one 4-5. Jane wins the next two holes 6-4 and 4-3. Hermie gets a hole-in-one on #4 while Jane gets a 3. They tie the next two holes at 4-4 and 4-4. Now the pressure is on.

Jane wins the last three holes and projects a loud screech throughout the golf course. She jumps up and down for joy, while Hermie has to stand there and take the abuse. They finally leave the golf course and check out the arcade for a few minutes where Hermie hides just to get some peace from Jane and her victory.

As they leave the arcade and walk to the car, Hermie tells her. "I'm famished. Do you wanna stop somewhere and grab some dinner? I think I know a place."

"What? You're hungry again? If you wanna stop, that's fine," says a surprised Jane as she rolls her eyes.

He tells her, "I know a cool restaurant that I go to … that my parents take me to … when they are in town." Hermie catches himself and hopes that Jane didn't hear that near slip up. After about 15 minutes of driving, they find the place Hermie was looking for.

This steakhouse looks fancy, too fancy for two teenagers wearing jeans and t-shirts. They put their name on a waiting list and have a seat. Hermie is just sitting there like a bump on a log while Jane is busy taking in all the sights. She has never been to a restaurant this elaborate and cannot sit down. In fact, she can't breathe properly because she is so excited and intimidated by the whole environment and ambiance.

They wait for about 15 minutes and finally get a table. After they sit down, they are handed very large and bulky menus. Both are impressed by the size of the menus and the prices, and think that the President must eat here.

Hermie says, "They don't even serve hamburgers here unless it's a kid's meal; and they still want $8 for it. Yay."

Jane has lost her breath after seeing the prices. She says, "This place is expensive. We can eat somewhere else if you want." Hermie shakes his head, indicating this is where they will eat.

Jane then says, "I can't even pronounce some of this stuff and it's in English."

Hermie replies, "I just want a steak and fries. That's enough to make the belly happy." Jane agrees and nods her head with her eyes wide open and a hungry grin.

They finally order their dinner: a steak, fries and a side salad. Hermie cannot decide whether to have water or soda, since a soda will keep him awake all night; he settles for a soda. They have small conversation but both are too busy looking around at this upscale establishment.

Twenty minutes later their dinner arrives and Jane practically faints from the size of the portions. The steak covers most of her plate and the French fries are piled very high. She has no idea where to start. Hermie started to laugh at her but quickly realized that he is in the same predicament. He grabs a few fries and starts eating.

During dinner nobody is talking very much. Both kids are busy trying to find a way to clean their plates. In the end they end up eating half of their meals and can barely move from being over stuffed. They completely forgot that they also ordered an extra side dish.

Hermie gets the bill and Jane notices that it's over $60 and she tells him, "I promise to pay you back," as Hermie shakes his head refusing her money.

Hermie jokingly says, "No sweat, it's my treat. Actually, it was the sodas that put us over the edge. They charged us $3 for each one. That's crazy," but Jane does not get his joke.

At 10 o'clock, they leave the restaurant very full and content. They get into Hermie's car and begin the one-hour drive back to Jane's house. Both are relaxed and mellow. Hermie puts the radio on an oldies station and hears music from the 50's.

On the way home Jane begins talking about how sweet and kind he was all day and how he paid for everything. She has a big smile on her face and is getting into the music Hermie is playing. Hermie is just happy that she is happy.

"I know you spent a lot of money on me today and I really appreciate it. I will make it up to you somehow. If you ever need some money, I have some at home and I can give it to you. I know it took you a while to save it up," says a satisfied Jane.

"Well, I save it so I can spend it once in a while. Today was that day. What good is money if I can't spend it on a friend or on my chick? Don't worry about me. With my job and my allowance, I'm doing just fine," replies Hermie.

Then he pauses and says, "Also, my parents throw me some extra bread to cover the bills, and I keep the change. The money is nice, but I still miss them."

Jane puts her arms around him as they drive on a dark and sparsely populated highway. He puts in a cassette from Pink Floyd and goes into his own zone. Jane is not too familiar with this band, but listens intently and begins to get into a groove.

Jane cannot believe how mature and grown up Hermie acted today and tells him so. She is very impressed with how he knew his way around the big city and with the certain level of confidence he carried with him. Not bad for a 16-year-old. She also noticed how mentioned that she is "his chick" and she likes the sound of that.

Jane tells him, "How did you know all those streets in the city? I guess with your parents being out of town so much, you had to grow up fast."

Hermie tells her, "That's exactly what happened. My father and grandfather showed me around the town and that got me prepped for my road trips. I had a choice. I could sit around at home or I could be mobile and see the world."

They arrive at Jane's house at 11:30. Once inside, Hermie quickly goes for the couch and lies down as if about to pass out. Jane looks around the house and suddenly looks puzzled. She notices the furniture has been moved and there is some trash on the coffee table. Now she is starting to fume.

She goes into the kitchen and sees dirty dishes, food containers, and empty wine cooler bottles and spills on the counters. Now she knows one of her sisters was here with some friends, partied, then left. Jane is visibly enraged and screams. She is about to throw a monster fit.

Hermie cautiously follows her into the kitchen, looks around, and asks her, "Are you okay? It looks like you're about to pop a cork?"

She tells him, "Somebody has been in here and they didn't clean up after themselves. It's probably my pig sister and her pig friends. Look at this mess, there's crap everywhere. Do they live in a barn? What's wrong with them? They always do this."

Hermie stands there with nothing to say. He's afraid he'll get slapped. Quickly he says, "I'll help you clean it up."

Jane starts to panic and breathe fast, then blurts out, "My dumb sister is a slob. She does this all the time. If my parents see this mess, they will never leave us alone again. And she knows I will clean this up. I can't stand when she does this to me!"

Hermie calmly tells her, "Don't trip. Just take a deep breath. We'll clean up tomorrow. I promise. Tonight, let's just kick back and enjoy."

Jane cools off and offers him a wine cooler. Hermie does not drink wine coolers that much, but hates turning down a free drink. Jane grabs one for herself and slams it down. The two kids sit in the living room and watch TV.

Jane sits closer and closer to Hermie. From out of nowhere, Jane kisses Hermie and he returns the favor. They begin to make out. Hermie is so busy with Jane that he does not realize that "The Legends of Bowling" is on TV. And this is a good episode.

After a few coolers and mundane television programming, Hermie finds himself lying on the carpet, playing strip Monopoly and missing half of his clothes. He looks across the game board and notices Jane is in the same situation as both kids are giggling. He does not remember how they got this way, but they keep playing.

The carpet feels very comfortable and the house is not too warm and not too cool. He has another drink and rolls the dice. He hears some laughing as his eyes are getting heavy. He looks at his watch and it won't stay still. He looks at Jane and she is asleep face down on the carpet; that's unfortunate because he wanted to keep playing. His eyes are very heavy and he closes them for a split second.

When he opens his eyes, it's the next morning and he wakes up on the living room carpet. He has a slight headache, but it's not that painful. There is a huge blanket on top of him. Next to him is Jane. Both are still half-dressed and there are several bottles on top of the coffee table. He looks at the Monopoly game and cannot tell who won; not that it really matters. Cards and game pieces are scattered about. But he thinks it was fun … from what he remembers.

He looks at his watch and it finally stays still. It is 11 o'clock and the house looks more trashed than it did the night before, at least he thinks so. He gets off the carpet and lies on the couch. He turns on the TV and flips through channels until he finds a show he likes, "The Bowling Battle on the Beach," also one of his favorites.

Half an hour later Jane finally wakes up and notices that she is wearing only her underclothing and does not know how she got that way. She looks startled and confused.

Hermie notices her puzzled look and says, "Don't worry, my clothes are missing too." They both have a small laugh.

Jane gets up, finds her clothes, and starts getting dressed. She walks to the kitchen and sees Hermie there. Hermie is trying to assess the damage and it does not look good. He thinks a tornado ripped through there.

After the two kids are clothed, they start cleaning up the house. Hermie turns on the stereo in the living room to get motivated. He finds a garbage bag in the kitchen and begins to fill it with all kinds of trash.

Jane's first task is to put the furniture where it belongs. Then she puts away the blanket and the Monopoly game. After Hermie takes out the trash, he finds a broom and sweeps the kitchen. Jane stands there and watches Hermie, adoring him and his effort to help out. After he sweeps, he cleans the tables and countertops. She begins running water in the sink to wash dishes. She is not as upset about cleaning as she was last night.

It's about 2 o'clock and the kids just finished cleaning up the house. Jane is putting away the vacuum cleaner and likes the condition of the house. It is spotless and she thinks it looks better than it did before her parents left.

She puts her arms around Hermie, gives him a kiss, and tells him, "Thanks a lot for helping me clean up this place. I was so mad last night that I could've screamed. I was kind of embarrassed because my sister trashed the place and I didn't want you to see this pigpen. But it's all better now."

Hermie replies, "No problem. Glad I could help."

Jane says, "My parents will be home about 8 tonight and they won't even notice that my sister and her friends messed up this place. They won't even know you were here either."

"Let's hope not," replies Hermie.

She walks Hermie to her front door, opens it, and tells him, "Thanks for spending this weekend with me. I had the best time ever. I really love the shirt you got me and I liked that restaurant we went to. I had a great time and I wish you didn't have to go."

Hermie replies, "I had a great time too. Maybe we can do this again someday."

As he walks toward the front door, she stops him and gives him a long kiss and then another one. She begins to breathe heavy and kisses him faster, all over his face. She is also starting to make some strange noises.

Between kisses she says, "Oh, this feels so good. I can't seem to get enough."

Hermie reminds her that her sister may be around the corner and could blow their cover. He tells her, "We don't have too much time for this stuff, maybe later."

She tells him, "I'm going to miss all of this," as she stops herself but is panting and her face is getting flushed.

Hermie tells her, "Well, now you have some homework." Jane looks puzzled. He adds, "You know, you need to find ways for us to see each other in private since you can't date right now. I work at the store every day and I bowl on Saturdays."

They hug each other and say goodbye. They will see each other in school tomorrow but decide to keep it cool for a few days, if that's possible.

Hermie walks to his car, gets inside, and waves to her as he drives off. He cannot believe the great weekend he just had. It was incredible being with only her for almost two days. He learned so much about her and how she lives.

He is very anxious when he will get to spend more time with her. He also hopes he didn't give away his secret by letting her see that small stack of cash. It does not matter anymore, it is the past. Hopefully she bought that excuse of getting an allowance.

He goes home thinking, "Imagine that, this whole thing started when I shot that 725 series on Saturday and when her parents were out of town. What would have happened if I would have shot 800? Who knows?"

Chapter 5

Front Row Window Seat

The following Monday, Hermie sees Jane in the hall a few times and they both say hello. Today, they are pretty busy and do not have a lot of time for their usual hallway talk. Both want to keep things cool for a few days since their wild weekend together and do not want to blow their cover.

In addition, Jane's older sister, Kelly, is a senior at the same high school. Jane does not want to get caught kissing Hermie, because she has no idea of what Kelly might say. The two kids still talk during their Home Economics class, but they do not discuss their private lives, and their conversation about last weekend is brief.

Hermie asks Jane, "So, did you get in trouble with your parents or sisters about the weekend stuff?"

Jane is smiling and replies, "Oh my gosh! They were so impressed on how clean the house was, they offered to be out of town more often. They thought me and my sisters spent the whole weekend cleaning up and they even liked the smell of the house. It was totally awesome!"

Jane adds, "As for my sisters, they know I cover for them a lot by cleaning the house when they mess it up, so they never give me a hard time. And sometimes they do small favors for me. It all works out good for everybody." Hermie nods his head in acceptance and in relief.

"Do you have any plans for Spring Break this year?" Jane asks.

"I don't have any plans. I might hang out with my grandparents for few days. I will probably play some basketball with the boys and get some bowling practice. What about you?" answers Hermie.

She replies, "Some of my friends are going to the beach for a few days, but I am not allowed to do that yet. Maybe I can go next year. If you're not doing anything, maybe you can come over for a visit … or two."

She mentions that her parents will be out of town again, which would reduce the chances of getting caught. He doesn't realize that their break is less than two weeks away but is excited to see her again.

"Yeah; I might check it out," says Hermie.

For the next few days, Hermie and Jane try to play it cool and not make a scene when kissing in the hallways. They usually have one or two per day and leave it at that. Hermie senses the anticipation building up in both of them and they cannot wait to see each other. Hermie is not sure why they are trying to be discreet. He laughs at that.

On the Friday before Spring Break, Jane tells Hermie that her parents are leaving on Tuesday afternoon and will be gone until Saturday. However, Kelly, her middle sister, will be in and out of the house starting Wednesday night. So she invites him for a window visit as early as Tuesday night. Hermie chooses to visit her on Wednesday night, regardless if her sister is there or not. She says she cannot wait to see him again.

That Saturday, Hermie and his friends play some basketball at the nearby middle school. They begin their game as HORSE and eventually get a bit more aggressive and start shooting balls at the basket. Before too long, they pick teams and play until somebody scores 20 points.

After their game, they go back to Hermie's house to cool down and just hang out. All the guys are pretty tired and cannot believe they played as hard as they did. They help themselves to the contents in the pantry and refrigerator.

"So, do y'all have any plans for Spring Break," asks Hermie.

Hank says, "I have to stay in town because the football coach wants some of the players to train for some track and field events for the upcoming track season, even though the track season already started. That makes no sense."

Hank is starting to get upset and adds, "I was a bench warmer for most of football season, but I still trained for some track events. The coach said I should try out for the discus and shot put because of my strong arms. So I practiced my butt off and the coach ended up choosing some skinny runt whose father was a buddy of his. What a load." Hank is visibly upset and stops talking.

Charlie says, "That sucks. I was invited to the coast with some ex-classmates, but I can't go cause I'm broke, so I'll just stick around town and check out a couple of parties. You guys should think about going. There's gonna be sex, drugs, and rock and roll!" Hermie and Scott look scared as their jaws drop.

Hank announces, "I probably won't attend because of the strict drinking and drugs rules made by the coach. If I get caught one time, I could be kicked off the football and track teams … even though I'm a bench warmer anyway."

Scott says, "I don't have any plans and nobody invited me anywhere. My parents might be going to Houston and they might make me go. I don't know."

Hermie tells Scott, "If you go, bring your bowling balls in case you have time. That way you can find an alley and get some practice. Also, keep your eyes and ears open for any upcoming tournaments." Scott is now excited to go to Houston.

"What about you? What do you have goin on?" asks Charlie.

"I'm probably gonna work. Jane wants to get together so we might do that. Some dudes from school were talking about going to the coast, but they're all talk," says Hermie.

On Sunday and Monday, Hermie visits with his grandparents. They talk about living alone and Hermie does like the privacy, but sometimes he gets lonely. Hermie mentions that he does not feel as scared as he used to be. Grandpa reminds him that they are only a phone call away and he should never be ashamed to call. His grandfather takes him to the garage for another lesson on fixing the car.

On Wednesday, Hermie sleeps in late. He is scheduled to work today but is not in the mood. He is busy thinking about seeing Jane later that night, and that motivates him to eventually get dressed and go to the store. He's noticed that each time they meet at the window they get a little bit closer. He wonders what will happen this time.

He shows up at the grocery store and begins his day of work. He does not want to be there because this is his Spring Break week and he would rather be doing something else; anything else. The store is very empty and there are too many bagboys. Today will not be good. He goes through the motions but keeps Jane on his mind.

He finally finishes up his workday at the store and merrily goes home at 6:30; two hours before the store closes. After a nice shower and another TV dinner, he leaves his house around 9:15 and is feeling a bit sassy. He decides to drive his car to her house and park it in front. He does not care what the neighbors think anymore.

He arrives at 9:30 and attempts to be as quiet as possible, so not to cause a scene. He accidentally slams the door of his car and quickly gives himself a "shhhhhhhhhh." He walks properly up the sidewalk and makes it to the front porch. He sees Jane's half-opened window and gives it three gentle taps.

The curtains are pulled back slowly, revealing a young lady in a dimly lit room wearing what looks like a bathrobe. She smiles at him and extends her head out of the window and gives him a long kiss, which takes his breath away.

Jane softly says, "Hi." Hermie notices her breath smells funny but is not sure what it is. It doesn't bother him because he has other things on his mind.

Hermie loves the greeting, but in his mind she looks like she is either ready for bed or ready for a bath. He laughs to himself thinking of how funny she looks. After all, this is the first time he has seen her in a robe. Anyway, it's still good to see her. He asks her if anybody is home and she turns her head from left to right indicating the coast is clear. His eyes light up as he bobs his head in acceptance.

Just before he asks how she is doing, she slowly opens the window all the way, grabs his two hands, and quickly jerks him toward her, pulling him in through the window.

Hermie was not expecting this and goes flying through the window into her room and lands on his butt, making a loud thud. Hermie is in shock while Jane apologetically giggles and shows her innocent eyes as if she were about to say "oops." Hermie is not sure if he is going to laugh or cry, but he slowly gets up, wincing and holding his lower back, just like the pro wrestlers do after they get flipped onto the canvas.

As Hermie stands up, Jane approaches him and gives him a hug and says, "Sorry about the fall. Maybe this will take your mind off the pain" as she slowly disrobes only to show off her birthday suit. She stands there and lets him look.

Hermie quickly forgets about that silly back pain and lays his eyes on what he believes is the mother lode. The room is barely lit, but with the help of some moonlight, that's enough to reveal the shape of Jane's body. He already knows she has soft skin but now he can see a nicely shaped body. She has a little bit of thick skin in

47

some places, but that's fine with him. He has no more pain and is now thinking about something else.

He has never seen her like this before and studies the specimen without looking too obvious, even though that's tough. Jane slowly walks toward him with a big smile on her face, looking up at him while he stands there in a daze. She begins to kiss him.

Jane notices Hermie is motionless and is blankly staring at her. She asks him, "Hermie, are you there?" She closes her window about halfway. Hermie mumbles and nods his head. He shakes his head and closes his eyes for a minute, then closes his mouth and takes a gulp. He has a nervous smile on his face and kisses her back.

She kisses him several more times and moans. At the same time Hermie is in shock; he is in heaven. He thinks "Wow, this naked girl is all over me, what a score!" He kisses her back, presses his lips against hers, then feels her tongue touch his.

He pulls back and says, "I got it, have you been drinking 'cause you're acting different and your breath smells funny."

A silence fills the air as Jane hesitates to speak, then she tries to approach him again. She quietly answers, "Yeah, I had a couple of drinks."

Jane looks scared, as if Hermie is about to pop a cork. Hermie says he is not mad at her but keeps asking questions just out of curiosity.

Jane eventually tells Hermie, "My dad left his liquor cabinet unlocked and I was curious and found the whiskey. I was really nervous about tonight and that stuff settled me down. I probably shouldn't have done it."

Jane puts her robe back on and sits on the bed feeling rejected, as if about to cry. She says, "All I wanted to do was surprise you and now you didn't like it."

Hermie sits next to her and tells her, "Are you kidding me? I loved it and I'm very surprised. It blew my mind!" as he tries to peel off the robe.

She tells him, "I was really scared about being naked in front of you, but the shot made the stage fright go away. And another shot made me feel even better. I did all this for you." She begins to cry.

Hermie puts his arm around her and tells her, "Don't cry, that was an ultimate gift. I could never get mad at you for having the courage to show me the complete package from out of the blue. You're a brave little chick."

He kisses her on the cheek and tells her, "You can blow my mind anytime you want. I wasn't mad, I was just worried you might get sick from that booze cause you usually don't drink it. That's all."

He kisses her again and she kisses back. The two kids are rolling around on the bed laughing and giggling. They have appeared to make up.

She gets up and walks to her dresser. Hermie is following her with his arms around her. She picks up the whiskey bottle, pours a shot, and hands it to him. He hesitates, takes a deep breath, and then takes the glass from her hand. He knows she is expecting him to drink this stuff and he is not looking forward to the taste.

He sarcastically says "thanks" and chokes it down, almost gagging. Instantly he feels the warm elixir make its way down his esophagus with a small stinging sensation as it lands in his stomach. Within seconds he begins to feel lightheaded.

Jane stands there and watches Hermie go through a chemical reaction. He is looking for a soda but cannot find one, so he sips on her glass of water.

She pours him a second shot and tells him, "You need to catch up, so drink it." She hands the second shot to a timid-looking Hermie who slowly takes the small glass from her hand and just sits there staring at it.

Hermie shakes his head and says, "Oh no, not again," as he tilts the glass into his mouth and closes his eyes, making a sour face. He swallows the brown liquid and exhales loudly. Another minute later he says that his body feels warm and his head feels funny. He has a relaxed smile on his face.

Just then, Jane sits on his lap and puts her arms around him. She smoothly and effortlessly pulls off his shirt. They begin to kiss and she starts to kiss him all over his face and neck. Suddenly Jane's robe slides down her body exposing her epidural layer. They look at each other in surprise as she says "oops" and they continue kissing.

Before long they are making out and there are four hands moving in all different directions. There is heavy breathing and some occasional moaning. After a while, Hermie is on Jane's bed, flat on his back and she is lying on top of him. There is a bed sheet covering the two kids as they take a break from the action and begin giggling.

Jane looks at him and gives him a big hug. She tells him, "I feel so comfortable around you the more I'm with you. I used to be scared to kiss you; now I want to kiss you all the time. I'm not afraid to do these things anymore. It actually feels pretty good and those shots helped too."

Hermie says, "Wow, those shots did help. I'm feeling as loose as a goose right now. When I first met you, I was a little scared too. But every time I saw you, it got better and better. I didn't know what was around the corner, but I knew it was something good and I started to melt every time we got together. I don't know what to do now, but I don't mind 'cause I can't stop anymore."

They hug each other and roll around in her bed having some more fun, laughing, and chatting about things. Although it wasn't planned, Hermie ends up spending the night as the kids fall asleep around 2 o'clock in the morning.

Hermie wakes up at 9:30 the next morning. He is in Jane's bed and she is snuggled up next to him. He looks under the sheets and all he is wearing is his underwear and socks. He looks at Jane and she is in the nude! He looks at her one more time and still cannot believe all this was his the night before. He has a big smile on his face.

He wonders how long they can live this way before they get caught. He gets this strange feeling every time he visits that her family will catch them in the act. But the way he feels around her, he doesn't care if they get caught; it would be worth it.

He covers her with the sheet and just looks at her. Her coarse but straight dark-blonde hair is slightly messy and her cheeks do not have that usual red glow on them. Her lips have the continual slightly chapped look, but only during the cooler months. He lets her sleep as he slowly leaves the bed to look for his clothes.

He finds his clothes on the floor and hastily gets dressed. Although he is being very quiet, Jane tosses and turns, moves her arms around feeling for him, and eventually wakes up. She opens her eyes, looks under the covers, and gets a surprise.

"How did I end up this way?" Jane asks in a very surprised tone.

"What do you mean how did you end up that way? That's how you started out last night. Just you and the robe ... and that nasty paint thinner you made us drink," quickly replies Hermie.

Being embarrassed, she completely covers herself with the blanket until she finds her robe. Then she puts on her robe under the covers.

She asks Hermie, "So, what happened," as she finds her clothes on the floor and gets dressed underneath the robe.

Hermie looks away and slowly replies "You know, we talked ... and kissed ... and messed around. That's about all. We got crazy a couple of times, but I don't remember all we did. A lot of it was like a blur, but I know it felt real good."

"Did we do it?" she nervously asks.

Hermie quickly gives her a scared "no" gesture, even though he has no idea what happened. He does not want to say "yes" or "I think so" and scare the both of them, but he has a different gut feeling about it.

She looks relieved and says, "I don't remember very much from last night but I remember that it felt real good. That whiskey is some crazy stuff. I feel really tired and my head hurts and I want to go back to bed."

Hermie tells her, "I think you're hung over. Just take some aspirin for that headache and go back to sleep. It's still Spring Break, so take it easy. I gotta go home and get ready for work later. I don't wanna go, but it's been a very light crew this week and they need me over there. I will probably work my butt off, but I can make some serious bones."

As Jane walks him to the front door, she asks him if he will come by this evening or the next. He is not sure but will think about it. He tells her he will call or come by later tonight to see how she is feeling. Before she opens the front door, she gives him a kiss goodbye and hugs him for a long time. She doesn't want to see him leave, but he has to go to work. She stumbles back to bed.

Hermie walks to his car and drives home. He tries really hard to remember what transpired last night but draws a blank. He really didn't have to work today but didn't feel like hanging around Jane's house doing nothing all day. He feels tired too, but didn't want to admit it. He makes it home, takes a three-hour nap, showers then goes to work.

He works all afternoon thinking about last night. It makes the workday go by smoother. At the end of the day, he drives to Jane's house and wonders how she is feeling from her first hangover ... at least the first one that he knows about. He hopes tonight will be a bit smoother. He normally leaves the store about 6:30 on weekdays, but because of Spring Break week, the store was shorthanded and he ended up leaving at 7:30.

He arrives at Jane's house at 7:45 and rings the doorbell. Jane opens the door in a secretive manner and sticks her head out to greet him. She looks more coherent and smiles, but is talking in a soft voice. With the door open, he can smell food and can hear people talking in the background. She asks if he wants to come inside. He agrees if she won't get in trouble. She says it's not a problem and he steps inside as his belly rumbles.

On the couch is a girl that looks like Jane but a little older. He is re-introduced to Kelly, Jane's sister, who is a senior at their high school. He remembers seeing her before. She is very pretty. Sitting next to her is a tall guy introduced as Kerry. He is also a senior at their high school. Hermie sits on the second couch next to Jane. Jane puts her arms around his arm, not realizing what she is doing.

Hermie notices they are watching some car race on TV. Hermie is not really into car racing and cannot see how anybody can watch a TV show about cars that go in a circle over 200 times. The cars he likes are muscle cars, but that's the extent of it.

They begin to exchange small talk about school and school activities. Kerry is planning on going to college in New York to study political science and perhaps go to law school afterwards. He wants to be a politician and run for a public office; but also thought about being a judge.

Hermie realizes the conversation is way above his head and tries to think how he can discuss his topic. He decides to just say what he wants to say, and tells Kelly and Kerry that he plans on trying out for the school bowling team next year and hopes to help the team make it to the playoffs, which is an area where previous teams have failed. He mentions that he has been practicing hard and is learning more about the game every day. They can tell he is excited about his quest. Hermie also mentions that he eventually wants to bowl professionally, but he is not sure if he wants to go to college or not.

Jane stands up and volunteers to give Hermie a tour around the house, since it is his first time there formally. They excuse themselves from the living room and begin the tour. Kelly reminds Jane not to go into Kelly's room and to feed Hermie if he is hungry, since dinner is ready. Jane takes Hermie toward the hallway and bedrooms.

Jane quickly shows Hermie the bedrooms, passing up all the bedrooms but hers. They enter her room. She quickly but quietly closes the door and pins Hermie against the wall, much to his surprise. She puts her arms around him and pushes her lips against his.

She exhales and says, "I have been waiting for that all day. I feel better now. Wait, I need just one or two more." Hermie stands there in shock but does not complain.

From her bedroom they travel to the kitchen where Hermie gets a whiff of some freshly made spaghetti, meatballs, and garlic bread. He notices an open bottle of grape juice. As he stares, Jane pulls him away from the kitchen and toward the back porch.

Hermie's stomach rumbles, because it just saw dinner and can't wait to eat. They enter the backyard and she pushes Hermie into a lawn chair. Then she sits sideways on his lap and kisses him a few times. He compliments Jane on a very nice house while she hugs him. Eventually they get up and enter the house to eat dinner.

During dinner they sit across the table from each other and both are very quiet and cautious. Jane cannot keep her eyes off Hermie and catches several glances of him as she smiles. Hermie just nods his head in appreciation. It appears that Jane and Hermie would rather have the whole house to themselves since her parents are away, but they have to share it with her sister. After ten minutes and total silence, they finally start talking about school and upcoming Home Economics assignments.

After dinner, Jane peeps her head into the living room. She sees the TV is still on and realizes that that Kelly and Kerry are not going anywhere anytime soon. Jane and Hermie finish their meal, clean up the kitchen, and slowly sneak into her room.

In her room, they both sit on her bed. She is all smiles as she sits next to him. Hermie looks around and the room looks a lot neater than it did this morning.

Hermie is wondering how soon it will be before she opens the whiskey, so he asks her, "So, are you ready for a shot of that nasty crap?"

"No way; it's going to be a long time before I taste that stuff again," she quickly replies. "That stuff made me forget things and it gave me a headache. I was in bed all day today. It's a good thing my sister didn't come by and bother me. I would have slapped her silly."

They both laugh and begin talking about things they want to do for next year's Spring Break. Both want to go to the beach with their friends and both think they will be able to go next year.

They stay up until about midnight talking, and eventually Hermie decides to go home. Jane leads him to the front door and onto the front porch, and they kiss goodnight. Hermie gets into his car and drives home.

As Hermie plops into his bed, he thinks about the last two nights and how his relationship with Jane is changing. Although they do not consider themselves as "steadies," it sure feels like it when they are alone. He does not know what tomorrow will bring, but he sure likes what he had today.

On Friday, the boys play some basketball in the morning, just hang out at Hermie's place all afternoon, and do nothing. Hermie decides not to go to work since he worked every day during his week off. Later that afternoon after the guys leave, Hermie visits his grandparents and catches up on all that is going on and has dinner with them.

On Saturday, Hermie goes to work and discovers it's a busy day due to Spring Break week. He works hard and makes 2 pocketfuls of money, then goes directly to his grandparents' house for some fried rice because he is too tired to cook.

During dinner, he talks about his workday. They ask about Jane and he tells them that she is a really nice person. They tell Hermie to bring her to the house sometime so they can meet her.

After dinner, Hermie goes home. He takes a shower and watches some TV. Later in the evening he gets a call from Jane and they talk for about an hour. She thanks him for visiting her during the week and tells him that he made her feel so good. He invites her over to his house, but Jane is too scared to tell her sister where she is going, even though Jane thinks that Kerry spent the night with Kelly. She tells Hermie that she will see him on Monday.

As he lies in bed, he reminisces about the great week he had and all the activities he was involved in. He made a pretty good chunk of change at the grocery store and he got to hang out with his good friends. But the week started off on a good note when he saw Jane and got a front row window seat.

Chapter 6

Summer Slam

During the second weekend in April, Hermie and Jane have a window visit. Jane has mentioned trying to have a window visit during the week, but Hermie thinks it's too risky, even though he likes her daring attitude.

Tonight's visit is like all the other visits; Hermie parks his car at the far end of the block and walks all the way to her house and makes a beeline to her window. However, tonight, after she opens the window, he enters without any hesitation.

Jane, being excited to see him, quickly hugs and kisses him. She is in a frisky mood and starts to tickle him. Hermie returns the favor and she makes a loud squeal sound and laughs. Then the couple gets quiet. Jane thinks she heard a noise coming from the living room. They stand perfectly still in Jane's nearly dark bedroom.

"Jane, are you okay?" asks her mother from outside of the door.

A surprised Jane nervously says, "Yeah, I … I just coughed a little, that's all."

Hermie is scared that her mother is two seconds away from opening the door and catching him in the act. He feverishly looks around the room, trying to find a place to hide. He cannot risk jumping out of the window. He sees her bed and decides to hide beneath it. He quickly throws himself on the floor and slides under it in a matter of seconds. Unfortunately, he is a bit clumsy and hits his head against the rail on his way under, making a "klang" sound.

"What was that?" asks Jane's mother.

Jane is speechless for a couple of seconds and says, "I just threw my shoes under the bed," hoping that her mother will leave her alone.

Just then, her mother opens the door and walks in. Jane, who is not very good at having a poker face, has the look of somebody that got caught in the cookie jar. She stands about three feet from her bed, not moving a muscle.

Her mother looks around the room, seeing if anything is out of place and listening for anything odd. After a few seconds of scanning the room, she walks to the window and notices that it's open all the way. Jane knows she is busted and begins to sweat.

"This is why you have a cough. The window is open and it's a little chilly outside. Goodnight," as her mother closes the window.

A relieved Jane tells her mother "Goodnight" in return, as her mother leaves the room and closes the door. Jane practically faints from excitement and falls on her bed.

Just then she remembers that Hermie is still under her bed. She jumps off her bed, gets on the floor, and whispers, "The coast is clear."

Hermie sticks his head out from under the bed and tells her, "Hey, you need to clean under here more often; I got a face full of dust and a shoe up my butt."

She laughs, gives him a couple of kisses, and says, "Wow, that whole thing kinda turned me on. You know what I mean? My heart is pounding real fast."

"It's pounding because we almost got busted," Hermie quickly replies. "How can you be turned on? I was so scared I think I pissed my pants. If your mom would've seen me, she would have shot me right here; then your dad would have lynched me!"

Hermie finally climbs out from under the bed and Jane gives him a towel to wipe his face and arms. She wipes off the back of his neck and starts kissing him. Eventually both kids sit on her bed and make out. Jane is really in the mood and Hermie really thinks her mother is still in the hallway listening. He plays along with Jane's advances but remains cautious.

At the end of a steamy night, Jane wants him to spend the night but he refuses. He thinks Jane's parents are on to her and know when he comes and goes. He finally leaves around 1 o'clock in the morning. It was a good night and, once again, she made him feel wonderful. He still cannot believe that Jane got excited for almost being caught.

On the first weekend in May, Hermie and his buddies go to the city of Austin to bowl a tournament. Hermie has been thinking about this one for a while. He has a good feeling about this tournament and feels confident ever since he shot that 725 series.

They all pile into Hermie's car and get ready to make the one-hour trek. They listen to rock music and talk about what they call "The 4 Bs," which are: Bowling, Babes, Booze, and Beef. They arrive an hour later and exit the car.

They grab their equipment and go inside to sign up. Hank chose not to bowl this tournament but decided to hang out with his good friends for the day. Hermie's grandparents follow the boys in their own car. They are excited to watch Hermie bowl again. They remember how excited John was when he first began bowling while in college.

Hermie finds a seat and sits down to change his shoes. He looks around to see if he recognizes anybody. The guys get their lane assignments and Hermie will be sharing a pair with Charlie. The practice lights come on and everyone begins to throw practice shots.

As in fine fashion, Hermie performs poorly during practice. He uses every ball he brought and gets a different reaction. Now he is really lost. He knows that he must get his act together because the tournament is a four-game qualifier. Then the qualifiers bowl a three-game block to determine the top 5. Then, the top 5 bowl one game to determine the winner.

He begins the first game with his solid black ball, which has been dulled with some sandpaper in case the lanes are slick. He is playing a medium hook and starts off with first five strikes. In the 6th and 7th frames, he leaves a single pin and makes the spares. He gets another strike then finishes with spares for a nice 235 game. Charlie was close with a 215. Scott shoots a 200 after complaining of all the single-pin spares he shot at. Hermie's grandparents are cheering.

For game two, they change lanes and Hermie notices an arrogant young man named Sam. Sam is also a left-hander and has very good form and style. He does not hook the ball very much and usually plays from the outside of the lane, pointing the ball toward the pins. The rumor is that Sam is usually the person to watch out for.

Hermie starts off the same way as the first game and watches Charlie and Sam shoot at several single-pin spares. After a few spares of his own, Hermie leaves a split in the 9th frame. Sam begins to clap his hands loudly after getting three strikes in a row. In the 10th frame, Hermie gets a strike and a spare; he shoots a 220.

Sam has a chance to beat Hermie, throws his shot, and leaves a solid 7 pin. He is a little bit steamed up. He rushes up for spare and misses it. Sam shoots a 211 and Charlie shoots a 200, while Scott improves with a 216. Hermie notices that Sam does not like to lose or shoot a bad game.

During the third game, Hermie is getting a different ball reaction. That dull black ball he is using is hooking too much and forcing him to throw it harder to delay the hook. This typically results in a weaker hitting ball which reduces pin carry. He changes to a shiny blue ball and watches it skid further down the lane. He makes a few adjustments and shoots another 220. Charlie gets his game together and shoots 225, while Scott gets no breaks and shoots a 189.

In the final game, Hermie continues to use the shiny blue ball and begins with four spares in a row. He strikes from the 5th frame up to the 10th frame, then gets a spare in the final frame to shoot a 244, and a 919 series. He thinks his scores are high enough to be the tournament leader, which gets an automatic bye into the final 5. He is watching Sam to see what his final score is. Hermie knows that Sam might be the leader.

Charlie threw a couple of splits in the final game and shot a 185 game for an 825 series. Charlie is pretty sure he didn't make the cut. Scott finishes with a 248 game and an 852 set. Scott is pretty sure he made the cut. Everybody paces the floor, waiting for the official results.

They announce the cut for the top 16 and it is 815, so Charlie barely made the cut and is very shocked but happy. As they announce the higher finishers, everybody guesses that Sam is the leader by the way he is walking around in his typical arrogant manner. They announce second place with an 890 series is Sam, which makes Hermie the leading qualifier with a 919. Sam cannot believe he got beat and is upset once again; he thought he was the top dog. Hermie is in shock and cannot believe the news either.

The semifinalists begin their competition. They must bowl three games, and the top four bowlers will play in the finals with Hermie. Charlie and Scott begin a bit nervous and are too afraid to take chances, but they make their spares. Charlie starts with a 206 and Scott shoots a 210. Meanwhile, Sam finds a hot streak and strokes a nice 258 game.

Hermie and Hank are eating lunch with Hermie's grandparents while watching the action. Charlie and Scott come by to nibble while they bowl. After lunch, Hermie gets some practice just to stay loose and warm up. Hank decides to coach him, if necessary.

In game two, Scott finds a good groove and shoots a 230, while Charlie encounters problems with his release and ball reaction, and shoots a 178. His chances are about gone. Sam shoots a very loud 225 and looks lined up. Hermie starts to take note of Sam.

In game three, Scott misses two spares and shoots a 205 to end up with a 645, while Charlie regroups a bit too late with a 219 and a 603 series. Nobody knows what Sam shot because he was rather quiet that game, but they guess he probably made the final 5.

The tournament director announces the cut to make the finals is and it is 645. Scott makes the cut and is jumping up and down. Sam is the high semifinalist, shooting a 685. Charlie already knew he didn't make the cut and is dejected, but knows today was not his day.

The finals begin and it's a one-game show. The top score wins a $2,000 scholarship. Hermie practiced for about 30 minutes and feels warmed up and loose. Sam is looking at Hermie with his nose in the air. Hermie just shakes his head and laughs. All five bowlers will shoot on one pair of lanes, lanes 19-20.

Charlie congratulates Scott and tells him, "Wow, the lanes were not that bad today, but I had thumb problems from the get-go. I should have monkeyed with it some more. Good luck in the finals."

The five finalists begin practice and Hermie looks lost again. But this time he has a plan. He decides to use his sanded ball and play the same area as Sam to see what kind of ball reaction he gets. Maybe he will get better pin carry. Hermie's ball hooks too much from that area, so he decides to use his shiny blue ball. Sam is still striking, while Scott is changing balls and targets, as well as shooting at some spares.

The lights come on and Hermie begins with a spare. Scott and Sam start with a strike. After four frames, Hermie has three strikes in a row, while Scott has a double and two spares. Sam is keeping up with Scott, but only a few pins behind Hermie.

The second half of the game is a bit more exciting than the first. In the 6th frame, Sam hooks the ball too much, leaving a split. He almost kicks the ball return machine. After that, Sam connects a few strikes starting in the 7th frame. Scott is shooting more spares than usual and eventually misses one. Hermie gets a string of spares and finally gets a strike in the 9th frame. Sam throws a powerful strike in the 9th frame and slaps his hands and yells, because he caught up to Hermie to make the game close.

Scott strikes out in the 10th frame for a 203 and knows the contest is between Hermie and Sam. He figures that he has third place locked up unless disaster hits both Hermie and Sam, which he doubts. The other two finalists shot 190 and 185 each.

Sam gets up in the 10th frame. He has to finish first because Hermie, as the top seed, chose it that way. Sam makes his way past Hermie, and Hermie mumbles, "Don't throw it flat." Sam puts his nose in the air as he looks to the scoreboard.

Sam is losing to Hermie by five pins, so matching Hermie's shots will not be enough. If Sam strikes out, he forces Hermie to strike out to win the tournament. Sam throws his first shot. He throws the ball a little bit too far to the left but it hooks back and carries a light but sloppy strike. He slaps his hands and yells "Yeah" as he walks around with some attitude.

Sam quickly gets up and throws his second shot but it hits flat and leaves a 7 pin. He screams loudly in disbelief, because he really wanted that strike. That would have made Hermie throw two strikes to win it all.

Sam makes the spare and shoots a 223. He doesn't even look at Hermie and is licking his chops, because Hermie has to finish on the left lane; which has caused him problems today. His chances of striking are slim. Hermie, being the top seed, chose to finish last, not even realizing he would have to finish on his bad lane; a typical rookie mistake.

Now it's Hermie's turn. He looks at the scoreboard and realizes that he needs the first strike and five pins to win. A spare will do no good. The bowling center is quiet, even some of the open bowlers stopped for a second to witness this final frame. Hermie is ready and a little nervous. He knows what he needs. He takes a deep breath.

He gets up, throws his first shot and it looks good. It hits half pocket but kicks out the 7 pin for a strike. With his fists clenched, he screams out a loud "Yeeeeeaaaaah!" toward the pins. He hears some applause and his heart is pounding a mile a minute. He paces around the floor as if he were lost. He is beginning to tremble and his eyes begin to water. He sees his grandparents and his buddies rooting for him. He needs a few pins but forgets how many. He cannot add right now. He can't even breathe.

Charlie comes up to him and says, "Great shot! Now calm down, all you need is five pins. Get that shiny ball and chunk it down the middle and this tournament is yours." Hermie nods his head, still trembling.

Hermie gets up for his second shot and knows this is for all the wheat. Now he is very nervous and throws his second shot down the middle and gets seven pins. He just won his very first tournament! The small crowd cheers as Hermie stares at the pins, falls to his knees, shakes his head, then puts his hands over his face.

Hermie says, "Oh my God. Oh my God. I don't believe it." He stays on his knees as his eyes water up some more. His head is spinning as he starts to smile.

He gets up and throws his spare shot then realizes he just beat "the man to beat." He walks back with a huge nervous grin on his face and puts his hand over his mouth. His grandparents rush out to hug him. Hermie has a small cry as he looks exhausted and out of breath.

Sam is upset again as he loses 227–223. Sam quickly packs up his equipment and practically runs out the door. He does not even congratulate Hermie or the other finalists. The other three contestants shake Hermie's hand and thank him for beating Sam. Hermie tells everybody that he felt great ever since he woke up this morning.

Hermie wins a big trophy and a $2,000 scholarship. Sam finished second and got a $1,000 scholarship, and Scott got a $750 scholarship for his third-place finish. The other two finishers each got a $500 scholarship.

Hermie's grandparents are very excited to see Hermie win his first tournament. They take Hermie and his friends to a nice restaurant for dinner. All the boys do is talk about bowling and how it was Hermie's day. As they leave the restaurant, Hank volunteers to drive home, because he knows the bowlers are tired from a busy day.

The following Monday is the last week of school before the summer. Hermie sees Jane in the hallway and tells her about his bowling. She is very proud of him and hugs him. She says she wants to be there to watch his next tournament.

They talk about their plans for the summer. Hermie wants to bowl more tournaments since he has the fever. Jane says she hangs out with her friends and they end up at the pool or the movies. The two kids will try to see each other over the summer.

It's finally Friday, the last day of school before the summer. Hermie sees Jane in the hallway and says he wants to see her during the summer. He tells her to call or visit anytime. Since she is not allowed to take phone calls, he gives her his phone number and directions to his house. He tells her he will be working at the grocery store and maybe she can come by and visit. She tells Hermie she will try to stop by the store.

That Saturday is the last day of Hermie's morning bowling league. His team made a serious charge in January and February, which resulted in many wins and vaulted them into first place by a huge margin. In fact, they are so far in front that they could lose all of their games today and still get the crown.

After the league is over, the final win-loss numbers are tallied up and all the places are announced. Hermie's team wins first place, and Hermie also wins the Male High Average award. Hermie and his teammates are excited because this is the first time any of them have won first place in any of their leagues.

After the trophies and awards are handed out, the league director tells the kids that there will be a pizza party for them, right now at the local pizza parlor. He is hoping everybody will be there. Hermie and the boys jump into Hermie's car and drive over there for the free food. They talk about their first-place accomplishment.

During the party, a few people approach Hermie and congratulate him on winning the league and the high average award. Hermie was not expecting the high average award because there were other guys that were right behind him, but he won't complain.

Somebody asks him, "I heard that you weren't on this year's school team. Are you going to try out for it next year?"

This is a sore subject for Hermie, but he stays cool and says, "I tried out for the team last year and I finished in 7th place out of the 12 guys they were gonna pick. But at the last minute, the coach decided to take only six guys instead of 12, and I was pissed. I thought that was unfair and I was kinda mad at him. But I'll try out again next year 'cause I really wanna make the team."

Someone else asks Hermie, "Are the coach's nephews good bowlers?"

Hermie bites his tongue and says, "They're not that great. I think if they would have bowled the qualifier tournament, they wouldn't have made the team."

Hermie just realized that he slipped up by blabbing. Now he hopes that this person doesn't go running to the coach to tattle. That could make next year very tough.

As the summer begins, Hermie and his friends play basketball at the elementary school courts. After their game, they usually get something to eat then go to Hermie's house to cool down. They watch TV and play video games, then leave after a few hours. Hermie notices that Charlie is usually not in a hurry to go home and always ends up being the last one to leave. It doesn't bother Hermie because at least he has some companionship for a few more hours.

One day the four good friends go to the mall in San Antonio just for a change of pace. They are hanging out, looking at the girls that walk by, and they visit the electronic stores as well as the arcade. They finally pass by a large department store and happen to see a large Jacuzzi in the Home and Garden section. This catches everybody's eyes.

Everybody gathers around it, dip their hands into the warm water, and begin imagining having one of these in their backyard. The first thing that comes to mind is wet and wild parties with lots of girls. All their heads begin to spin.

Hermie really likes the large model and says, "I would love to buy this right now! That would be so awesome. We could have chicks over every night!"

Hank replies, "Sure and I bet your wallet is full of money too!" The others laugh, knowing that Hermie can't afford that as a high school student with a part-time job.

Charlie says, "You get that tub, then we gotta change it to 'The 5 Bs': Bowling, Babes, Booze, Beef and Bubbles! That's got a nice ring to it."

Hermie knows that he could buy it right now, if he really wanted to, but he cannot give away his secret. He makes up a story that he will tell his dad about it and will see if it's cool with him. The boys are on pins and needles, hoping that Hermie's father will let him buy the tub, because they will soon be on their way to a wet and crazy summer.

Two weeks later, the second Saturday in June, Hermie and his buddies find themselves bowling in a tournament at their local bowling alley. They guess there won't be very many entries, because it's a small town and not many bowlers from the big cities drive all the way to an old center that produces very low scores.

They enter the building and look around. They are correct; only 25 bowlers showed up. Scott isn't bowling due to being with his family this weekend. Hermie, Hank, and Charlie pay their entry fee, get their lane assignments, and begin changing their shoes.

The practice lights come on and Charlie is striking with everything he throws. Hermie puts his usual signature on practice and does everything wrong. His timing is poor and his speed control stinks. Hank is busy fishing all over the lane but is throwing the ball very well. He is playing the lane incorrectly, but makes some adjustments.

Hermie looks for his new buddy, Sam, and sees him in the distance. The lanes in this alley are very dry on the outside area and could pose problems for Sam because he throws the ball from outside part of the lane. Hermie is curious.

Practice is over and the competition begins. Charlie and Hermie start off striking the first five frames and dot their games with a few spares after that. Charlie finishes with a 221 and Hermie shoots a 217. Hank gets a late rally and finishes with a 210 game. Everybody changes lanes and begins the second game.

Charlie runs into trouble early in the game, but rallies back with a strong finish and a respectable 200 in this tough bowling center. Hermie shoots a 211 after a split in the 10th frame, while Hank finds a good line and shoots 220. The boys are feeling pretty good about the lanes and about their scores. They have no idea who is leading.

In game three, Charlie decides to change equipment after that near disastrous game and finds a good line to shoot a 231 game for a 650 series. He knows he made the cut. Hank gets close to his target score and shoots a 208 for a 638 series. He thinks he barely made the cut. Hermie loses his good line and began shooting lots of spares and ends up with a 197 and a 625 series. He is sweating bullets and thinks the last game messed up his chances to advance. He is just shaking his head thinking it's over.

Hermie sees Sam and figures he made the cut because he is still hanging around. He also sees Lou, who is the nephew of the bowling coach. Hermie cannot stand Lou because he didn't have to qualify for last year's team' even though he is a nice guy and a good bowler. He is not really mad at Lou, he is just angry at the situation and the coach.

The results are in and Lou is the leader with a 655, Charlie is in second with a 650, Sam is third with a 646, while Hank is in fifth place with a 638. They announce the eighth spot and the cut is Hermie with a 625. Hermie breathes a huge sigh of relief.

Hermie was expecting better scores from himself because he just won a tournament last month and is still riding high with emotions and confidence. But he made it to the finals and that's fine with him. Besides, all the pin fall totals are erased for the finals. Everybody starts with zero and is paired up in a bracket format.

The bracket finals are one-game matches, and they begin. In the top half of the bracket, the #1 seed Lou will face the #8 seed Hermie. The #3 seed Sam will face the #6 seed Wally, who is Lou's teammate. In the bottom half of the bracket, the #2 seed Charlie will face the #7 seed, who is on the Antler High school team. Finally, the #4 seed, who is a female bowler from Austin, will face the #5 seed Hank.

In the first match, Lou and Hermie start off even. Lou is throwing the ball well but is having lousy pin carry. Hermie is getting more strikes than Lou, but got a split early in the game to keep Lou in the match. Every time Hermie watches Lou throw the ball, he thinks that he should be on the school team, instead of Lou. Right now, he is not impressed with Lou's skills, but somehow Lou seems to get the job done.

In the end, Lou gets a few spares for a 209 and opens the door for Hermie. Hermie gets a 9-spare-strike to win 214–209. Hermie knows that he is just as good as Lou but isn't on the school's team. Lou congratulates Hermie and leaves quietly.

In the second match, Sam pounces all over Wally, Lou's teammate, with a 224–179 victory. Sam started off hot with five strikes in a row, then settled for a few spares, while his opponent never got on track. Perhaps Sam's loud and flamboyant antics intimidated Wally into throwing bad shots. Sam will face Hermie in the second round.

In the third match Hank takes on the female bowler from Austin. Both kids are not striking very much, and shooting spares is an adventure. By the look on their faces, both want this match to be over. The match is close until she opens in the 9th and 10th frames to give Hank the lead. Hank spares in the 10th frame and wins the match 188–180.

In the fourth match, Charlie is challenging the guy from Antler High. Charlie is packing every shot and striking a lot. Meanwhile, his opponent gets nervous and has difficulty releasing the ball. He struggles the last four frames and shoots a disappointing 188. Charlie marks the 10th frame and wins with a 220.

Charlie goes to the scoreboard to see his next opponent. He is bummed out because he faces Hank in the second round. They both look at each other and say, "Wow." Hermie looks at the board; he will face Sam, as he already knew. He is excited and nervous at the same time because he beat Sam last month. Maybe he can do it again.

Sam starts off striking and clapping loudly while Hermie makes a few spares. In the middle of the game, Hermie begins to strike and notices Sam is getting quiet as he shoots more spares. In the 9th frame, Sam throws a split; he ends up losing 226–214. Once again Sam is really frustrated and leaves the building without saying a word. Hermie is going to the finals, and unfortunately he has to face one of his good friends.

In the buddy match, Charlie and Hank really do not want to beat out the other person and casually bowl the match. In the end, Charlie edges out Hank 190–188; neither of them really cared who won. Now Charlie will face Hermie in the finals.

Charlie knows that he is throwing the ball well, but he also knows that Hermie is riding high with emotions because of his first win just last month. Charlie is not looking forward to this match and wishes he was facing somebody else, even Sam.

Charlie shakes Hermie's hand and tells him, "Well, buddy, it's just the two of us. Let's just keep it casual, unless you're out to whip me."

Hermie replies, "Yeah, we can keep it casual and see what happens."

The final match begins and each bowler starts off with five strikes. Hermie is throwing the ball near the gutter and watching it hook back at the last second. Charlie is doing what he does best: throwing the ball down the center with lots of speed. Both guys are trying to keep it casual by talking and cracking jokes, but Hermie senses that Charlie is really trying to win it. That's fine by Hermie because he won last month.

The game is practically neck and neck. Hermie leaves single-pin spares in the 6th and 7th frames, while Charlie throws two bad shots in a row to fall behind. Hermie strikes in the 8th and 9th frames while Charlie gets a spare in the 8th frame and a strike in the 9th frame. Both boys look at the scoreboard and Hermie is up by 13 pins. They are not talking very much now. Hermie is semi-cool but Charlie is really pacing the floor.

Hermie is up first in the 10th frame. He knows if he strikes out he wins it all. He throws his first shot a little fast, the ball skids a bit further down the lane but hooks back to the pins and leaves a "pocket 7–10" split. He falls to his knees and sits down on the approach staring at the pins in disbelief. His quest for a second tournament win is basically over. He gets one pin and ends up with a 234. He slowly walks back and sits down, not even looking at Charlie. Hermie is in shock and looks like he is going to cry.

Charlie looks at the scoreboard and realizes he needs the first strike and seven pins to win it all. He takes a deep breath and throws his first shot very well. The ball hits flat and leaves a solid 10 pin. Charlie falls to his knees as if he was in great pain and screams "No!" very loudly. Hermie falls out of his seat because he cannot believe he just won his second tournament in five weeks. Charlie makes the spare and strikes, only to lose 234–232.

Charlie hangs his head down as if all the wind was knocked out of him. He threw the ball great all day long and even started thinking about winning the tournament after making the first cut. He felt it was his day. He felt it was his time.

Charlie approaches Hank and says, "Geez, everything was going great for me, then along came Hermie and he started winning matches and I knew I was doomed. Why me? Why did I have to face the hottest bowler in the area, and he's my buddy?"

Hank tells him, "Both of you threw the ball great. But in this center, it's a matter of carrying the pins. Throwing the ball good here doesn't guarantee a strike; look what Hermie left. You did the best you could and you were that close. You can do it again."

Charlie is happy for Hermie, but was hoping that he would have won instead. Charlie shakes Hermie's hand and tells him, "You threw the ball better than me, but I thought that 7–10 ended it for you. Then I got bit by that stupid 10 pin. Wow."

Hermie says, "My 10th-frame ball really sucked and it didn't surprise me that I left a split here in this dump. I didn't know the match was that close and I thought you won, even with your stone 10. It's been a crazy day."

Hermie still cannot believe he won but wants to celebrate. Hermie invites his friends to the arcade and says it's his treat, which raises some eyebrows. The boys are surprised because Hermie usually does not treat a whole group of people.

At the arcade, the gang decides to have a couple of pizzas and play some video games. They walk inside, find a table in the back, and order their food and drinks. Hermie gets a few rolls of quarters and puts them on the table.

Scott asks Hermie, "Where did you get all this money, did you break your piggy bank or what?" as the crowd starts to laugh.

Before Hermie can answer, Hank interrupts and says, "No, he sold his bike; second thought, after seeing its condition, Hermie paid somebody to take it!" and the laughing continues. Hermie is just shaking his head, barely smiling but knowing it is a little funny.

Hermie gently retaliates, "My parents give me an allowance plus I have a job, so there. What do you gotta say about that?"

He hands each boy a roll of quarters and shouts out, "Who is ready to lose first? Pick any video game?" Nobody raises a hand and Hermie says, "Chickens, pawk, pawk!"

They play video games and eat for the rest of the night. Charlie eventually forgets about the tournament because he knows he did his best and the match could have gone either way. Now he knows that he can throw strikes with the rest of them. Charlie has a good physical game and his attitude is great, but sometimes he has a problem with confidence. Today was a huge step in building on that confidence. He looks forward for the next tournament.

After the arcade mania, everybody goes their separate ways. Hermie goes home feeling great. He wishes he could call Jane, but she can't receive phone calls yet.

At home, Hermie decides to go upstairs and have a nice hot bath. He pours a tall glass of lemonade. He brings his portable stereo into the bathroom and turns up the music. He soaks and sips until the wee hours of the night, then gets out and goes to bed, thinking of everything he won during his summer slam.

Chapter 7

Rate the Date

The following Tuesday, Hermie arrives home from working at the store and gets a phone call. It's Jane and she invites him and his buddies to her birthday party this Saturday at 7 o'clock at her house. She is turning 16 and tells Hermie that she will finally be able to officially date him. Both kids are excited and cannot wait for their first date.

That Thursday, the boys play a brisk game of basketball at the courts at the junior high school. After the game, Hermie says, "I got a call from Jane on Tuesday. She's inviting all of us to her house for her birthday party this Saturday. Let's check it out."

Charlie asks, "I wonder if I can bring a few friends I met during Spring Break?"

Hermie says "It don't bother me cause it ain't my party, but I think she meant to invite us only." Charlie gets the hint.

Charlie is curious and asks, "Do you think Jane would mind if I brought some juice to her party? You know, for a celebration or something."

Hermie frowns at Charlie and says, "Her parents are kinda strict, so I doubt they'll serve booze at a 16-year-old's party, but if they do, bring your stash and start pouring the junk.

Otherwise, keep cool so I don't ruin my chances with dating her." They all agree to attend the party and will meet at Hermie's house at 6:30.

On Saturday, the day of Jane's birthday party, Hermie is getting up to go to work. The morning is cool but it is quickly getting humid and muggy; typical for June.

All day long Hermie is thinking of the party and what to expect from Jane, now that she is old enough to date. He quickly starts thinking of the window visits and wonders if there will be anymore of them. All that thinking makes the day go by faster and he does not even pay attention to how much money he makes even though it was a good day financially.

He sneaks out of work at 5:45, which is about an hour early. At first he feels a little guilty because the baggers that remain are short handed and the store is packed with customers. But later, he feels better because he has been stuck working late while others left early; it's a trade-off.

He casually walks out the door and quickly hops on his bike and takes a different route away from the store, so he won't be seen by anybody. This means a longer ride home, but it's safer for him in case somebody tries to call him to come back.

He arrives at home and throws himself on the couch from exhaustion. He pulls out a huge wad of crumpled dollar bills and about two handfuls of coins and throws them on the coffee table. He turns on the TV and watches some old reruns of bowling shows as he gets comfortable. He forgets that his buddies are showing up in 20 minutes.

Eventually he goes upstairs and takes a quick shower. He gets dressed and runs downstairs just five minutes before his friends show up. He realizes he forgot to eat and hopes Jane's party has some kind of chow.

Just as he sits down, the doorbell rings. Hermie opens the door and invites Scott inside. A few minutes later, Hank and Charlie show up. Charlie smells like booze, but that's nothing new. Everybody sits down in the living room and waits until 7 o'clock, because Hermie doesn't like being the first one at a party.

Charlie asks Hermie about Jane and he tells the group, "We usually hang out in the hallways, but now we'll officially get to date and do stuff, so that's gonna be cool."

Charlie says, "Geez, the way I've seen you guys make out in the hallway, I woulda thought y'all were heavies already."

The guys leave Hermie's house and drive to Jane's house. They arrive at her house about 7:15. Hopefully Jane won't notice their tardiness. He knocks on the door and Jane's mother answers the door. Hermie introduces himself and his friends as she smiles and lets them inside.

Sybil, Jane's mother, tells Hermie, "It's so nice to finally meet you, Hermie. Jane has told us so many nice things about you and how you are helping her in Home Economics. She said you are very smart." Hermie smiles as the boys roll their eyes.

Hermie replies, "She said that about me? That's very nice of her." Hermie quickly scans the living room and thinks he sees Jane. He compliments Mrs. Leuistan on having a very nice house and thanks her for inviting him over.

Jane appears from a small crowd, and greets Hermie with a small hug and tells him he's late; his belly rumbles. Jane greets the rest of the guys. Hermie tells her that he's late because he had to work, then he had to shower and change clothes. He approaches her and says, "Happy Birthday." He gives her a rectangular gift-wrapped box.

Jane's eyes open like a child in a toy store, and an appreciative smile comes across her face. Without opening the gift, she thanks him with another small hug and looks at him with her big blue-green eyes.

As she gets closer to him, she whispers, "I have been missing your kisses, so you owe me plenty!" Hermie nods his head in agreement.

She opens the box to reveal a new ladies watch. She thanks him again as she puts it on her left wrist, not even realizing that she threw the box and wrapper onto the floor.

She takes Hermie by the hand to meet some of her friends. He has seen some of them before at school. Scott, Charlie, and Hank get the hint and do their own thing. They walk around the living room and hallway, and peep into a couple of bedrooms, but act like they didn't see anything. They eventually make their way to the kitchen.

A few minutes later Jane and Hermie go to the kitchen to get some punch and some snacks. Hermie quickly gazes in the kitchen and there is a huge assortment of food. There are finger foods, chips and dips, smoked meats, cheese, and lots of crackers. Charlie, Hank and Scott are hovering around the food, helping themselves to this delicious trough of chow in their usual hungry manner. Charlie even started making pig noises and snorted.

Just as Hermie stretches his right arm to pick up a "pig in a blanket," Jane pulls his left arm and leads him to the backyard. She tells him her father is outside and she wants Hermie to meet him. Hermie's belly rumbles again as he takes one last look at the food.

Once outside, Hermie meets Mr. Leusitan. Paul is a bit short and stout with thinning hair. He strikes Hermie as being a minister and seems like a very nice guy. Hermie shakes his hand and notices Mr. Leusitan's powerful grip and feels his own knuckle being popped. Hermie notices a grill full of decent vittles cooking up real nice.

Mr. Leuistan tells Hermie, "Don't mess with that junk food in there, have one of these instead," as he gives Hermie a double-meat hamburger.

Hermie salivates as he gets his hands on the block of meat, then takes a huge bite and lets out a light moan. Mr. Leuistan tells Hermie, "Slow down, son, there's plenty more on the grill that the good Lord has provided us."

Hermie replies, "Sorry, but I worked all day at the store and I didn't get to eat lunch because the bagger crew was understaffed.

We were running around like crazy. Then I got to the party and Jane introduced me to her friends and I still didn't eat."

Mr. Leuistan tells Hermie, "Yeah, you do look familiar. I think I have seen you at the store. That's not easy work. Please, make yourself at home and dig in. There's no reason to go round hungry."

During the party, Hermie sees more schoolmates but eventually finds his gang. He waits until Jane's mom leaves the area and tells the guys to gather around. Hermie pulls out a brochure for that Jacuzzi they saw at the store. Now they know Hermie is serious about this item. They are all very secretive, like a football huddle.

He tells them, "Check this out, I got permission to buy the tub. I'll probably order it tomorrow," and everyone's faces light up as their jaws drop.

Then Hermie adds, "By the way, I am having a party at my house on July 4th. Invite who you want and it's BYOB. I should have the tub by then, so bring your trunks and bring some chicks. It's gonna be wet and wild."

The guys are salivating as they nod their heads in acceptance with a zombie type of look in their eyes. They cannot believe the news. It's like a life-changing event. Charlie's mind is spinning and he looks like he is about to faint. During the rest of the night, they boys practically invite everybody they speak to.

Later in the evening, Hermie sees Jane outside mingling. He casually strolls by as if looking for somebody and she notices him. She grabs his arm and quickly hugs him.

They sit down in the porch and he tells her, "Hey, I'm having a party on July 4th. You should come and bring some friends. Also, bring your swimming suit."

She asks, "A party? That sounds pretty neat. I'll be there, but why do I need to bring my swimsuit? Do you have a pool?"

"Trust me," Hermie confidently replies.

Jane tells Hermie, "Ugh! I wish I could snuggle up with you and kiss, but there are too many people watching, including my parents. I just don't want my parents to think I already have a boyfriend because that could blow our chances of dating."

"Well … let's do something tomorrow, just the two of us, and we'll take care of that problem. We can go to the movies, arcade, library, whatever," says Hermie.

The party finally ends around 10 o'clock. No one realized it was that late, including Jane's parents. The party was a success and everybody had a good time.

Charlie's friends from Spring Break eventually showed up, and they got along great with Jane and her friends, even though her parents frowned. Finally, the partygoers leave and Charlie leaves with his other gang. Jane tells everybody "goodnight" while she and Hermie are both excited that they will finally get to do things together in public.

As Hermie is about to walk out the front door, he feels a strong hand on his shoulder as Mr. Leuistan tells him, "It was a pleasure meeting you, son, and I would like to speak to your parents first to make sure it's okay with them for you kids to date."

Hermie's jaw almost drops as he sees Jane behind him with an open mouth as well. Nervously, Hermie reassures him that it's not a problem. Mr. Leuistan insists on calling Hermie's parents, just because he wants to meet them first.

Hermie quickly thinks and tells him, "My father travels a lot and is hardly home. I will tell him to give you a call when he gets home next week." Mr. Leuistan nods his head in compliance. Hermie feels like he just got busted.

Jane gives Hermie a generic hug as her parents look on. She thanks him for the gift and for attending her party. She whispers that he still owes her some kisses.

Hermie leaves the Leuistan house wondering how he will ever get to have a date with Jane. Now Mr. Leuistan wants to talk to his parents. Hermie is afraid to reveal his secret to her parents because he may never see Jane again. Or should he come clean and tell them the truth? He goes home and is awake practically all night long thinking of a solution to this new dilemma. He finally falls asleep from exhaustion at 5 o'clock.

The next morning, Hermie is awakened by the telephone and it is Jane calling him. She tells him, "My parents will let us go to the arcade or the library or bowling, but that's all. They still want to talk to your parents first. And today is not good because I am busy all day. Maybe tomorrow or Tuesday we can go. Is that good?"

Hermie is half asleep and mumbles, "Yeah, that's cool." They end their conversation and Hermie quickly goes back to bed to continue his beauty sleep, barely remembering the phone call.

Hermie wakes up a couple of hours later feeling refreshed. He is shocked to see that it is now 2 o'clock. He goes downstairs and sees two messages on his answering machine. The first message is from Charlie. Charlie sounds bummed out but serious. He wants to come over and talk. The second message is from Scott. He wants to know if they are playing basketball today. He calls Charlie, but his father says he is not home. He calls Scott and tells him that they are not playing basketball today, but maybe tomorrow.

As he sits on the couch to watch TV, Hermie knows that he spoke to someone earlier this morning, but does not remember who it was. Then it hits him. It was Jane and her dad still wants to talk to his dad. Wow, what is he going to do?

Just as he settles in to watch baseball, another sport that does not interest him unless it's the playoffs, he hears a knock on the door.

Hermie opens the front door and it's Charlie. He looks a little confused and unresponsive. Charlie is also carrying what's left of a 12-pack of beer. Charlie hands Hermie a beer as he enters the house.

Charlie tells Hermie, "Sorry to walk in, but me and pops had an argument and I just walked out on him. I'm gettin pretty tired of his whining crap. It's always the same old stuff; bitchin and moanin about nothin. Wait till he sees that I took his 12-pack. He's gonna flip his lid. Forget him." Charlie slams his beer and grabs another one.

"Wow. That's crazy," Hermie replies. He hesitates then says, "Hey, listen to this. Jane's dad wants to talk to my dad before Jane and I can date."

Charlie, being confused, asks, "So, what's wrong with that?"

"My dad might be gone for another month and I can't wait that long to see Jane. He's pretty busy and I don't know when he'll call. I wanna go out with her now. What am I gonna do?" moans a concerned Hermie.

Charlie confidently says, "Give me the phone, I'll call Jane's father and act like your dad. I'm not scared, besides, he doesn't know me. He also doesn't know what your dad sounds like either. No sweat."

"Whoa," says Hermie. He loves the idea and looks for some paper to write on. He decides to write up a script, similar to a flowchart that maps out all possible outcomes of the conversation between Charlie and Jane's father. Charlie adds his own ideas.

At 4 o'clock, Charlie calls Jane's house with a deep voice and asks for Paul Leuistan. About ten seconds later, Charlie is having a conversation with Jane's dad about Hermie and Jane. Charlie is very supportive and very positive about Hermie, and is aware of all his actions. He also informs Paul that he is out of town a lot and that he can call Hermie's grandparents if there are any concerns, since they live a few blocks away.

The conversation ends with Charlie saying, "Well, it's okay with me if it's okay with you. The kids will be just fine. Have a nice day. Bye."

Charlie hangs up the phone with a huge smile on his face and gives Hermie a high-five as he grabs another beer. He excitedly tells Hermie, "Man, you can write your own ticket with that chick. That old man practically gave away his daughter. Damn, am I good or what?"

Both cannot believe what just happened. Hermie thanks Charlie for his part in this, and both agree never to tell anybody about their prank. Both boys watch TV for the rest of the afternoon. Charlie goes home around 9 o'clock feeling pretty good. Hermie is thinking of what to do first with Jane and hopes nobody finds out about the phone call.

On Monday morning, Hermie calls Jane to invite her to go bowling. She asks her parents and they quickly approve. Hermie picks her up at 11 o'clock in his car and they drive to the lanes. She is excited because she really wants to get out of the house. She is not a good bowler but likes to play anyway.

They bowl a few games and Hermie spends time teaching her the basics. They also sneak in a few hugs and kisses. She absorbs the information like a sponge and is already showing signs of improvement. After an hour of practice, they have lunch at the snack bar and talk about their pre-date date and their activities for next time.

Jane tells Hermie, "I don't know what your dad told my dad, but he was very pleased after the phone call. My dad said I could go out with you anytime I want. I guess he likes you and trusts you."

Hermie smiles, nods his head, and tells her, "That's cool. That makes one less thing to worry about. I guess we're in the clear. Where do you wanna go now?" They pack up their stuff and leave the bowling center holding hands.

They end up at the library, because Hermie is looking for a book on drilling a bowling ball. Jane thinks he is strange. After walking around for a few minutes, Hermie finds the location of the sports books but does not find the book he is looking for.

In the meantime, Jane has found a secluded corner in the remote part of the library, and she slowly corrals Hermie into that area. She corners him, puts her arms around him, and kisses him.

She exhales with excitement. The kids begin to make out but quit when a librarian walks by, giving them a dirty look just as Jane was getting into it. The kids grab their things and leave the building. Both kids feel they were cheated out of a good session.

After the library, they decide to hang out at the arcade to see who is there. Hermie plays a few games while Jane watches him, sometimes hugging on him. She sees one of her friends and starts talking to her. After an hour of playing video games and drinking soda, Hermie decides to take her home. She tells Hermie she had a great time and both start thinking about what they will do on their first real date.

He drops Jane off around 4:30 and goes home to lie on the couch. Suddenly, he feels lazy, more than he does tired. He turns on the TV and flips through channels to see what is on. He eventually falls asleep on the couch dreaming of Jane and how much fun she is to be around. She is cute and is always upbeat.

He wakes up from his nap at 6 o'clock and decides he wants to visit his grandparents. He drives his car over there and he is just in time for dinner. What impeccable timing. He has dinner with his grandparents and they chat about a few things, such as his summer plans and Jane.

His grandparents would like to have her for dinner one day so they can meet her. They think she is a nice girl from what Hermie says about her. After dinner, they watch some TV until about 9 o'clock, when grandma retires to bed. Hermie bids them good-night and drives home. He feels very tired and goes to bed quickly.

The next morning Hermie gets a call from Scott. He wants to play basketball and the other boys are ready to play. Hermie gets dressed and rides his bike to the elementary school just in time to meet with the boys. The play their usual game of two-on-two, then follow it up with some HORSE. They end up playing for almost three hours, then travel to Hermie's house to cool down and hang out.

At the house, Hermie sees one message on his answering machine. Jane called wanting to know if he thought any more about their date and when it will occur. While the rest of the guys are in the kitchen, Hermie calls her back and tells her that the following weekend would be great, since this week is half over already. She agrees to the following weekend upon her parents' approval. Hermie tells her he already thought of some things to do and will give her a choice of what she wants to do.

The rest of the week is about the same as usual. Hermie and his gang practice bowling on Thursday, play Basketball on Friday. Hermie and Jane call each other about every day and sometimes twice a day.

Saturday finally arrives—the day of Hermie's big date with Jane. He works only a half day at the store so he has time to prepare for the evening. He is nervous and excited at the same time. He is rehearsing what he will tell Jane's parents about where they are going and having her home by 10 o'clock.

He gets out of the shower and starts getting dressed. He bought some new clothes and shoes for this big event. As he walks out the front door, he sprays some cologne on himself and gets into his car.

He arrives at her house at 4:45 and rings the doorbell. Jane answers the door with a happy face and her big blue-green eyes wide open. She is dressed up too.

Just then her mother approaches and greets Hermie. She is also dressed up. They invite him inside and he sits on the couch. A short while later Mr. Leuistan comes into the living room and greets Hermie. He is wearing a coat and tie. Now Hermie is confused and thinks that Jane's parents are also going out.

A few minutes later, Hermie gets up from the couch and says, "Well, I guess it's time to go," as he walks toward Jane and motions her to get up.

Jane stands up and her parents suddenly stand up too. As the kids make their way to the front door, Hermie notices that her parents are following them. Hermie is not sure what is happening but is already starting to fear the worst.

Just then Mr. Leuistan says, "Yes, it is time to go. I know this great restaurant we can all go to. They have a huge selection and the food is heavenly; no pun intended."

Jane and Hermie stop in their tracks and look at each other as if they had seen a ghost. They can't believe what they just heard. Jane's mouth is wide open. Her parents are tagging along. Now what are they going to do?

Just to be cool and get the real story, Hermie asks, "Does that mean the both of you will be joining us tonight?"

Mr. Leuistan replies a bright and cheerful, "It sure does. You don't think that I'm going to let you kids go out alone into that crazy world without any supervision, do you? Well, Sybil and I will be with you all night to provide just that."

Now Hermie knows that he and Jane will be chaperoned by her parents all night. What a dirty trick. As the foursome walks out the door, Hermie acts as if somebody knocked the wind out of him. He is starting to develop an "I don't care" attitude.

They get in the family car and drive 15 minutes to the small nearby town of Antler. They find a quaint and hidden Mexican restaurant called "Manos Pintos" (Painted Hands). They get a table and sit down. Hermie and Jane are seated across from each other and look at each other with controlled but cautious expressions the entire time. Both are quiet and stunned.

Suddenly, Hermie is not very hungry and cannot believe how her parents deceived him and Jane. He continually shakes his head in disbelief and pretends to have a good time conversing with her parents. He hardly gets to talk to Jane. Although Hermie doesn't know it, Jane's parents are watching both teens very closely.

A waiter comes by and takes their orders. Mr. Leuistan does his best to speak Spanish to impress his family but he doesn't have a clue about the accent. He orders for himself and Sybil and completely hacks the Spanish pronunciation of the menu items. He also orders Jane some tacos, much to her surprise. He asks Hermie if he is ready to order and Hermie orders something simple; tamales. He figures they are pretty harmless and will rate the restaurant on this plate alone.

About 20 minutes later, dinner is served. Jane's parents got the enchilada plates and Jane got her taco plate. She is disgusted that her dish was prepared in a very sloppy manner with refried beans splattered all over the place; including on her tacos. She just picks through the tacos to get to the meat. She looks disappointed.

Hermie gets his food and is not too crazy about his cold and soggy tamales. It looks like everybody else is enjoying their meal except him and Jane. He wonders what Jane's father likes about this place. Hermie has never seen this place and now he knows why. He only eats his rice because that's the only item that looks edible; besides the tortilla chips.

After dinner, the groggy foursome slowly waddles back inside the small family car and drive. Hermie notices that they are not going back to Pibb just yet, but are staying in Antler for a little bit longer. Hermie wonders what is next on Mr. Leusitan's agenda.

Hermie asks, "Where are we going?"

Mr. Leuistan answers, "It's a surprise, but I guarantee you will love it," as he shows off a large grin.

Hermie looks down and shakes his head in defeat. He quietly laughs as if going crazy, telling himself, "I can't win. I just can't win." Jane puts her arm around Hermie to console him. She has an idea of where they are going but isn't sure.

A few minutes later they arrive at a small Baptist church with a very full parking lot. Hermie knows his night is shot and that he is doomed. Mr. Leusitan runs toward the building like a child in a toy store and practically knocks down the front door.

They enter the church and they are just in time for a Saturday night worship services. Hermie and Jane walk very slowly into this building, as if they had broken legs.

"What a stroke of luck!! There are some seats left," says an excited Mr. Leuistan as he finds a pew of seats near the back and leads the group toward them.

Hermie looks at Jane as if he were about to jump off a cliff. She has an "I can't believe this is happening" type of smile as she shrugs her shoulders and raises her hands, palms up, with a dumbfounded look on her face. She comes up to him and whispers, "I am so sorry," as she sneaks in a kiss. Everybody sits down.

After 90 minutes of sermons, singing, prayer and happiness, Hermie can't take it anymore. He is about to pop a cork and walk out. Just as he stands up, the mass and celebration is over. Hermie and Jane are both relieved. Hermie looks as tired as if he just ran a marathon.

Hermie and the Leuistan family get into their family car and drive home. This time Hermie does not ask where they are going. He already learned his lesson. He decides to keep his mouth shut while Mr. and Mrs. Leuistan discuss the evening's festivities. He listens to Jane's parents talk like excited children.

Hermie looks out of the window and is a bit upset about tonight, but not at Jane. It's not her fault, she didn't know either. He shakes his head over the whole situation and cannot believe the string of bad luck tonight. The whole night was a complete waste of time. He could have been at home doing nothing; that would have been better.

Just then he feels a warm head press against his shoulder. Jane softly tells him, "I feel really bad about tonight. I will make it up to you somehow," and she reaches over and kisses his neck and then his cheek. That makes him feel better. She doesn't care if her parents saw that or not. She is a little perturbed too.

They finally arrive at the Leuistan house about 10 o'clock and Jane's parents invite Hermie inside. Hermie is not sure what to expect if he steps inside the house. Maybe it will be another hour of religious chanting and raving. Maybe he will get to watch church on TV. Either way, he is expecting to get another unannounced treat.

Mr. Leuistan tells Hermie, "I hope you had a great time. We enjoyed having your company and we would love to have you again. If I sounded like I was pushing the church on you, that's because it's my job. Nowadays, kids need a direction in life and the church helps provide that vehicle. I'm sure your father would understand."

Hermie is polite and replies, "Yes he would. I had a good time tonight, and Jane is fortunate to have parents that care for her this much. I am pretty sure you will see me again. Good night everybody."

Hermie gets up to leave for the night because it's getting late. He shakes Paul's strong hand and bids Jane's parents goodnight. Hermie walks out through the front door.

Jane gets up to walk Hermie to his car. As the kids walk toward Hermie's car, Jane tells him with a chuckle, Oh my gosh! I had no idea all this was going to happen."

"Hey; that ain't funny. Your parents pulled a fast one on us. I was getting so torqued, I was about to kick something. Geez," Hermie replies.

"I can't believe they made you go to church with all of us. I am so embarrassed and I hope you're not mad at me," says a giggling Jane.

"I'm not mad at you," Hermie responds. "It wasn't your fault. We were like mushrooms, sitting in the dark. I just hope our next date isn't this way. What a dirty trick they played on us to tag along. I know they had this planned. What's so funny?"

"The look on your face every time we went to a different place. You had your pouting face on and it was cute. You had it at the restaurant and at the church. Was it that bad?" Jane asks.

He pauses for a moment then adds, "Yeah it was. Tonight started sucking ever since they joined us. Then it went super suck when I had them stupid rubber tamales. Then it went total blow when your father started shoving church down my throat. That's how bad it was." Hermie is starting to fume up.

Jane reassures him by saying, "I will make it up to you, and I promise that my parents will not be with us on our next date. My father really likes you; otherwise he would have treated you like dirt and asked you a million questions. He probably wants to be sure that his daughter goes out with only the best guys. And you technically are my first real date. He just wanted to be sure." Hermie rolls his eyes.

When they get to Hermie's car, Jane gives Hermie a small hug. She looks back to the house and doesn't see any sign of her parents, so she gives Hermie a goodnight kiss. She knows she wants more but is afraid that her parents might pop out at anytime. She does not care and just goes for it anyway. Her eyes light up after they make out.

They tell each other goodnight, and Hermie gets into his car and drives home. He cannot believe how he was deceived. Plus he thinks Jane's father became a jerk when he began to shove religion down his throat. He does not need that kind of preaching.

He arrives at home and goes up to his bedroom. He goes to bed replaying all the events that happened that night. He thinks about the botched date that he and Jane had with her parents. Then he thinks about the 90 minutes of singing and praying and being happy at the church. His blood is starting to boil again.

He closes his eyes and thinks about his next date with Jane, but without her parents. Then to really cool off, he begins to think about his bowling and how good he is throwing the ball on some days. He makes a mental picture of his delivery. He turns on the TV with low volume and slowly falls asleep.

Chapter 8

Wet Days and Buzzed Nights

The next day around noon, Hermie is sitting in his living room with his lunch and watching a classic movie channel. Just before he crunches on a big handful of pork rinds, the phone rings. He answers the phone and it is Jane.

Jane says, "Hi Hermie, I am really sorry about last night. I had no idea that my parents were coming with us and that they were going to take us to those places and preach to us. I understand if you're mad at me."

Hermie replies, "I'm not mad at you. I'm kinda mad at them. You didn't know either. I was kinda surprised when your parents tagged along and took us to all those places, but I didn't like your dad shoving religion in my face. He might be right, but it doesn't mean he has to rub my nose in it. That's where he started to bother me."

Jane, defending her father, says, "Yeah, it is uncool the way he does that, but he does that to all of my friends; especially all the boys I know. I've heard that speech a million times and you're the first guy he's said that to on a date because you were my first date ever. It's like a test. He wants to see how people react and I guess you did well because he didn't preach anymore and he didn't say anything to me after you left."

Hermie is not impressed and replies, "Whoopee, I passed. So what do I get; a free bible?"

Jane is trying not to laugh and tells him, "Well, we can still date. My father is very religious and he thinks everybody should be the same way too. I'm his daughter and I'm not like him. I don't like going to church all the time and sometimes the lectures are sooooo boring. But what can I do? Don't worry about that speech. You're okay with him, otherwise he would have said something to us or he would not let us date anymore. We're in the clear."

Jane senses that Hermie is about to lose his cool because it is very silent on his side, so she says, "On our next date I will make it up to you. I promise that my parents will not be there."

"Okay," says a bored Hermie.

Jane adds, "If it makes you feel better, my father really likes you and thinks you are very smart. Don't tell anybody this but I think he is a little scared of you because you know a lot about a lot of things. I think he is intimidated by you. But he does like you."

"Wow, that's pretty deep. I don't think I'm that smart. I guess that's kinda cool," says Hermie.

"Of course you're smart. You know how to do lots of things like fix your car, wash clothes, sweep and mop and you can cook. You see? You are smart; even though my dad says you need a haircut," Jane responds.

Hermie is flattered but hopes that she keeps her promise by keeping her parents at home. They have a few laughs about how disastrous and crazy their date was. Hermie mentions that he could not handle another night like that one.

Before the conversation ends, Hermie tells her, "Check this out, I got permission to buy a Jacuzzi, so I might do it this week. Maybe I can get it set up on Saturday. I will call you to come over so we can test it."

"A Jacuzzi? Are you serious? Isn't that like a pool?" an excited Jane asks.

"Yup; but it's smaller and the water gets hot," Hermie answers. "If all goes well I'm gonna have a July 4th party with this new tub. You need to come to the party and bring all your friends."

"Okay. I will start asking around," Jane is very excited and promises to show up for the party. She says she will start inviting friends to attend.

That Wednesday Hermie goes to his grandparents' house. He tells them that today he wants to buy that Jacuzzi he has been thinking about. His grandparents do not have a problem with Hermie's desire to purchase this large item, they just want to be sure he does not start a spending spree with high-dollar merchandise.

Grandpa gets Hermie's checkbook from a secret hiding place and hands it to him. They all get in grandpa's car and drive to the big city of Austin. Hermie can barely contain himself. His mind is racing and his heart is pumping.

They arrive at the store about an hour later and Hermie is ready to run to the Pool and Spa department. His grandfather reminds him to look interested but not desperate. This could land them a better deal such as a lower price or more freebies. Hermie is so excited, and his grandmother reminds him that this item is a major purchase and will require lots of maintenance and lots of responsibility. The only thing on Hermie's mind is how crazy his July 4th party is going to be with this thing.

The salesman arrives and shows them a few models. Hermie already knows which one he wants but plays the game even though the suspense is killing him. Hermie has thought of a few questions and asks the salesman, who is impressed by Hermie's interest and knowledge. In the end, they locate the model that Hermie loves. It is a large "eight-seater" with dual motors, oxygen infuser, lights, a wooden gazebo, and the color is a nice sky blue.

Grandpa senses Hermie's hyperactive behavior and asks the salesman a few questions to slow Hermie down. He tells the salesman they will buy one today if they can get a good deal on it. The salesman reduces the price by $400 and throws in a cover and an extra filter. Grandpa shakes hands with the salesman and says, "We've got a deal."

They travel to the checkout counter and the salesman starts the purchase. The Jacuzzi, gazebo, chemicals, cover, water toys, tax, and twenty-year warranty come up to a little over $3,200. Hermie is almost shaking. He forgot about the tax and warranty. He pulls out the checkbook and slowly writes the correct amount. He hands it over to the salesman, who checks his grandparents' ID cards to help validate the signature. The salesman calls a manager to validate the check and the manager approves it. Hermie hears the register say "cha-ching" and knows the sale is complete. The tub is now his!

The salesman gets Hermie's address and says the Jacuzzi will be delivered to his house on Saturday, possibly before noon. Hermie is excited and cannot wait. The salesman recommends hiring an electrician to connect the electrical wires that will power the tub. Hermie's grandfather will contact an electrician when they get home. Everybody leaves the store happy, but Hermie is wearing the biggest smile.

When they get back to grandpa's house, Hermie goes to the living room and begins reading the owner's manual. He looks over the Care Kit that came with the tub and reads about all of the chemicals and how to test and maintain the water. He spends the afternoon there and tells his grandparents everything he read from the owner's manual. His grandfather contacts an electrician, who will arrive Saturday around noon.

During the week, Hermie hangs out with his buddies and they play basketball and end up at Hermie's house. They still practice bowling one day out of the week, even though their league has already finished up. He believes it is good off-season practice and tells everybody that he plans on shooting in tournaments this summer and wants to keep his form. Scott is the only one that takes Hermie seriously.

Hermie is anxious about the hot tub and wants to share the news, but chooses not to. The subject of the tub finally pops up and Hermie spills the beans. He tells the boys he got permission to buy the tub. In fact, he tells them he already bought it and it will be delivered on Saturday. Everybody drops their jaws and can't wait until the big day.

After a long and emotionally draining week, Saturday finally arrives and Hermie gets a call from the delivery crew. They wake him up at 9 o'clock and will arrive sometime before noon. Hermie is so excited that he forgets how tired he is and starts getting ready. He also calls grandpa to tell him the good news. Grandpa is on his way.

The delivery crew arrives at noon and places the tub in a section of the backyard that Hermie and his grandfather have already marked. While the crew is leveling the tub, the electrician shows up and grandpa is right behind him. Everybody is working, and Hermie is watching it all.

An hour later the delivery crew leaves and Hermie begins to fill up the tub with water. He starts to add the chemicals to the water as the electrician finishes up the job. Grandpa pays the electrician and then Hermie starts the motors and heater to make sure the electrical connection is working properly. Hermie spends the next two hours watching the tub fill with water and notices there are about a dozen bees circling the hot tub area.

Around 4 o'clock, Hermie cannot take it anymore and calls Jane and his buddies to come over and to bring their swimming suits. Charlie, Hank, and Scott know exactly what Hermie is talking about and tell him they will be there in a few minutes. Jane will have her mother drop her off if she is able to make it.

In less than 15 minutes, all of boys arrive, run to the back yard and look at the new playtoy. Everybody is in love with Hermie's new tub and Charlie is already envisioning the upcoming July 4th party next week. He gets up and grabs a round of beers from the ice chest that he brought with him.

Charlie says, "Dude, this is a major score and I'm thinkin' about that party so much, I can't even see straight. Here's to a killer time."

Scott says, "I still can't believe you got this. This is so cool."

Charlie runs inside the house and comes out with five shots of rum, with Jane right behind him. Jane greets Hermie with a kiss as the group toasts another good time.

The kids soak and talk and have a few drinks. Jane has only one beer, while the guys have a few more. Charlie and Hermie have about three shots of rum and are feeling real good. Hermie stops after a while, but Charlie has a couple more before the night is done.

At 9 o'clock, Jane's mother picks her up. Hermie and his troops stay in the tub for another hour and eventually go home. At the end of the night, Hermie puts the cover on the tub, sits in a lawn chair, and just looks at it. He can't believe he has a hot tub.

The following week starts off with basketball practice and a couple of phone calls to Jane. Everybody is talking about the upcoming July 4th party and the hot tub and how crazy it's going to be.

On Wednesday morning, Jane is bored and brings Angie, Suzi, and Belinda to the basketball court to watch the boys play. All of the guys are hamming it up, including Hermie. They play and talk for about two hours then quit. The girls even shoot some baskets.

Around 1 o'clock the gang ends up at Hermie's house and everybody happened to bring their swimwear, including Jane and her friends. They all jump in. Charlie sees some extra wine coolers in the fridge and hands them out to the "tubbers." Jane sits next to Hermie, while the rest of the girls sit across from the guys.

After a couple of drinks, everybody is mingling, especially Hank and Charlie. Jane reaches over and kisses Hermie a few times. Everybody says, "Woooooooooo … get a room!" as both kids looked surprised as if they got caught.

Hermie and Jane go inside the house to make some snacks. He finds some finger foods in the freezer and puts them in the oven. Just as quickly, Jane puts her arms around him for another kiss. Jane pours two shots of whiskey and gives Hermie one. She tells Hermie that this is the only one she will have today. They make a toast and slam their juice.

She tells him, "I can't wait for the party this weekend. We are going to have a blast. I still can't believe you got a hot tub. It makes your yard look more fun."

"That's true. I can't believe how big this thing is. It's massive," says Hermie.

The kids eat, drink, and soak until 5 o'clock, when Jane has to leave. She tells everybody she will see them on Saturday. Jane and the girls leave.

The guys run out of booze and Charlie is in the mood to party but is too young to buy alcohol. Hermie tells him to mellow out and save that festive mood for Saturday.

Hermie reminds him, "On Saturday, bring plenty of booze. And whatever we don't drink we can save for days like this." Charlie promises to help stock up Hermie's house with liquor. Scott and Hank also agree to pitch in.

Saturday finally arrives and Hermie goes in to work early. The store does not open until 8, but he is there at 7:30 because he was awake nearly all night. The only thing on his mind is the party.

Even though Hermie wasn't scheduled to work today, he chose to show up so he would not go stir crazy sitting at home waiting for the party to start. He plans to work until about 1 o'clock so he can have time to take a shower and a nap. All morning he wonders how crazy this party will be, if anybody shows up. Soon, the day begins and it looks like another busy one.

At 1 o'clock he sneaks out of the store and pedals his bike fast to get away from the mania. He keeps looking back, hoping that nobody sees him escape. He makes it home and dives onto the couch for a nap, not even paying attention to the answering machine. He takes out the cash from his pockets, throws it on the table, and falls asleep within minutes.

At 2:30 there is a loud pounding on the door that is strong enough to make your heart skip a beat. Hermie wakes up and opens the door. It's Charlie, Hank and Scott. They are loaded with meat for the grill and a variety of beer and liquor. Hermie is so groggy that he forgot he gave them some money last week to go shopping. He helps them unload the car and has no idea how they bought the alcohol. Charlie starts the party by passing out a beer for everybody.

At 3:15, Jane and three of her friends arrive and make a bee-line to the backyard. Hermie and his bowling buddies are hanging out, watching TV on the back patio, and talking about "The 5 Bs," as usual. The girls get a drink and jump in the tub. An hour later, Hermie fires up the grill and begins cooking some chow for the soon-to-be-hungry guests.

Between 4 and 6 o'clock is when most of the people trickle in. Some people look familiar. Some of Charlie's biker buddies show up and they look pretty rough. Hermie sees some of Jane's friends, and their friends show up and they look really nice. By 6:30, there are about 25 people, which is the party's maximum count.

The partygoers are having a great time and they eventually get the munchies. Hermie's cooking is barely keeping up with the demand. It seems that as soon as he finishes cooking something and puts it on the tray, some grubby hands swipe it. It's a good thing he was nibbling while he was cooking or else he would have starved.

Jane hops out of the tub and hugs Hermie from behind. As he turns his head she gives him a kiss. She tells him that she and her friends are having a great time. She says that Scott and Suzi are talking. Charlie is chatting between Angie and Belinda, while Hank is playing the field and talking to any girls that will listen to him. A few already know him as the football player and stick around.

Just as soon as Hermie finishes cooking and closes the grill, Jane drags him inside. There are some people playing quarters on the kitchen table, and others are hanging out by the kitchen counter, drinking shots of whatever they can find.

She and Hermie join a small foursome drinking whiskey shots. They pound their shooter and Hermie begins to have memories of that interesting night several weeks ago when Jane made him drink that nasty jet fuel. Now he is getting a good buzz, but Jane looks like she is already there. After their next drink they go outside to watch some of the firebugs light up some Roman candles and other pyromaniac goodies.

By 10 o'clock, the party has thinned out to about a dozen people. Charlie and his biker gang take off. Belinda and Angie tag along. Before Charlie leaves, he asks Hermie if he can spend the night, just in case. Hermie tells the partygoers that he would prefer them to spend the night instead of driving. Hank drives a couple of girls home then drives himself home. Some of the unknown faces leave the party a few minutes later.

Jane finds Hermie in the kitchen and tells him, "Wow, you have a great big house! How come you never gave me a tour?"

Hermie replies, "I don't know. I guess I never thought about it. Wanna check it out now? It's no biggie."

Jane is excited as she grabs his arm and tells him, "Okay, let's go!"

The two kids stumble to different rooms on the lower level, giggling on the way, then they walk upstairs for the final few rooms. They are both drunk and struggle to stand up straight. Hermie shows her the extra bedroom, his father's office, and his parents' bedroom, all in pristine condition. Jane is amazed on how clean the rooms are. He tells her the rooms are very clean because his parents are out of town a lot.

The final stop of the house tour is Hermie's room. Overall it's pretty clean too, but messy compared to the other rooms. Jane notices the computers on his desk and the computer parts on the carpet next to the desk. She also sees a pile of clean clothes on top of his dresser that he has not been put away just yet. She even notices a couple of bowling balls against the far wall.

Jane stops the tour in his bedroom and slowly pushes Hermie onto the bed. She kisses him once then kisses him again. They begin to make out as she smoothly takes off his clothes. Hermie is too caught up in the moment to notice what is going on. There is heavy breathing and much kissing and moving going on. Jane seems very excited and Hermie is not able to keep up. Jane locks the door, dims the lights, and both kids roll under the covers for the rest of the night, not even worried about the party downstairs.

The following morning Hermie wakes up with only his shorts on and Jane is in the bed next to him. His wall clock shows 9:15. He gets dressed and walks downstairs. He sees Scott on the couch cuddled with Suzi. Now he believes Scott when he says that a few drinks loosen him up and help him talk to girls. He must have said some nice words.

He sees Charlie asleep on the carpet with a few other unknown people near him, including Belinda, who is in his arms. There are a few glass bottles and beer cans lying around, and the TV is still on. He walks around the unconscious party animals and makes it to the kitchen. To his surprise it is rather clean, except the sink full of dirty dishes.

He goes to the backyard and it's in good shape except for a few plastic cups. He is surprised that the tub is also clean. He walks to the rear of the backyard and notices several shards of paper and wooden sticks from the fireworks. He does not see any fires or burned areas. He is impressed that the drunken party animals were also responsible and considerate of his property. He walks back inside knowing it was a great party.

Once inside, his belly rumbles, which is nothing new. He opens the fridge and finds some eggs, sausage, onions, and bell pepper. He takes out a skillet and a cutting board and starts cutting everything into small pieces, then throwing it into the warm skillet and hearing it sizzle. It creates a really tasty aroma.

Scott immediately smells the food cooking, wakes up, and joins Hermie in the kitchen. He is now cutting while Hermie cooks. A short while later Suzi comes in with her messy hair and a blanket wrapped around her. She can't stop looking at Scott.

Eventually Jane joins the crowd, just in time to eat. She gets the plates out of the cabinet and the silverware from the drawers. Everybody serves themselves and compliments Hermie on his cooking as they make quick work of the chow.

After breakfast, the crew helps clean up the rest of the house. A few people grab garbage bags and clean up the fireworks shrapnel in the backyard. Hermie is testing the pH of the water and cleaning the filter. Suzi, Jane, and Belinda are washing dishes, cleaning the counters, and mopping the floor.

At noon, the partygoers begin to disassemble. They thank Hermie for a great party and convince him to do it next year. They offer to bring the food and drinks, and they might even cook too. All Hermie has to do is provide the house. He agrees and promises that next year will be bigger. As they leave, Jane gives Hermie a big hug and a kiss and says she will talk to him later. He closes the door behind his last friend and watches them leave. He goes back to bed and sleeps a few more hours.

During the rest of the summer, Hermie and his friends play basketball two to three times per week and bowl once or twice a week. They play basketball early in the morning due to the heat. And they practice bowling because they are motivated to make the bowling team this coming school year. They tried to play tennis once, but it became a circus so they quit.

Once in a while Jane and her friends visit the boys at the basketball courts or at the lanes and play also. The guys do not mind the change of pace and the company. Plus, it's also good to see a girl once in a while. And after their practices finish, everybody usually ends up at Hermie's house and relax in the warm Jacuzzi water.

Sometimes the group will "tub it" as many as three or four nights per week, and every so often, cold adult beverages happen to appear, with Charlie's persuasion. On some weekends, a few people show up unexpected and form a small party. These people usually bring lots of beverages and food for the grill. Hermie does not mind cooking or having the company. He typically hoards the unused food and drinks for the next time.

Hermie and Jane tried to date every other week. They had their second date, and this time her parents didn't tag along. They started with miniature golf then headed to the movies followed by the arcade. For Hermie, it was a bittersweet experience because the places they visited were the same places she was allowed to visit beforehand. The only difference now is they can hold hands, hug, and kiss without worrying about who is watching.

Hermie notices that Charlie has been hanging all over Belinda whenever she comes to the house. He suspects they are dating, but Charlie insists they are friends because she claims to be dating somebody else. Hermie has a hard time believing that an assertive Charlie is backing off from a girl that is spoken for. Hermie knows that the real Charlie would go after a prize, even if it means fighting for it.

Hermie also notices that Scott is also hanging around Suzi when she shows up. Scott says that he would like to date her, but her parents won't allow her to date until next year. In the meantime, Scott is very happy with seeing Suzi at the courts or wherever.

Hank dated Angie a few times, thinking there was a spark. Hank told Hermie that the spark almost caught fire until Angie mentioned she had a boyfriend from out of town that she keeps up with. Hank did not believe that story, but he backed down and never asked her out again. Hank thinks it is Angie's way of not dating anybody. Either way, Hank had a good time with her and would not mind seeing her again.

When Hermie is not playing basketball or bowling or having cold drinks in the hot tub, he is working. Somehow he has managed to work fewer and fewer hours during the summer months without being caught.

He knows he does not need the money and would rather do other things besides bagging groceries and loading them into the trunks of cars. At the very least, it's a cover-up because sometimes he spends lots of money and he doesn't want people to think his parents give him a salary instead of an allowance.

Hermie and Jane had another date during the last week in July. They started off at a barbecue place and ran out of ideas from there. Jane wanted to get in the hot tub and mess around, so Hermie went along with the idea, thinking they would have some privacy. After they got to his house, she had too many drinks and fell asleep. Now he is not sure if he wants to drink alcohol when they date, or if he should just limit her drinks.

Hermie visits his grandparents about once a week and hangs out with them for the afternoon. They give Hermie an update on the pending Acme Chemical lawsuit whenever they receive correspondence from their lawyer handling the case. All of them believe Acme has their back up against the wall, but Acme continues to find ways to stall the lawsuit and investigation. This is possible because they are a large company and have their own staff of expensive lawyers to use delay tactics in the courtroom.

Hermie does not understand the judicial system but he believes that it should not take this long to bring a guilty party to justice. He listens to his grandparents talk many times about the case and knows that Acme Chemical is guilty of what they did. Since Hermie's father, John, is not there to defend himself, Hermie's grandparents and the evidence the John left behind is all that is available to bring down Acme. Unfortunately, this process will take some time.

Hermie's grandparents ask him what he wants to do for his upcoming birthday, and Hermie just wants to spend a quiet evening with them and some friends. He has been so busy working and dating and enjoying the summer that he never gave it a thought. His grandmother says she will bake a cake from scratch, make his favorite red punch, and have a celebration. Hermie likes the idea.

Hermie and Jane have another date in early August. He was hoping for a window visit because they seem to be more fun, but they also increase their chances of getting caught. This time they go to a party hosted by one of Jane's friends. The party ends up being lame, so the kids go to Hermie's house. This time Hermie watches Jane's alcohol intake. She does not go overboard and they have a great time in the hot tub.

Chapter 9

Not So Green 17

It is the middle of August, the morning of Hermie's birthday. His grandparents call him to wish him a happy birthday and to remind him to come over after work for some cake and punch. They also mention that a couple of his friends will be there. Hermie thanks them for the birthday wish and will show up as soon as he can. Today he works a split shift from noon until 5 o'clock so he can be at their house shortly after.

At the grocery store, it looks like a normal day. The weather is good and cooperative, and the size of the crew is just right. He begins thinking of tonight's party and having some cake and punch. He feels the need to slow down from the fast pace of his crazy summer parties full of girls and drinks. This should be a good change.

During the course of the day, he makes a few dollars and sees some friends, then decides to leave early at 4 o'clock since it is his special day. He sneaks out of the store unnoticed. He rides his bike home, looking forward to a good night.

He arrives at home and falls into the same routine of emptying his pockets, lying on the couch, and watching the tube. Today he gets a bonus and falls asleep while watching some college swimming.

This is not his favorite sport unless the swimmers are female. This boring sport puts him to sleep for about 45 minutes.

He wakes up feeling a bit refreshed and slowly walks upstairs to take a shower. During the shower he thinks about being 17. He tells himself, "Wow, I am 17. I'm getting older and becoming a young man now. I'm not a little boy anymore. Things are going to start changing."

After his motivational speech, he gets out of the shower and goes to his room to get dressed. He puts on a pair of jeans and a knit shirt. He thought about getting dressed up fancy, but it's only a small party. No big deal. He gets into his car and begins the short drive to his grandparents' house.

He arrives at his grandparents' house about 6:15 and knocks on the door. There is no answer. He knocks again, still no answer. Now he is puzzled. He turns the doorknob and the door is unlocked. Now he's really stumped. He opens the door and sees a dark living room, but there is a night-light that is active in the kitchen. He walks in cautiously.

He calls out, "Hello ... anybody home?" and there is no answer. He closes the front door and continues to walk forward wondering where everybody is.

Just as he enters the living room, the light suddenly comes on and about 12 people stand up and yell "Surprise!" Hermie nearly wets his pants. He is very surprised. The crowd surrounds him and everybody is patting his back or hugging him. His grandparents are watching from the kitchen, laughing loudly.

The crowd consists of his grandparents, Scott, Charlie, Hank, Jane, Belinda, Suzi, and some of their friends who he doesn't remember. Also attending are two of Charlie's biker friends. Jane comes up to him and wishes him a happy birthday, giving him a huge kiss in front of everybody. The crowd says "woooooooo," and both kids just smile.

Just as Hermie's heartbeat goes back to normal, his grandparents walk to the living room carrying a cake with lit candles on it. Everybody sings "Happy Birthday" as the cake is placed on the table. Hermie blows out all 17 candles and gets a round of applause from the guests. His grandparents present him with two square boxes, both the same size. He has an idea of what they are because his grandparents won't lift them.

Hermie opens the first box and it's the new blue Deep Driver bowling ball that he's wanted for a long time. And it's already drilled to fit his hand. He opens the second box and finds another new ball. This one is the red Twist, another ball he's been wanting for a long time. This one is also drilled and also fits his hand perfectly.

His grandparents tell him, "We know how much the school tryouts mean to you and we hope this equipment will help you qualify." Hermie gives them a hug and thanks them for the gifts. He cannot wait to use these new tools of destruction.

Jane approaches Hermie and gives him a small box. He opens it and it's a new watch with the correct time. He thanks her and gives her a kiss.

She tells him, "I was at the store and saw that watch and it looked really neat and I wanted to get it for you. I hope you like it."

Scott comes up to Hermie and gives him a box too. The size of this box is somewhere in between Jane's gift and the bowling balls.

Scott tells Hermie, "Me and the boys pitched in to get you this."

Hermie unwraps the box and it's the newest expansion module of a science fiction game for his computer. He loves the game and knows he will really enjoy this new module. He thanks his friends, saying he was getting bored with the old game.

The group assembles in the kitchen and enjoys some cake and punch. After feasting for a few minutes, Charlie says, "Let's move the party to the lanes so we can watch the birthday boy throw some strikes." Everybody likes the idea and the party moves to the lanes, much to Hermie's surprise.

At the lanes, Hermie is using his new equipment and notices the balls are hooking very aggressively and he is striking every three out of four shots. Some of the partygoers did not know that Hermie was that good. They are very impressed with his game and begin to watch in awe. Charlie, Hank, and Scott also brought their equipment and are throwing some strikes too, but Hermie is getting most of the attention.

After 30 minutes of bowling, Hermie's grandparents and their friends leave. It's about 9:15 and they are feeling a little tired. Hermie thanks them for the wonderful gifts and tells them he will not let them down in his quest for the bowling team tryouts. His grandparents know he will do the best he can.

After another half an hour, somebody decides to finish the party at Hermie's house. Hermie has no problem with that, and soon a caravan forms and makes its way back to Hermie's house. Jane is hugging all over Hermie and seems very happy for him.

She tells him, "I know you will do great in the team tryouts."

Hermie replies, "I'm gonna give it my all 'cause this might be my last chance. If I don't make it this year, I don't know if I'll tryout out next year. I'm not sure if I wanna be a senior and be on the team for the first time. I don't know; I gotta make the team first."

Then Jane says, "Just remind me of when the tryouts are, and me and some friends will come by to cheer you guys on."

Hermie says, "That would be pretty cool. The tryouts are in October from what I heard, but I will let you know as soon as I find out for sure."

The gang arrives at Hermie's house and Charlie already has a beer in his hand as he exits his friend's car. Somehow he seems to be ready every time he comes over. Of course, it helps to have friends that can help in a time of need. That's why Charlie invited these people to the party. Everybody exits their cars and goes inside.

Once inside, everybody makes themselves at home. Hermie just sits on the couch and watches TV. He is a bit tired but is too nice to tell his friends to leave. He has a beer and talks to some people. As he talks, he notices there are some professionals in the kitchen already pouring shots. He thinks they are crazy and shakes his head thinking, "No thanks, I won't be doing that tonight."

Hermie looks around at the party in front of him. Tonight, he is not in the mood to get smashed even though it is his birthday. But he has a strange feeling he will crumble under peer pressure, like he usually does. And the person usually applying the pressure is Charlie. He will play it by ear to see what happens.

He sneaks out of the living room and slowly slithers his way past the crowd in the kitchen. He opens the kitchen door, steps outside into his backyard, and takes a big breath of fresh evening air. He finds a lawn chair in the patio, picks it up and moves it about 30 feet away from the house, turns it toward the rear of the yard, sits down, and stares.

A few minutes later Jane finds him outside and brings a chair from the patio to join him. She notices that he is blankly staring at the far end of his backyard.

She asks him, "Hi Hermie, what are you looking at?" She cannot see anything except darkness, a clear sky with stars, and some trees way in the back of the yard.

"Nothin," he says. "I'm just enjoying the air and the silence. Did you know there's a small stream at the end of this yard? You can't hear it from here but it's there. It's hidden by those trees and bushes. That stream separates this yard from the county property. I don't know where the water comes from, probably some big lake to the west of us, but it flows all year long. Pretty cool, huh?"

Jane is in awe. She doesn't know what to say, but that's nothing new. She is usually not very verbose or wordy, so she asks him, "Can we go see it?"

The kids get out of their seats and walk toward the dark side of his yard. Jane is holding on very tightly to Hermie's arm as they walk, feeling cautious and excited at the same time. She has never been to this part of the yard before.

Hermie tells her, "As we get closer to the stream, you'll hear it. And because of the moonlight tonight, the stream looks shiny, even some of the trees are lit up. It's like the light from the moon hits the stream and reflects it to the trees. And on the other side of the stream, it's nothing but fields forever. Sometimes you'll see a few cows or horses out there. The stream flows to the right and goes into a big lake where people like to party. I've never been there, but I heard it's cool."

They finally arrive at the stream and Jane looks around. She notices the stream is small, about five feet wide and moving at a slow pace. She cannot tell how deep it is, but it looks shallow in most places. She gets closer to the stream and looks in both directions. The stream is flowing from left to right, which is really northwest to southeast, and to Jane, it looks like the stream runs forever in both directions.

The area is covered with short grass, similar to the grass on a golf course. There are several small shrubs that dot the area. There are a few types of trees that line the path of the stream. Jane cannot identify all the trees, but some look like oak and some look like cedar. As she gets closer, she can clearly hear the sound of the stream and see the light splashing sound as the water hits the rocks. She touches the water and it's very cool.

As Jane turns around there is a small handmade wooden bench that faces the stream. It could probably seat four people, or one person lying down. Behind that bench there is a small "wall" of bushes that provides privacy from the house.

She walks toward this bench and asks, "Where did this bench come from?"

As they both sit down on the bench, Hermie tells her, "My father built this bench right after he bought the house. Whenever he had a tough day at work, he would come here, hang loose, and forget everything. He didn't watch a lot of TV, but he loved being here when he got the chance. Maybe it's the quietness or maybe it's the water splashing around; either way, I'm kinda digging it too. Not a bad deal."

Jane is a little excited, being all alone with Hermie. She looks across the stream and notices fields as far as the eye can see. Since the bushes are taller than the bench, she stands up and looks to the slight left and sees the house way in the distance. She does hear the light splashing of the flowing stream.

Hermie tells her, "Don't sweat it, nobody can see or hear us right now."

Jane sits back down and has a particular look in her eyes as she gives Hermie a long and slow kiss. She tells him, "Happy Birthday, Dreamer."

Her hands immediately begin moving all over his body. She begins to breathe heavily while Hermie is too busy kissing back to reply to her sudden advances. The two embrace and continue to get very intimate. This lasts for about 30 minutes; there's some heavy breathing and a few pieces of clothing have been removed.

The kids end up lying on the bench next to each other with flushed faces and looking at the pieces of sky obscured by the small forest above them.

Jane says, "Wow, this feels so good out here. I wish I could stay out here all night," as she sits up and puts her clothes on. She's wearing a big smile.

Hermie replies, "I should have birthdays every week. That was double prime!" He sits up and begins getting dressed, then slowly stands up and looks toward the house to see if anybody is coming. Luckily, nobody missed them.

As they walk back to the house, Hermie is in the talking mood and tells her about his off-season training, "Me and the boys play basketball two or three times a week and bowl once or twice a week. We used to bowl just once a week, but with the tryouts coming in the Fall, we want to be ready. For the summer, I was gonna bowl lots of tournaments, and after I won those two, I was feeling pretty hot. But I got that Jacuzzi and the tournaments got sidetracked."

Jane responds, "I bet winning those two was awesome. Some guys don't win two in two years. Plus your Saturday team won 1st place. You've had a great year."

Hermie replies, "I have never been so excited about bowling before, and every time I pick up a ball, I want to shoot 700. I know I can do it."

They enter the house and there are a few lights on. In the living room the TV is on with a few people talking. Charlie is sitting very close to Belinda on one couch and Hank is sitting next to Angie on the other. Charlie says that his buddies are in the front yard, Scott took Suzi home, and Belinda called Angie to show up and hang out.

It's about 10:30 and Jane asks her friends to take her home because it's getting late. As the girls leave, she tells Hermie she cannot wait for their next date. Hermie now has to think of a time and place to go. He tells her he will call her. Hermie walks Jane to Belinda's car and tells her goodnight.

Before Jane gets inside, she kisses Hermie and tells him, "I hope you had a great birthday." Hermie smiles and nods his head, like a little boy rewarded with candy.

Shortly after Jane and her friends leave, only Charlie, Scott, and Hank remain. That does not surprise Hermie, and he likes hanging out with his good friends. He had a great birthday and is thankful he has good people to share it with.

Hermie sees a familiar glow in Charlie's eyes and asks him, "Hey man, what's up with you? You got a big smile on your face."

Charlie walks toward to the kitchen and pours two shots of rum. He replies in a very excited tone, "Wow dude, check this out. Belinda and I were just talking and having some drinks. I asked her if she wanted to walk and talk and she did. That blew my mind. I wanted to hit the backyard, but you and Jane were already there. So we sat on the couch and talked. I went for broke and put my hand on her face and kissed her. She kissed me back, then we made out! Talk about a score of the year! If the living room woulda been empty, we woulda made it for sure."

Hermie says, "Whoa! That's cool. I thought she was seeing somebody."

Charlie replies, "The way she mugged me, I'm the only dude she's seeing. I gotta check her out some more. She's heavy but she ain't green. Ask Scott about his night." The two friends lift their glasses of rum into their mouths, toasting "good times."

Just before Hermie queries him, a lightly inebriated Scott blurts out, "Whoa, me and Suzi lit it up tonight. At the lanes, she spanked my ass, so I returned the favor and she liked it. When we got back here, we did a couple of shots in the kitchen and that junk made her crazy. We went outside and talked and hugged a buncha times. That was awesome! Now it's easier to talk to her."

Hank takes his turn and says, "Angie and I started talking again and I finally asked her out again. She wasn't drinking much because she had to wake up early tomorrow, but we're going out on Saturday. It's been a good week. What about you, birthday boy? How was your night?"

A lightly toasted Hermie says, "It was a super day. I went to work, made some serious money, got to hang out with my friends, got some new tools, and sipped some more jet fuel. It was a blast. Then Jane and I went to the bench and she got super hot and practically raped me! That's a cool bench and it was a great birthday."

About 11:30 everybody gets the hint that Hermie is tired and they leave. Charlie was the only one drinking heavily, but that's no surprise. They all wish Hermie a happy birthday and say they will see him at the courts tomorrow for another game of basketball … if they are able. If not they will play another day. Hermie walks upstairs to his room and lies on his bed thinking about his great day. Changes are coming.

Chapter 10

Junior Daze

It's the last week of August and school starts up again. Hermie and Hank are both juniors, while Scott and Jane are sophomores and Charlie has to repeat another year as a freshman due to many missed days. Everybody is looking for old friends to talk about what they did during the summer. Some people are not so happy to come back.

As the summer wound down, Hermie and Jane didn't date very much, but called each other a few times. They ended up doing the same old stuff such as mini golf, the movies, bowling, and the arcade. They tried to do new things and were not in the mood to get drunk all the time because of the hangovers. Both still explored their sexuality. They had one more window visit, but they still had intimate moments in other places.

Over the summer, Hermie experienced some physical changes. He is now 5'8" tall and weighs about 155 pounds. At school he also noticed that many of the girls have also grown in some areas and have filled out nicely. That gets Hermie's attention.

Hermie and his teammates signed up again for their usual Saturday morning bowling league. In the first week Hermie used his new equipment and shot a 750 series for an incredible 250 average.

The other guys did about average except for Hank. He was a bit sore from a hard football practice and shot 520.

In the second week of September, a schoolmate invites Hermie to a party. His name is Vinny and he is a senior. He attended Hermie's July 4th party and remembers what a smash it was. He tells Hermie there will be some college students and an older crowd. Hermie decides to attend and tells Charlie about it, since Charlie probably goes to parties like this and Hermie doesn't want to attend this thing alone. He has no idea what to expect, but it sounds like fun and he might get to meet new people.

On the night of the party, Charlie arrives at Hermie's house and picks him up in his car. They drive to the other side of Pibb, to an area that Hermie is not very familiar with. It is a very old neighborhood with cracked streets and large trees, but the houses are still in good shape. They notice many cars parked in the vicinity of this house. They park the car and as they approach the house, somebody at the side of the house tells them to enter though the gate and into the backyard. They follow the directions.

They enter the backyard and see about 30–40 people spread out all over the place. There are many small groups talking, laughing, smoking, and drinking. They find the keg and get a cup of beer, then go inside the house only to find more people talking, laughing, smoking, and drinking. They cannot believe their eyes at the size of this party and decide to look around the whole place. They discover it's a "back-to-school" party and they smile.

After a few beers, Hermie is in dire need of the restroom. He finds a long line for both downstairs restrooms and decides to sneak upstairs to use that one. The pressure in his bladder is building up as he locates the restroom. As he opens the door, he sees two naked people on the floor having sex.

Hermie stands there in shock as the guy tells him, "Get outta here freak, this ain't no peep show!" The guy slams the door in Hermie's face.

Hermie rushes downstairs forgetting the pressure and decides to find an obscure corner of the backyard to find relief. He already knows this is a crazy party. He cannot believe what he saw.

He meets up with Charlie and they go outside to see the keg again. Vinny runs into them and invites them to the rear of the backyard, which is where he is going. They meet a few people smoking in a small group and decide to hang out. Hermie gets a whiff of some funny smelling smoke. Someone passes a strange homemade cigarette to Charlie and he takes a drag and passes it on. Hermie gets another whiff of the funny smoke.

A few minutes later, Hermie is sitting on the lawn giggling at nothing. Charlie is next to him joining in the laughter. Neither of them knows what is so funny.

Vinny tells Hermie that he and Charlie are stoned, but Hermie tells him, "How can I be stoned, nobody threw any rocks at me, maybe I dodged them all," as he laughs again.

The next morning Hermie wakes up on the couch in his house; Charlie is on the other couch. When Charlie finally wakes up, Hermie asks how they got home. Charlie has no idea. He looks outside and Charlie's car is parked in front of the house. Now they know that was a crazy party, but are not sure if they will attend next year.

During the week, Hermie runs into Jane and she invites him to her oldest sister Sheryl's wedding. The wedding will be on Saturday at the local church, with a reception following shortly afterwards. Sheryl graduated from college about three months ago but has been dating her boyfriend, Javier, for about three years. He also graduated in May.

That weekend, Hermie attends Sheryl's wedding and it seems nice. The couple looks happy. Jane is a bridesmaid and has to be up front, while Hermie takes a seat as a regular spectator. It's a medium-sized crowd and there are many ladies already crying. There are more people on Sheryl's side than Javier's, because he is from California.

After the ceremony everybody goes to the country club for the reception. Hermie takes Jane in his car and drives to the club. On the way there, Jane changes clothes, which really gets Hermie's attention, seeing a partially nude body. She is in the front seat stripping down in broad daylight. It doesn't seem to bother her.

Upon arriving at the reception, it is full of people, music, food, and champagne. Hermie's first thought is, "Oh no, it's time to start drinking again. Why me?" and does not look forward to another weekend of alcohol. He is still trying to recover from Vinny's party last week.

As a self-fulfilling prophecy, somebody comes around and gives out glasses full of champagne. Apparently there are many cases of this bubbly liquid that is destined to be drunk by all the attendees including Hermie and Jane. Hermie shakes his head as he slams the first glass. He and Jane experience a head rush after their second glass.

About two hours later, Hermie finds himself in his car with Jane and has no idea how he got there. Both are in the back seat making out like maniacs. Jane seems pretty turned on, while Hermie is in a euphoric state and feels like he is in a dream.

Both of their shirts are partially unbuttoned and some of the windows are fogged up. He doesn't remember how long they have been in there, but he keeps doing what he's doing; embracing, kissing touching and giggling. He closes his eyes for a moment because they seem very heavy.

When he opens his eyes, he is lying on his back in the back seat. Jane is partially on top of him with her shirt missing and she is sound asleep. He looks around and it is almost dark outside. At least an hour has elapsed since he was last awake. He guesses he was in the car with Jane for almost two hours! He has no idea what happened.

He slowly rolls her off his chest and starts to get dressed. He tries to get her dressed, but it's very difficult. Finally, she slowly wakes up and gets herself dressed with her eyes closed, while Hermie hops to the front seat and starts the car to take her home. He thinks they are still drunk because his head feels funny.

He makes it to Jane's house a few minutes later. Before he can get out and help her, she opens the car door, stumbles to her feet, and tells him "bye." She waddles to her front door, fumbles the keys, and goes inside. She doesn't even kiss him goodnight.

Hermie drives himself home and stumbles upstairs to his bed for a good night's sleep. He looks at his watch and it shows 10 o'clock. He thinks to himself, "How long can this madness go on? I can't live like this forever. What a crazy way to go."

He wakes up the next morning at 11, only because it seems the phone keeps ringing. He finally answers it and it is Scott calling about their Sunday basketball game. Hermie is too tired to play and cancels the game. But Scott reminds him that tomorrow is a school day. Hermie agrees to play and will meet the boys at noon.

Hermie finally arrives at the court and they begin playing. Hermie is playing very slow today, missing shots, barely running, and sweating like a pig.

Charlie notices the change in Hermie's game and asks him, "Hey man, are you alright? You're moving pretty slow today. This ain't you."

"Jane and I went to her sister's wedding and reception yesterday, and we had a little too much champagne. We had a great time, but it was crazy," Hermie replies.

Charlie speaks up and says, "Dang boy, you're becoming a party animal. First it's Vinnie's place, now the wedding reception. That's two weekends in a row. Where are you going to this weekend? A frat party?"

"Nothing for me, man; I'm all partied out. I can't live like this forever, it's hard work. Look at me. I'm wrecked," says Hermie.

Hank chimes in, saying, "Hey Charlie, Hermie might be taking your title away for being the party animal. He's making you look like you're in training wheels." He and Scott begin to laugh.

The boys cut their basketball game short due to Hermie's lack of ability today. They end up back at his house and lounge around while Hermie lies on the couch. Scott and Hank enjoy the hot tub while Hermie lies on the couch and Charlie takes a quick shower and eventually leaves the house to see Belinda.

The following week, Hermie and his grandparents go to court against Acme Chemical for a preliminary hearing. Even after 18 months, the company does not have any solid answers and claims the investigation is still being conducted. The judge is not happy with that answer and indicates that the momentum is swinging in favor of the plaintiffs. This might get Acme's attention, but they will still probably take their time.

Hermie is a bit upset at the delay tactic by the chemical company and he's had enough. He eventually blurts out, "We have documentation that will put Acme away for a long time. Our documentation shows who the guilty people really are! It was no accident."

This gets the attention of many people as they look at Hermie and start talking and causing commotion. The judge pounds his gavel and warns the courtroom to be silent. The judge gives Hermie a warning to keep quiet. Hermie finally calms down and gets quiet.

As Hermie and his grandparents leave the courthouse, their lawyer tells them, "I think the judge is fed up with Acme's delay tactics and wants to get this case underway. We all know that the big rich companies can afford to hire expensive lawyers and delay the trial because the average Joe can't afford to sustain the length of a long trial."

He says the judge hinted at making an example of Acme Chemical, but didn't disclose any details about his plans. This is a small glimmer of hope for Hermie and his family. Perhaps soon this ugly case will finish up.

Hermie has noticed that with his social status growing unexpectedly and with working and everything else going on, he is seeing Jane less. They still say hello in the hallways and sneak in a few hugs and kisses, but most of the fire is fading fast. They have not been on a date in almost a month and their window visits have practically disappeared. He wants to try to see her again, but she informs him that she just joined a book club at school. Now both of them have become busier than ever.

It's the last week of September and Hermie and his teammates find themselves at the lanes for some practice. They have been practicing two times per week, because the school team tryouts are next week and they are determined to make the cut. They have been practicing for about two months. Hermie wants to show the coach that they are for real. Hermie even talked to the lane mechanic and found out what oil pattern will be used.

After practice Hermie invites the guys for a sleepover Friday night. He tells them he bought a new game for his computer and it will support four players simultaneously. He describes the game and how it plays and wants to see how the four-player mode looks. Scott is the only one interested but Charlie and Hank decide to tag along and bring their sleeping bags.

That Friday night, the usual gang shows up around 7 o'clock and begins the night by jumping into the hot tub and drinking some iced tea that Hermie made. He does not realize the amount of caffeine in the tea, but the boys drink it up. They all get wired and do not even realize it.

At 8:45 they go upstairs to play Hermie's new computer game. Game play starts off slow because they are learning the rules and how the game controllers work. They keep starting over until they all get the hang of it. They play for a couple of hours without even knowing it and nobody feels tired. In addition, Charlie brought up a 12-pack of beer and a bottle of whiskey, and the thirsty foursome start making quick work of it.

Around 2 o'clock, Hermie thinks he hears a noise and says, "Shhhhh. Did you guys hear that? It sounded like it came from downstairs."

Charlie tries not to laugh and tells him, "You're a big boy now, and there's no such thing as ghosts. That tea has gotten you wired and you're hearing stuff … it's probably the ringing in your ears. The booze is probably kicking in too."

Hermie claims, "No. It sounded like a door opening and closing somewhere downstairs, and then I heard a crunching sound, sorta like leaves."

Hank says, "Before we went upstairs, I checked the front door and it was locked, but I never checked the back door after we left the hot tub."

He tells everybody to be quiet and to listen. They all put their joysticks down and turn down the volume of the TV speakers. Now, all of them think they hear something too as they all stop moving and barely breathe.

Hermie quietly tells the boys, "Let's get up and sneak to the hallway for a better listen. If somebody is here, they'll move again." They hear a small crunch. Then they hear a smaller crunch and a "shhhhh."

Hank looks scared and tells Hermie, "Holy smokes! I just remembered that I accidentally spilled a few potato chips on the kitchen floor and forgot to clean them up. Now we know that somebody is here. But who could it be? And what do they want?"

They slowly walk downstairs and Hermie goes back to his room to get his video camera. He wants to record this event no matter what happens. He can't believe this is happening and hopes nobody gets hurt. He is a little scared but a little excited too.

Hank leads the way downstairs in this dark house with Charlie close behind. They all stop near the bottom of the stairs and wait. Hank and Charlie drank a few beers after exiting the tub and are feeling pretty tough and angry.

Charlie goes up to Hank and whispers, "It ain't fair that Hermie's dad busts his hump for his house and some punk wants to take it. Well, he ain't gettin any of it! I don't care how many there are, someone's getting a beatin'!'"

Those words seem to work because Hank is fired up and says, "Damn right! I'm ready to crack some skulls," as they give each other a low five.

Scott has been totally silent the entire time. He has been watching this event unfold and has kept himself at the rear of the line. He is pretty scared right now and doesn't know what to do. He is about two steps behind Hermie but is thinking about going back to Hermie's room and closing the door.

Hermie thinks the intruder or intruders are in the living room. He tells his friends to get ready because he will flick on the lights and Charlie and Hank will pounce and tackle whoever is in the living room. Hank is breathing heavy and Charlie sounds like he is growling. Hermie has his camera rolling and approaches the light switch for the living room.

Charlie whispers to Hank, "If you look closely, you can see two dudes and they ain't even moving. The light from the window is going through the curtains and hitting them and they don't even know it. They probably know we're home. I'll take the short dude on the right. You get the one on the left," as Hank nods his head.

Charlie and Hank get into their football stances and Hermie turns on the light switch. The lights come on and there are two grown men in the living room looking at each other in shock, frozen, like a deer looking at headlights. Hank aims for the taller, medium-sized guy while Charlie goes after the shorter, older-looking guy.

Hank and Charlie belt out a loud charging scream, run toward the two men, jump, and tackle them in a matter of seconds. Charlie jumps in the air, not even worried about getting hurt; he just wants to hit the other guy really hard. As Charlie jumps, his leg hits the side of the coffee table and makes a "thud" sound, but it does not affect his jump.

The intruders are so scared by Hank's size and Charlie's speed, that they didn't even have time to move as they get wrapped up and hit the floor hard with their heads and shoulders first. They land on their backs and get the wind knocked out of them.

Hank is breathing heavy as he is lying on top of one and Charlie is on top of the other. Charlie wants to hit this guy real bad and can almost taste a beating. Charlie is so fired up that he is sweating and shaking. He has a fist ready.

Hermie shouts, "If they move a muscle, pound 'em!"

He tells Scott to call the police and Scott runs to the kitchen and dials the phone. Hermie still has his camera running and gets a close up of the two intruders. He is still shaking because he does not know what's going to happen next.

Hermie yells at the intruders, "What are you guys doing in my house? What do you want? Let's find out who these guys are," and tries to remove the wallet from the man underneath Charlie.

The man lying beneath Charlie tries to protect his wallet and moves his hand to cover his rear pocket. Charlie gives him a solid punch to the kidney. The man lets out a small moan as if he was hurt by that punch and does not move anymore.

Charlie tells him, "Dumb move, buddy. Try that again and I'll aim for the face. There ain't no law saying I gotta be nice to you … so don't push it!" The man stops moving and looks away while Charlie nods his head in acceptance. Charlie breathes on his face just to annoy him to see if he will flinch.

Hermie retrieves the wallets from the two older men and opens them up in front of the camera. Hermie shouts out, "So do you guys work for Acme Chemical or did somebody pay you to break into my house? Tell me!!"

Nobody answers. Hermie notices the silence and responds, "My friend Charlie has a short fuse, and he's been drinking. He's waiting to smash your face in and doesn't need a reason. Why don't you talk and save yourself a beating," as Charlie shows that he has a fist ready to use by waving it in the air and has a snarl on his face.

Hermie adds, "My other friend Hank plays football and is trained to hurt people. He's the biggest one here and could really hurt both of you. What do ya say?"

The man under Charlie identifies himself as Shannon. He is a bit short and thin and seems a little mousey. He looks clean cut but is pretty weathered and smells of cigarette smoke. He decides to speak up after Charlie grabs his hair and rubs his face into the carpet. Hank gives the other man a punch to the stomach.

Shannon pleads, "Okay, Okay, I'll talk. Just cut the camera and get the psycho off me."

Hermie is not sure why this guy wants the camera off, since he already got his driver's license recorded on camera. Charlie lets Shannon get up and then gives him a bonus shove, causing Shannon to hit the wall. Charlie tells Shannon to sit down and start talking. Shannon sits in the corner, with his back to the wall, and begins his story. Charlie is eyeballing him as if Shannon were a prisoner.

Shannon tells Hermie, "Me and George were secretly hired by some mystery person over the phone to search this house for evidence about some Brambleweed case. We were told to look for any evidence in the house and either take it or destroy it. I swear I don't know who called me, but they offered lots of money and it sounded real good. And the more evidence we found, the more we got paid."

Hermie and the guys are in shock to hear what Shannon has to say, but they have a feeling that Shannon has more to say so they let him continue.

Shannon says, "I took the case thinking it was gonna be a simple break in and looting job. Then I was told to go to a secret location to pick up the payment. At first, I was skeptical, but after I found a fat envelope with the money, I knew the caller wasn't bullshittin. Now I had to search the house and find something."

Hermie asks Shannon, "Do you guys work for Acme?"

Shannon quickly denies it, as does George. Shannon adds, "We're private investigators and usually accept cases like cheating spouses, fraudulent will executions, and deadbeat child support; small crap like that. This case was different because it sounded too easy and the money was nice, so we took it."

Just as Hermie is about to ask another question, there is a very authoritative knock on the front door. Hermie thinks it's the police, walks toward the front door and opens it.

The police walk in and see two older men surrounded by three teenage boys. The police ask whose house it is and if anybody is hurt. Hermie says that nobody is hurt and the police report begins.

Hermie tells the police it is his parent's house but they are currently out of town. The police tell him that since all the guys are underage, the police would like an adult present to assist with the report. Hermie provides the name and phone number of his grandparents, whom the police call most urgently. The officer explains the situation to Hermie's grandfather and reassures him the boys are not hurt. Grandpa says he will be there in five minutes.

Grandpa shows up and asks Hermie how they are all feeling. He can tell they are a little shocked, even Charlie is trembling a little. Everybody is quiet and the two robbers are sitting on the floor looking down. The police report continues.

After 30 minutes of blabbing and answering questions, Hermie looks for Scott and he is in the kitchen being very quiet and looking very pale. The police ask him how he is feeling and Scott is in shock as he takes a drink of water.

The police eventually handcuff the two men and put them in the police car as they call for a tow truck to impound Shannon's car. Hermie goes inside the house, closes the door, and looks through the window as the two trespassers are taken away in police custody. Suddenly he feels cold and starts to shiver.

Grandpa lectures Hermie and his friends and says, "You boys should consider yourselves lucky. You all could have been hurt if they were carrying weapons. They might be small-time crooks, but those guys have lots of street smarts and sometimes, that is better than muscle and anger. I'm just glad that nobody got hurt."

Grandpa asks the boys again if they are feeling better and they reply that they are. He tells Hermie that he will look for a security system for Hermie's house and his house as well. Grandpa goes home. It is 4 in the morning.

Hermie is shaking a little as he slowly makes his way to the couch. He has a blank stare and is acting very spacey. He puts his head inside his hands and looks as if he is about to cry. He just breathes heavily and repeatedly says, "Wow … unbelievable. There were two strangers in my house and we could have gotten hurt. Oh man."

Just then Charlie hands him a beer and a shot and tells him to drink it to calm his nerves. Hermie slams the shot and takes a large swig and suddenly feels better. In fact, everybody is having a drink after that ordeal as they move to the kitchen to talk about it.

Scott, who has been quietly sitting in the kitchen during the entire event says, "I think I believe their story."

"What proof do you have," Charlie asks.

Scott walks to the lower cabinet, opens the door, and pulls out a fat manila envelope with no writing on it. Charlie and Hermie drop their jaws because they have a good idea of what's inside. Hank is not so sure of the contents.

Scott puts the envelope on the table and everybody stares at it as if it were a creature from outer space. Nobody tries to touch it, not even Charlie.

Scott explains, "After I called the police, I was too scared to look at those guys, so I stayed in the kitchen, but I could hear them talk. After I heard Shannon talk about the nice payday, I wanted to see if he was dumb enough to leave the cash in the car. So I snuck out the back door and went to his car. I looked around and found nothing. Then I looked under his seat and saw the envelope. Yup, he was dumb enough. It was too easy. I've had algebra problems that were harder than this."

Charlie laughs loudly and says, "Who woulda guessed that quiet little Scott would rob the robbers," as he gives Scott a high-five. "Let's see how much money is in there for the party fund," as Scott tears the envelope and pours out the cash on the table.

Everybody stares at the small pile of paper money in awe. Scott says, "Wow, that's a whole bunch of money, let's count it." He hands out small piles to each person.

They all agree to tell nobody about this remarkable windfall because it could cause serious problems, especially if their parents found out about it.

They count almost $2,000 and agree to split it four ways. But now they have to keep this money a secret. Hermie tells his friends, "We can keep it in my room. Since my parents are gone most of the time, they will never find it in there. I also say that we don't purchase high-dollar items, cause people will talk."

"That's a good idea," Scott nervously says.

"You know, when we go out of town to bowl, now we can chow down at the nicer places instead of fast food all the time," suggests Hermie.

"Hey, what's gonna happen when them punks discover their money is gone? They'll be out of jail in a day or two, and they'll be back with a vengeance and some friends. So we better be ready," says Charlie.

"Their car has probably been impounded and it won't be cheap to get it out. They probably don't have any cash on them so the car may stay in the lot for a few days," says Hank.

"By the time those goons come back, this house will have a security system installed. They won't come back no more; it'll be too risky," replies Hermie.

Charlie looks around the house and says, "There's something in this house that's very important to their mystery boss and I think they'll keep poking around until they find it. If I ever see them goons again, I swear I'll bust 'em up real good!"

Hank sounds a little bit excited and tells the gang, "Me too! I don't care if I see them on the street. They're dead meat!"

Charlie adds, "Yeah, what's their big boss gonna do when his stoolies show up with no evidence and no money? He's gonna flip his lid. Talk about ass beating deluxe. Coming back to this house will be the least of their problems. They might as well pack their crap and move to Mexico. Their days are over, man."

There is a short silence, then Charlie asks, "So … tell me about this Brambleweed case. Does it involve you or your parents or what?"

Charlie, Hank and Scott all look at Hermie for an answer. Hermie stalls for a minute. He quickly thinks about what he will say because this can quickly become a life-changing discussion. Does he tell the truth? Does he spill the entire can of beans? Does he lie? It is time to step up to the plate.

He takes a deep breath and says, "Well, I don't know the whole story because it happened when I was real little. My dad used to work at Acme and he got hurt on the job one day. He had a ton of doctor bills but the company didn't wanna pay. He was on some top-secret project that could make the company rich."

"Wow! What kind of project was it?" asks Scott.

"I don't know, but it had to do with radioactive stuff," Hermie answers. "Acme was scared that if they paid the bills, they would have to assign the medical bills to a project. Then the word would hit the streets that Acme was working on a new product and the competition would try to find ways to steal those secrets. Acme told pops they would send him cash instead of telling the insurance company, but he never got the bread."

"That sucks," replies Charlie.

Then Hermie adds, "My dad heard that one of his coworkers was pretty angry for not getting that project when it was promised to him. This dude started to tell other companies that he had a new product that could make them rich and showed them some designs. This company, called TriCity, liked the idea and offered this dude a VP job. All this dude had to do was make the project work, but he had to steal my dad's secret papers he was working on. TriCity was a small-time company, but this new product could make them real big."

Everyone is in suspense as if watching a scary movie. Nobody is moving and all eyes are on Hermie as he continues his story. Charlie is starting to get angry as he passes out more beer. He takes a big swig to calm down.

He continues, "My dad figured out this dude's plans too late and the dude secretly replaced the laboratory equipment with cheaper stuff to fail the experiment. The dude knew the project would fail but never thought it would hurt my dad. Well, it did fail and that's how my dad got hurt."

"Rotten bastard. Is your dad okay?" asks Charlie.

Hermie hesitates and says, "He's okay now. My dad suspected foul play but now nobody was talking. My dad knew people that had information, but those people suddenly disappeared."

"Disappeared? Like how," Hank asks.

Hermie answers, "It's like they got fired and moved to a different state or something."

"You know they're coverin up somethin," adds Charlie.

Hermie takes a big drink and adds, "The crook left Acme with the secrets and took the VP job at TriCity as promised. But Acme already filed for a patent and this crook didn't know that. So the joke was on him because this messed up TriCity's plans for getting rich and they had to fire that punk 'cause they had no use for him."

"Damn! What a roaster!" snaps Charlie.

Hermie adds, "The case is real crazy now because TriCity's name has been mentioned in court and this VP dude is splitsville. It's like he vanished or somethin'. TriCity says they never heard of this dude or ever hired him. Acme has the dude's old address and phone number, but it's no good no more. With that dude gone, it's hard to prove these things happened."

All the guys are looking at Hermie with their jaws dropped. They look as if they just fell off the planet and none of them seem to be breathing. They want to hear more.

Hank asks, "What kind of product was this that everybody wanted? It sounds like a hot item that could change the world and make people rich."

"I don't know about changing the world or getting rich. Maybe. I'm not a chemist but I heard it involved atoms and radiation and isotopes. That stuff is way beyond me. My dad learned things really fast and that's probably why he got the project. It wasn't a simple product like a bicycle; I think my dad found a way to make something faster and cheaper. And he proved his way was better than the old way," replies Hermie.

"What about this evidence thing? Is there really some evidence left over and is that stuff in this house? What were them two goons looking for?" asks Charlie.

Hermie continues his story, "My dad took real good notes of his research and kept every memo that he got and wrote. He also kept a personal diary and it has names of people who were on that project and dates of when things happened. He also made copies of all this stuff and kept it hidden here in the house. When that dude split, he took all of the notes and design papers with him. We think there is enough paperwork to make Acme look like the bad guys. But Acme doesn't want us to show those papers because it could hurt the company and they could lose the lawsuit. That's probably why somebody sent those two dudes over here; to find these papers and destroy them."

"Those guys are going to pay. I hope they all go to jail," Hank says.

Hermie finishes his story, "Acme treated this project like one of those secret recon missions you see in the movies. If the mission was a success, then everybody was a hero. But if it failed, the company would deny everything. Acme tried to cover it up, but my father knew too many people that were about to talk. Acme figured that if they destroyed all the evidence, then my father would not have a case anymore. That's what they want. And TriCity Chemical is denying everything. It's gone full stupid now."

Charlie, Hank and Scott just sit there as if somebody just slapped them. They just heard the most incredible story ever told. Hermie was talking as if he experienced the drama first hand.

"So where's this stuff hidden? Are you allowed to tell us?" Scott asks.

Hermie leads everybody to the kitchen and gets four shot glasses from the cabinet and a bottle of rum. The boys are watching, pretty sure of what will happen next. Hermie fills each glass with rum and passes them out to each of his friends.

Hermie tells the guys, "There is one more piece of information. I know this sounds corny, but we all must be sworn to secrecy … for life. You guys are like brothers to me and I trust all of you. We must keep this secret like brothers. Do y'all agree?"

Everybody takes a glass and agrees to secrecy. They raise the glasses, make the toast, and take the drink. Now they are ready for the last piece of the story.

Hermie concludes, "This house has a basement. Not too many houses around here have basements because of all the clay in the ground and how it moves around. My dad liked basements because he could hide stuff down there and not have to show the world. He didn't like attics very much because they are too hot."

"Wow, a basement in this house? That's awesome," replies Charlie.

"In the basement is all the paperwork that my dad saved up from his project. There are boxes and boxes of stuff down there. The room is sealed tight and has an electronic wire just in case. I don't know who hooked it up, but it's live. I'm not even allowed to go inside there. All I know is that I have to protect the stuff in that room until the case is closed. My grandfather has a key, and I think there is a key hidden in this house. Our lawyer has to schedule a time to go in there whenever he wants to look through that stuff," Hermie says.

The whole house is quiet as Hermie finishes his story. Charlie shows up with a beer for everybody. He makes another toast, "Hermie, I will do everything I can to help you keep that stuff safe. It's too valuable."

They raise their cans, and Hank and Scott agree with Charlie and say, "Me too and the secret will stay in this house," as they all drink up.

Hermie tells the guys to follow him as he leads them to the closet beneath the stairs. Way in the back of the closet is a hidden left turn with a secret wall that is activated by pushing on it. The wall opens and reveals stairs down to the basement. At the bottom there is a thick large door with wires all around it and blinking red lights. Everybody thinks they are in a sci-fi movie after seeing this high-tech lock.

Charlie says, "Damn! Them crooks never would've found this basement. And even if they did, they ain't smart enough to get past them hot wires. Wow!"

Hermie tells them, "Behind that door is all of my dad's paper-work."

After the show-and-tell concludes, everybody climbs back up the stairs and to the kitchen. Everybody is in shock after hearing this story. Nobody is talking. Hermie has four small brown paper bags. He puts a name on each bag and puts an equal portion of the crook's money in each bag.

He says, "These bags will be in my room. Anytime y'all need some dough, you know where it is," as Charlie grabs about $100 from his bag and nods his head. Hank and Scott also grab a few dollars as well.

It's almost 5 in the morning and all the guys are tired from a night full of activity. They look at the computer that is still playing the new video game everybody came to see, but nobody is interested anymore. They just want to sleep.

As Hermie changes his clothes for bed, the boys do the same and unroll their sleeping bags to get ready for a hard sleep. Hermie knows his buddies have a million questions regarding the case, the money, and the basement, and is ready to answer them all the best he can.

He feels better for telling his good friends about the case and the basement. He feels less pressure to be so secretive about his life and his father's past. He knows he can trust them. He falls asleep instantly.

Chapter 11

Team This

It is Monday in the middle of October and this coming Saturday is the annual tryouts for the school's bowling team. Hermie and his friends have been waiting a year for this event and most of them feel it is their last chance. For some reason, Hermie doesn't want to be a senior and be on the team for the first time. Hank shares the same sentiments.

For Hermie is more than just a simple team tryout. It's a way to redeem himself and get past all of the disappointments and deception from last year. During last year's tryouts, Hermie finished in 7th place and was confident he had a spot on the second team. Then from out of nowhere, the coach decided to accept the top six players because he wanted to keep his nephew's team intact. Those six players would comprise the second team while the nephew's team would still remain as the first team. Hermie was one place shy of being on the team and that gave Hermie a negative image about the coach's integrity.

It took a long time to get that foul taste out of Hermie's mouth from that incident. But he vowed to get better and learn more about the game and his equipment. He also started to practice more. Over the last year, his hard work paid off after he won two tournaments during this past summer. Also, he is more confident with any bowling center he walks into.

Hermie feels that he and his friends have an edge because they spoke to the lane mechanic who will be applying the oil pattern for the tryouts this year. Hermie just asked him what the pattern was like and the mechanic told him exactly how the oil would be applied. In fact, the mechanic offered to apply the same pattern for Hermie and his bunch the next time they came to the lanes to practice. All Hermie has to do was show up and buy him lunch.

One day after school, Hermie's gang decides to get some practice. Hermie sees the mechanic and the mechanic tells the team to practice on the very last pair. He says that pair will have the tournament lane condition. He strongly recommends using dull equipment, not shiny. He also recommends playing near the gutter and watching the reaction they will get. Hermie slips the mechanic a few dollars and the guys begin their practice.

They throw their initial shots very apprehensively, but later get comfortable playing near the gutter. Once they are lined up, they are striking at will and some of their pin action is phenomenal. All are very excited and cannot wait until Saturday. All week long they watch bowling on TV and mentally envision their perfect strike shot.

Thursday night after work, Hermie goes by Jane's house for a surprise visit. He originally wanted to have a window visit and get close to her again, but this time he takes the more traditional approach. He goes to the front door.

After a short knock, Jane opens the door with a very surprised look on her face and lets him inside. Her mother walks by and greets him.

Jane's mother asks Hermie, "Would you like something to eat? We just finished dinner and the food is still on table."

"Thanks Mrs. Leuistan, but I'm okay right now," replies Hermie

Jane whispers to Hermie, "I think you should eat, otherwise you're gonna hurt her feelings and she went through a lot of trouble to make it." Hermie changes his mind and accepts her dinner invitation and Jane's mother is a bit happier.

Jane takes Hermie by the hand and sits him down in a chair in the kitchen. As her mother has her back to the two kids, Jane and Hermie sneak in a quick kiss and Jane's eyes light up as she smiles in pleasure. Jane's mother approaches Hermie with a plate of fish sticks, tater tots, tartar sauce, and small green salad. It looks like the fish sticks are the frozen type, but he won't say a word.

Jane's mother says, "The tartar sauce is made from scratch from my own recipe ... try it."

Hermie picks up a stick and dips it into the sauce and eats it. Meanwhile, Jane and her mother eagerly look on, anticipating his comments as if he were the judge for a $1 million baking contest. Hermie looks up while chewing and notices the two ladies eyeballing him.

He swallows his mouthful of food and makes a "mmmmmmmmm" sound.

Then he says, "This is really good stuff. Can I have some more?" as he dips his second stick, picking up a heaping pile of the sauce and takes another big bite.

Jane's mother is very excited as she rushes to the stove with a large spoon and a saucepan, and plops a large spoonful of this homemade emulsion onto his plate. She puts the pan back on the stove and pats Hermie on the back, then leaves the kitchen smiling.

Jane looks at Hermie and tells him, "Wow, I haven't seen her that excited about her cooking in a long time. You got her going for sure. Maybe she will be in a good mood for a while. So, was the tartar sauce really that good?"

He tells Jane, "Hey, I was all over that stuff. It's great to have a home-cooked meal once in a while." Hermie finishes his meal then puts the plate in the sink.

Hermie usually doesn't use many sauces or mayonnaise or gravy on his foods, but makes an exception once in a while. This was one of those exceptions.

Suddenly Jane gets an idea. She runs to the living room and her mother is putting away some magazines from the coffee table. Jane asks her mother if she can go riding around in Hermie's car for a little while. Her mother, still on Cloud Nine from the kudos that Hermie provided, approves the short cruise. Jane tells Hermie she wants to go for a ride in his car. Jane goes to her room to change her shoes.

When Jane comes back, she sees Hermie sitting on the couch and her mother is handing him a small plastic container which looks like it has tartar sauce inside. Hermie thanks her for the sauce, and the two kids walk out of the front door and get into his car.

As they leave Jane's house, Hermie asks her, "So where do you wanna go? Or do you just wanna cruise around for a while?"

"I don't care where we go, I just wanted to get out of the house for a while. I'm tired of homework. Let's just cruise," says Jane.

As they drive, Hermie begins to talk about the tryouts on Saturday and sounds excited, but nervous. He tells her that he feels so prepared and can't stop thinking about it. Jane tells him he will do just fine and wants to bring some of her friends to watch. Hermie likes the idea and hopes he can give the fans a show.

As they drive down "the strip," Jane takes off her socks and shoes, lies on her back with her head in Hermie's lap, and sticks her feet out of the window. Hermie stares at this display and continues driving. He also stares at her lying down, puts his right hand on her face, and just strokes her cheeks. He nods his head in appreciation. After they leave the strip, Jane tells him she wants to go to his house and hang out for a while.

They arrive at his house and Jane is carrying her shoes in her hand as they enter. Once inside, Jane goes to the refrigerator, grabs two wine coolers, and gives Hermie one. She begins to drink hers in large gulps. Then she walks right outside the back door into the backyard. It's about 7:45 and it's getting dark outside. Hermie finally catches up to her and sits on a chair under the patio. He does not drink wine coolers that often, but tonight he will go with the flow.

Jane seems rather fidgety and walks around the Jacuzzi and says, "Let's get in the tub ... just for a little while. Come on."

Jane begins to undress in the dark backyard. The only source of light is coming from the moon. Hermie can't get a good view of her because of the darkness, but he can tell she is stripping down. All he can see is a silhouette of her and can tell all of her clothes are off. He tells himself, "Geez, what's this chick doing now?"

Hermie cannot believe what is happening and is wondering how strong that wine cooler is because Jane is acting loopy and wired. He is also not amused on how she just helped herself to the wine coolers and the hot tub. Her behavior bothers him a little, but he isn't about to let that ruin a potentially good night with her all alone.

Hermie follows her lead and gets in the tub. Before long, the two kids are making out. There are hands moving everywhere, lots of splashing and heavy breathing. The kids move faster and faster. Eventually Jane ends up sitting on his lap facing him. Both are holding each other tightly. A few minutes later, they exit the tub and get dressed.

It's about 9:30 and Hermie is taking her home. They are not talking very much about what just happened, but both have very satisfying smiles on their faces every time they look at each other. Jane wishes him luck on his tournament and plans on being there with a rooting section. Hermie likes that idea and really wants to make the team. He tells her it would mean a lot for him and the boys. She reassures him.

They arrive at her house and she gives him a long goodnight kiss and will see him in school tomorrow. Hermie drives home feeling pretty good. The time he just spent with Jane took his mind off the tournament. He makes it home, changes clothes, and goes to bed thinking of Jane and bowling, but mostly Jane. That was one heck of a surprise he got from her. What a night; all that just for complementing some tartar sauce.

On Friday, Hermie has a quiet barbecue dinner with his grandparents and talk about alarm systems for the house. His grandfather already found one and bought it with his money. It will be installed early tomorrow morning. Hermie tells him to just use the money from his account to pay for both systems. After dinner, his grandparents wish him well on the tournament. Hermie goes home and tries to go to sleep, but is too wired.

It's finally Saturday morning and Hermie is awoken by his alarm clock very early. He gets up, showers, dresses, and eats. An hour later, he gives his equipment a final inspection and the boys show up. Soon they are loading their equipment in Hermie's or Hank's car. After a short and brief hello, they drive to their local bowling center.

They arrive a few minutes later, unload their equipment, and enter the familiar building. There are a several people already inside and they do not know if these people are bowlers, staff, or just onlookers. Hermie and his clan find seats and sit down.

Over the next several minutes, they watch as the place begins to fill up. It feels strange that they will not be bowling their usual morning league today, even though it also starts at 10 o'clock. Hermie wonders why they didn't hold the try outs after their league finished up.

At 10:10 the tournament director, who is also the team coach, announces over the P.A. for all tryout participants to meet in the lounge for a quick meeting. Hermie sees a small crowd walk toward the bar. He was expecting maybe 20 entries, but it looks like a dozen or so. He figures that the fewer people there are, the better his chances.

In the meeting room the coach announces that the school will have two men's teams this year, just like last year. He also mentions that one team has already been formed, so today's rolloffs will be for the second team. The rolloff competition will consist of four games. The top four finishers will be starters for the second team and the 5th and 6th place finishers will be alternates for the team.

Hermie is pissed off again, knowing that the coach kept his two loser relatives on the first team. He blurts out, "That's a bunch of crap. They're not doing the tryouts because they would never make it anyway. They can't bowl. This already sucks!"

"Hey man, save that energy for the lanes and take it out on the pins. In the end, the better bowlers will make the team," Scott reassures Hermie.

Charlie adds his two cents, "Just think, when we make the team, eventually we have to bowl against them pukes. Won't it be great to kick their butts all year long?"

Hermie says, "Yeah, I guess that would be cool."

The lane assignments are given out and there will be four bowlers per pair or two per lane. There are 16 entries, so eight lanes will be taken up. Hermie and his friends will occupy lanes 1 and 2. They take their equipment to the starting lanes and change their shoes. They are excited.

The lanes are turned on for practice and Hermie takes out his new equipment and is ready to see how they react. He begins the session with a "Big 4" split, followed by a few washouts and chopped spares. Hermie is already getting angry, but also knows his worst bowling always occurs during practice. The other guys are getting loose and lining up with the "gutter shot" the lane mechanic told them about.

Practice is over and the tournament begins. Hermie and his teammates want to start off very aggressive and sustain it all day. They have been thinking about this for a year and have practiced very hard. They are hoping that they are the ones to beat. Hermie looks behind their lanes and sees no one. He is not worried because he knows somebody will show up.

All four friends are really focused and Hermie starts with five strikes and feels very comfortable. He looks back again and sees his grandparents. As he walks toward them, he sees Jane and some of her friends just walking in. It looks like Jane brought Maria, Suzi, Belinda, and Angie to support the boys. She greets him with a hug and a small kiss on the cheek. Everybody wishes Hermie and his friends the best of luck. Hermie is fired up now.

Hermie gets a few spares in the middle of the game, then he strikes out for a score of 238 which makes him the current leader. Scott rolls a 221 for second place, while Hank shoots 209 for 5th place and Charlie had early struggles and winds up in 8th place with a 186. They all know where to throw the ball, but they are all a bit nervous and excited at the same time. They hope their nerves settle down for the next game.

After the first game ends, all of the competitors move one pair of lanes to the right and begin the second game. Scott starts off with six strikes in a row. Hermie has two spares followed by four more strikes. Charlie and Hank are shooting at a 200 pace. In the 7th frame, Scott leaves a "pocket 7–10" split then follows it up with a "Big 4" in the 8th frame. Scott looks like he is about to cry. Hermie tells him to stay strong.

Scott finishes strong for a 234, which keeps him near the top. Hank gets a surge and finishes with a 222. Hermie experienced an "over-under" reaction and didn't strike that much. He shoots a 219 and barely remains in 1st place. Charlie strings a few strikes in the middle of the game and ends with a 215 to move him up to 6th place.

The third game begins and Hermie and Charlie start with six strikes. Hank and Scott are going at a slower 190 pace. Neither can seem to get two strikes in a row, but they are making their spares and avoiding costly splits. Hermie's grandparents, Jane, and her friends are starting to cheer and are getting excited.

In the 7th frame, Charlie leaves a "ringing" 10 pin and there are many "ooohhh's" heard in the bowling center. He makes the spare. Hermie continues to strike and is really wired. In the 9th frame, Hermie leaves a "blowout" 10 pin, and another round of "ooohhh's" is heard again. Hermie has a slight letdown, but still remains positive.

In the end, Hermie shoots a 268 to give him a comfortable lead going into the last game. Charlie spares two more times for a 256 and knows he is in position for a spot on the team, depending on his final game. Hank strikes out in the 10th frame for a 215 and Scott follows close behind with a 209. Both do not seem too happy.

Jane is so excited, she rushes down and gives Hermie a big hug and tells him, "You are sooooo good!! I knew you were going to do great! You have one more game. You can do it."

While that is taking place, there is other hot action that the boys should be taking note of. Tyler, who was in 5th place after the second game, just bowled a 279 game and has moved up to 2nd place, about 30 pins behind Hermie. Paul was in 7th place after the second game, bowled a 257 to move up to 4th place. Unofficially, he is the cut to make the team.

This grabs Scott's attention and Scott tells the gang, "Wow, I thought we had the inside line on where to play. I guess them dudes saw us score from the gutter and decided to play out there for a while."

Hank adds, "I saw most of the guys play outside after about the 7th frame, but some of them caught up. We don't have that secret information anymore."

Everybody is now throwing the ball near the gutter, having discovered the secret to success. Now more high scores are being reported and this could change things.

After the last bowler finishes his third game, the tournament staff calculates the scores to determine an official ranking after the third game. Most of the bowlers who think they have a chance usually calculate their own scores, and sometimes the scores of their opponents to get a feel of where they stand.

After a painful 15-minute wait, the official results are in for the third game. In 1st place with a 725 is Hermie, second place is Tyler with a 695. Here is where it gets interesting. In 3rd place is Charlie with a 657, 4th place is Paul with a 656, 5th place is Scott with a 654, and the 6th and final spot is Hank with a 646 total for three games. They are reminded that 5th and 6th places are for the substitutes.

In addition, there is another bowler who has an outside chance of making the cut. Julio, who was in 3rd place after the first two games, is currently in 7th place with a 638 series, which is only eight pins behind Hank. If Julio were to shoot a huge game, he could grab up a spot on the team. Everybody now knows who everybody else is.

Hermie and his pals have a good idea on what score they need to make the team. Hermie knows that he is in as long as he does not "fall off the planet" and shoot below 150. And the way he feels, he thinks he may have a 150 by the 7th or 8th frame. But he also knows there are three other guys that could spell trouble for his friends.

Hank guesses he will need a 235 to make the team, even as a sub. His confidence in bowling is rather low compared to that on the football field. The only reason he bowls is to be with his friends. He wants to make the team but thinks that he probably won't make the cut because he has not shot a big game all day. Anyway, football is his primary focus.

Scott says, "I never would have thought that I would be this close to the cut and then start losing ground in the last two games. This is tough."

Hank says, "We both have lots of ground to make up, so let's do it."

The final game of the day begins. Hermie and his friends all begin with a couple of spares. Hank and Scott seem the most worried because they have the most ground to make up. They look around and nobody is throwing strings of strikes. Now they are even more nervous.

Hermie tells the gang, "Get away from the gutter and throw the ball closer to the center because the oil on the edge has dried up." They hesitate at first but then decide to take his advice, and suddenly pins are falling from all different directions.

Hermie is not really trying that hard, but is shooting at a 210 pace. He is spending time with his grandparents and Jane. Charlie is also taking the low-stress approach and is spending time talking to Jane's friends. Hank and Scott, who have more to lose, are suddenly stringing strikes and are feeling less pressure. Although they have the urge to peek at their opponents' scores, Hermie tells them to bowl their own game.

Hermie looks at Jane, and each time he sees her or hugs her, he thinks of last night, when they were intimate. That gets him excited; it also gives him an idea.

He tells Charlie, Hank, and Scott, "If you wanna bowl better, think of things that get you excited. If it's a pretty girl or a video game that gets your blood pumping, then think of that. It works for me and it can work for you."

It's the 10th frame and Hermie, the lead-off bowler, decides to slow play the tournament; he wants to see others finish before him and his friends. He goes into the restroom to wash his hands. After a five-minute delay, Hermie leaves the restroom to finish his game. If he strikes out, he will shoot 220 for a 945 set and probably be the leader.

He throws his first ball and strikes. Whoops. He begins to fidget with his thumbhole and buys time as he watches Tyler finish his game. Tyler gets a split in the 10th frame and shoots a 185 for a four-game total of 880. Tyler is not happy and almost kicks a chair, but Hermie knows he made the team. Currently, that's the score to beat. Now everybody starts doing math to see what scores they need to beat him.

Hermie gets up and throws his second shot pretty sloppy and gets a 9 count, leaving only the 5 pin. He plays with his thumbhole again, so to watch Paul finish up.

Paul, who is a junior, started strong but finished weak with a 211 game and an 867 series. Currently, this is second place. He made the team last year but got demoted to a sub because he had personality issues with the coach's nephews.

Miguel, who is a senior, bowls the 10th and strikes out for a 216 and an 858. This is currently 3rd place, but he may be out of luck this year with all the high scores. Miguel made the second team last year and took the 6th spot; one spot ahead of Hermie. Miguel would like to be on the team this year.

Joseph, who was also on the second team last year, was in 10th place before the fourth game started. He finishes his final game with a missed spare and shoots a 190 for an 823 set. Last year he shot 820 and got a spot on the team. This year it will not be enough. Joseph quietly leaves the center.

Hermie makes his spare and shoots a 210 game for a 935 series and knows he has a spot on this year's team. He is currently the leader and thinks he will stay there because Tyler was his closest rival. He lets out a long exhale, and closes his eyes and looks up.

As he walks off the lane, he covers his face with his shaking hands. He is so joyous and excited that he is about to cry. He can hear some clapping and cheering from his grandparents, Jane, and her friends. All of his buddies pat him on the back because they know he bowled great and led the tournament all day.

Hermie walks off the lanes and gets teary eyed as he hugs his grandparents, saying, "Oh my God. I did it. I finally did it."

"Yes, you did it! We knew you could do it. We are so proud of you. Your father would be proud too," his grandparents tell him.

Jane is standing close, hugs him next, and says, "You were so awesome today! You made it look so easy. Were you nervous?"

Hermie, who is still trembling, says, "Big time! I was shakin' the first game but it went away after I got loose. Wow, I am so glad it's all over. Now to see if the other boys make the cut. I think Hank is gonna need lots of help."

Hermie shakes his head and takes a deep breath. He is pacing like an expectant father. It's the end of a long road for him. All that practice, all that hard work, and all that training finally paid off. What a feeling; now to see if his friends will follow.

Charlie is up next and has strikes in the 8th and 9th frames. Striking out will give him a 235 and an 892 series, which would vault him into 2nd place for now. He throws his first shot and he is nervous; the ball goes high and he gets seven pins. He has to make it to beat Tyler, who is currently in 2nd.

He throws his spare and chops it so bad that he makes it. He stands there for a few seconds in sheer disbelief and just stares at the pins. On his "fill ball" he gets an 8 count for a 224 game and an 881 series. That puts him in 2nd place, just one pin over Tyler. Tyler is now in 3rd place and he shakes his head in disbelief.

Charlie knows he made the team and nervously walks down the lanes yelling, "Yeah, count me in too!!" He walks off the lanes and back to Jane's group where Hermie is waiting for him and gives him a "double high-five." Belinda steps in and gives Charlie a big hug and holds him tightly, almost like a baby. Charlie looks very tired and drained. Hermie can see a big smile and a big sense of relief on Charlie's face.

On lanes 1 and 2, Julio is finishing up his game. After the third game, he was in 8th place, only 19 pins behind Charlie. If Julio strikes out, he will shoot 245 and beat Charlie's total score by two pins. This will put Julio in 2nd place and drop Charlie to 3rd.

Charlie and Hank eagerly watch as Julio throws three strikes and finishes with a 245 game and an 883 series. He is currently in 2nd place. The only person left that could beat him is Scott. Julio walks off the lanes with his arms up in the air and he is very happy. Julio gets a round of applause from Hermie and the boys as they shake his hand.

Hank is up next and can strike out for an 870 series, which would give him the last substitute spot, assuming that Scott takes the last team spot. This could also knock Paul off the roster completely. What a complicated mess this has become. Hank won't be a regular starter on the team, but he can still try to be an alternate. He knows that the weekly bowling schedule would conflict with his football practice. And for him, football is his focus while bowling is just a hobby.

Hank gets up and "packs" all three of his shots and shoots a 224 for an 870 set. He just earned a substitute spot on the team unless Eddie knocks him off. Not a bad deal considering the high scores today. It's a bittersweet win for Hank, but he will take it.

Next, it's Scott's turn to finish his game. He is a slight bit nervous and completely forgot what score he needs to make the team. He looks around the center. It's so quiet that it seems everybody is watching him. Now he starts to sweat.

Scott has lots of physical talent, but his mental game needs improvement. He typically looks up at the scoreboard to determine the minimum amount needed to qualify. He often tells himself, "If I get a 9 count and miss the spare I will still shoot a score that qualifies." Hermie decides to intervene and thinks of something to tell Scott to get his mind off the 10th frame. He tells Scott to think about seeing and talking to Suzi.

Scott thinks about Suzi and that gets his mind off bowling. Hermie tells Scott, "You know where to put the ball, just roll it and let the ball do the work."

Scott throws his first ball and gets eight pins. He doesn't know it, but if he misses the spare, he will get the last substitute spot and Tyler will get the last starter spot. Hermie reminds Scott to "reach out" and Scott makes the spare. Scott, still nervous, throws his final shot and gets eight pins for a 236 game and an 890 series, which is 2nd place.

Tyler kicks a chair because he just got handed a substitute spot instead of a starter spot. Then Paul kicks a chair because he just lost his substitute spot, which he thought he had all wrapped up. Last year, Paul had a spot on the second team but didn't bowl due to an injury. Paul is not happy right now.

Just as Scott walks off the lane, he looks in the area of Hermie's grandparents and sees Suzi. She smiles at him as she claps for his efforts. Although she is one year younger than Scott and looks very plain, he still thinks she is hot and he smiles back. Scott is now very relieved after seeing her. Then she hugs him.

The last person that has an outside chance is Eddie. He was in 9th place after the third game and needs three strikes for a 240 game to knock Hank off the team. Eddie leaves a single pin in the 10th frame and shoots 220 for an 856 series. He comes up short.

Eddie is fired up because he shot about 860 last year, was the #3 seed, and made the team. This year, the scores were higher and he finished 8th. He is complaining to the director about the easy lanes. The director tells him that he has no control over the lane pattern. Eddie is also irate that the other team didn't have to qualify.

The bowlers that didn't fare too well know who they are and promptly leave the building. Hermie and his friends are sitting down changing their shoes. All of them are in a great mood, but they can tell Hank is not as cheerful.

Eddie walks by and tells Hermie, "Must be nice being left handed. The shot was so easy from there that a blind dog could have qualified. What a load of crap."

"I guess they weren't easy enough for you," Hermie retaliates, "If you didn't like the lanes then you shouldn't have bowled. I didn't like how the coach kept his loser relatives on the first team without makin 'em bowl. THAT'S the REAL load of crap. I bet none of them wimps could've shot over 800 cause they suck!"

Eddie shuts up and nods his head in agreement as he walks out of the building.

Hermie tells Hank, "I don't get it. Eddie, Paul and those guys are way better than the coach's nephews but they had to try out for the team. That just ain't right."

Hank says, "Miguel was telling me that the coach decided to break up the second team because they didn't perform very well. According to my math, they had a better record than Lou's team. That makes no sense."

149

Charlie adds, "This whole thing stinks. Hopefully we can make some changes this coming year; starting with a new coach. One that wants to win."

The director approaches the microphone and announces the official final results.

"Thanks to all who continue to support our school's bowling program. Here are the results of today's team qualifier. The tournament leader and captain of the second team is Hermie with a 935, the second qualifier was Scott with an 890, third was Julio with an 883, and the last team spot goes to Charlie with an 881. Congratulations to all of you. If any of these starters cannot bowl, then one of the two substitutes will take their place."

Then he adds, "The first substitute spot goes Tyler with an 880 series and the second spot goes to Hank with an 870. If any of these substitutes cannot bowl, then our alternate, Paul, who shot an 867 series, will take their place on the team. Don't forget that the first team meeting will be here in two weeks at 2 o'clock. Please attend. Thank you."

Scott is excited and says, "This is so cool! We all made the team. Hank, you came on strong and got a sub spot. That will work great with your football stuff."

Hank tells them, "I am happy about how I performed today, and at least I got a sub spot so I can still bowl with you guys on occasion. I guess it's a good thing I didn't get a starter position, because I would probably be missing a lot of weeks due to football and track. It was a good day overall. Plus Angie was talking to me, so that's cool too."

Julio comes up to Hermie and says, "Congrats on winning the whole thing. You threw the ball great and I had a feeling you were the one to beat."

Hermie replies, "Thanks. I think what helped me was starting off strong and losing those butterflies. Heck, you came back real strong. If there was one more game, I probably would have ended up in 3rd or something."

Julio is a junior and is a little taller and thinner than Hermie. He is of Hispanic descent and his skin is a little darker than Hermie's, even though Hermie's grandmother is also Hispanic. Julio was on the second team last year but didn't have much luck.

Julio says, "I was on the team last year and we finished dead last. We had some good players but we really sucked. I was a sub but I didn't bowl until January. The coach was desperate to win games and not finish last and put me in. I helped win games and we moved up, but some crybaby wanted to bowl every week, so they took me out and we lost games again."

Hermie responds, "That's pretty sorry. Why put a team together if you don't wanna win? You know? Then you gotta pull out the player that's suckin eggs. All the pros do it. You suck and you get benched. It's that simple."

Julio says, "I think we have a really good shot of making the playoffs this year. You guys bowl well together, and me and Tyler will try to help you out. I know we can beat Lou's team and win the district title. The coach would just freak out."

Charlie says, "I think we gotta pretty good chance too, but I just wanna whoop up on the first team. That will make a statement. I can't wait for the season to start."

All four bowlers pack up their stuff, and Hermie's grandparents offer them lunch as a victory lap. Hermie looks at his watch and it's about 2 o'clock. He says he is craving fried rice and wants to go to his favorite Chinese restaurant because of their buffet. The other guys like the idea and invite Jane, her friends, and Julio.

They arrive at the restaurant in the nick of time; a group of 20 walks in right behind them. The waitress takes them to a large table and points to where the food is. The boys practically run over the waitress as they grab plates and start to pile on the chow. They are so hungry that they pick food off their own plates and eat while standing in line.

Hermie's grandparents and Jane's posse watch Hermie's army make complete pigs of themselves and the boys don't care. It's okay because they did work hard today and put up with a lot. All those strikes took lots of energy and they have to refuel. Jane thinks she heard pig noises and some snorts.

After the gluttony is complete, Hermie invites his gang of pigs back to his house to relax. He tells them that his grandparents will be there, so they can't have any booze. Hermie invites Julio over and he accepts.

At the house, everybody is lazy and hanging out in the living room watching TV. Julio and the boys are getting along well, and Hermie notices they have a few things in common. Julio loves video games and bowling. Hermie also noticed that Julio was looking at some girls at the lanes. They do not talk about parties because of his grandparents. Hermie thinks Julio will be a great addition to the team.

Around 7 o'clock, Hermie's grandparents leave as well as some of Jane's friends. The remaining crowd opens a few cold drinks, and they have a mini-celebration and talk about the great day they all had. Hermie, Charlie, and Scott still remain, as well as Jane and Belinda. At 10:15 the party winds down and everybody goes home.

Hermie gives Jane a ride home. After they get out of his car, she wants to walk around the block. He does not mind. As they walk, she reaches for his hand and they hold hands while walking around her neighborhood.

She tells him, "You were so awesome today! You're my little pro bowler. I am so proud of you. I'm so glad you got a spot on the team because it means a lot to you. I know your team will kick everybody's butt this year. Maybe you'll win it all!"

He replies, "I tried not to think about the spot on the team, but it was hard. I just thought about throwing good shots one frame at a time. I used the new equipment my grandparents gave me and it felt great. Then the pins were falling all over the place and I was trippin' out. Maybe our romp in the tub did me some good cause it blew my mind and freaked the pins. Whatever it was, it worked."

Jane has a naughty grin on her face as she says, "Maybe the next time you have a tournament, we can get together and mess around again. It was fun."

The kids continue to walk around the block until they reach her house. He walks her up to the front door and holds her tightly. Both look into evening sky.

Hermie says, "Thanks for coming out with your friends and cheering us on. It was pretty cool having someone cheer for us. I still can't believe I finally made the team, and I promise to do the best I can. I also wanna show the coach and the other team that we're for real. I'm ready to show them all."

Jane tells him, "I had a great time. I'm not much into bowling, but you and your friends make it exciting. I'm going to start attending more of your bowling things. I know you'll do your best. You always do."

She tells him goodnight and gives him a goodnight kiss; then another. She tells him she will see him in school on Monday.

Hermie gets in his car and drives home. He quickly marches upstairs and goes straight to bed. He is very tired from a long day of activity and falls asleep within five minutes. What a great and memorable day it was.

Chapter 12

An Expected but Rudimentary Alteration to a Blissfully Busy but Predictable Lifestyle

It's the Monday following the monumental performance from Hermie and his friends on the lanes. They are still flying high with confidence and emotion about finally earning a spot on the team. This is a spot they should have had last year. Hermie and his buddies could not be happier. They also cannot wait for the season to start.

He sees Jane in the hallway and they have their usual hug and kiss. She congratulates him once again for bowling so well during the qualifier and reiterates how happy she is for him. He tells her that he still cannot believe he led the tournament all day and was the top seed. He thinks it was the new equipment his grandparents got for him. Jane has seen Hermie bowl before and knows he has some talent.

On Wednesday, Hermie sees Jane at school. When he comes up to her in the hallway for their usual hug and kiss, she looks bothered, as if something is on her mind.

As he greets her she tells him, "I've been thinking. Ever since I was a little girl, everybody called me Jane, which is really my middle name. I have decided that if people are going to take me seriously, then I need a serious name. From now on, people can call me Laurie, which is really my first name. I have to go now, I will see you later," as she hugs Hermie and quickly walks down the hallway.

Hermie is stunned, just like a housefly being grazed with a flyswatter. He doesn't know what to think, much less how to react. But he wonders what brought about this change. Maybe she is trying to change her image, but why?

On Friday, Hermie sees Jane in the hallway. He calls her Laurie and she seems so responsive. They talk about their week and Hermie asks her out for tomorrow. Surprisingly she accepts. He wants to play miniature golf and she sounds partially excited about it. He wants to ask her about a window visit but will wait until tomorrow.

On Saturday, Hermie and Laurie have a date. They go out and play mini-golf. They play nine holes but this time thcy do not make a bet. Hermie wins most of the holes. He notices that Laurie does not have her usual charisma and energy. He asks her if something is wrong and she just tells him she is tired.

After golf, they go to the local barbecue restaurant because he is in the mood for some smoked brisket. After they sit down to eat, he asks her about a window visit.

He asks, "So when's our next window visit? I can't wait."

She sounds distracted and replies, "Uh, I don't know right now; maybe November or December. It's too early to know right now."

That wasn't the answer he was expecting, but at least he got an answer. He notices she is still acting distant. He looks at her closely and sees a tired and worn-out face.

After dinner they drive back to her house. They are not talking much and that's driving Hermie crazy. He can't take it anymore, so he decides to lay it on the line.

As they arrive at Jane's house he asks her, "Hey, you've been pretty quiet all night and it's driving me nuts. What's going on? Is there something wrong?"

Laurie pauses for a moment and tells him, "It's my oldest sister Sheryl. She's the one that got married back in the summer. She doesn't like being married anymore. When she comes to visit, she spends the whole time complaining about her husband. She says he can't do anything right. He spends too much money, he's out with his friends too much, he's a slob, and she's tired of it. And I am tired of listening to her complain."

"Whoa, that's pretty heavy. But how did you get involved in all this riff raff? I know y'all are sisters, but she doesn't have to dump on you, does she? That junk would bring me down too," replies a surprised Hermie.

Laurie clarifies, "Well, she and I are very close. She taught me about school and college and jobs and money. She taught me a lot of things about growing up that my mom didn't teach me. So whenever she's happy, I'm happy too. Whenever she's sad, I'm sad too. I can't explain it, but it's like me picking up her feelings."

"Wow, that's wild. Sorry for nagging you, but you were making me trip when you were going silent movie on me. I thought you were mad at me or you got an F on a test or something. I got it now," says Hermie.

Hermie walks her to her doorstep and they both have a hug goodnight. He does not bother her for a kiss and will give her some space. Now he knows the truth but wonders how it might affect her in the next few weeks.

The following week at school, Laurie acts the same as last week. She has very little energy, she walks slowly, she is constantly looking down, her hugs are pretty weak and emotionless, and getting a kiss from her is almost a chore. This is starting to worry Hermie.

He is not sure whether to try to help her or just leave her alone. He decides to leave her alone and tries to keep their conversations to a minimum so he doesn't bother her. He knows she is going through a lot, but it's also affecting him too.

The following Saturday morning, Hermie and his teammates go to the lanes for their weekly league competition. They are excited about the school team meeting immediately following their league. They have been thinking about it for two weeks.

The meeting begins after their league session is over. The coach discusses the rules of competition and hands out a schedule for the entire season. Both school teams are in the same district with six other teams. The top two teams earn a playoff spot and fight for the district championship. The district winner advances to the regional playoffs in April. The regional playoffs and the quarterfinals are on separate weekends, but the semifinals and the finals are on the same day, also in April and in Austin.

Since Hermie was the high qualifier for the rolloffs, he was selected as the team captain. The coach mentions that the captains have an added responsibility of ensuring attendance. If he chooses not to be the captain, he can relinquish his duties to somebody else. He decides to be the captain. Lou is the captain of the other team; no surprise there.

The coach does not sound very excited because for the last eight years, his #1 team has made it to the district playoffs three times, only to lose in the first round. The second team hasn't even won 50 percent of their games in the last three years. He would like a different outcome this year. Lou's team is the #1 team and Hermie's team is the #2 team.

He reminds the teams that their competition starts next Thursday and runs every Thursday afternoon at 4 o'clock sharp. If anybody is late when scoring begins, then they cannot bowl that game. In addition, there will be a several weeks where travel will be required to Austin. Arrangements have already been made with their teachers and leaving the campus at 2:30 is highly recommended.

After the meeting, the boys decide to go to the arcade and invite Julio. Charlie is in the mood for some greasy pizza and nobody argues.

At the arcade, Hermie says, "Wow, the school teams have sucked hard for the last eight years. And the second team sucked even harder. I don't get it. Some of those guys that we beat in the qualifier were pretty good. Don't tell me that all these little towns have a team of pro bowlers and whipped our school every week."

Julio says, "I was on the second team last year and we had some good players. But some of us didn't get along. Then we had attendance problems and then some guys got hurt. Paul was on the team but hurt his hand and missed the whole year. The coach put this whiny brat on our team that couldn't spare but wanted to bowl every week. We were dead last in our district because everybody beat us. It sucked."

"That's stupid. Where did this whiny kid come from?" asks Hermie.

"He's a friend of the coach and was probably promised a spot," says Julio. "After the Christmas break, I finally got to bowl only because the coach didn't want our team to finish dead last at the end of the year. We won a few games and moved out of last, but it was too late."

"That coach's got a screw loose," says Charlie. "If he's complaining about his losing streak, why don't he put together a team of good players instead of making a team from his family? That don't win championships."

Julio replies, "I agree. I think you guys have that combination. You guys are pretty good and you all get along. Don't be surprised if the coach gets jealous."

"What do you mean jealous? Of us? How's that possible?" asks Hermie.

"I think if our team starts winning more games than his hand-picked team, he might be jealous and start to resent us. It's just a guess," answers Julio.

Charlie is fired up and barks, "I didn't know he's like that but it don't surprise me. I wouldn't put it past that bum to act like a big baby. I already know he hates us. He screwed a couple of us out of team spots last year. But this year the joke was on him. We all made the team. What's he gonna do now, drop our team and create another handpicked one full of losers? He'd be more pathetic than I give him credit for."

They eat, talk about the upcoming bowling schedule, and just hang around for two hours before finally going to Hermie's house. Hermie tells them that he has to mow the grass, and trim the bushes and trees. They boys offer to help him on Sunday if they can lounge around today. Hermie accepts their offer and everybody lounges around for the rest of the day.

The following Monday Hermie sees Laurie in the hall and they exchange hugs and he finally gets a kiss that feels like she means it. Laurie seems a bit more upbeat and Hermie tells her that next week he wants to have their next window visit. Laurie agrees and tells him she cannot wait. Hermie's mind and heart begin to race. Hermie is thinking that maybe she has snapped out of her spell and is back to normal.

That Thursday afternoon, the boys travel to the nearby town of Antler for their first week of team bowling competition. They find the center and it has only 16 lanes, which is smaller than their home center of 24 lanes. They walk inside; it's practically full. There are two districts of eight teams each that will be bowling today. Hermie checks the schedule and his team will be bowling Lou's team. He licks his chops and tells his team that he wants to whip Lou's team. This will prove which team is better.

Hermie and Charlie start off very aggressive and a little angry, while Scott and Julio are a little bit apprehensive and nervous. Hermie really wants to beat this team and get the mental advantage early in the season. Charlie just wants to see a good old butt kicking against the coach's team.

In the end, Hermie's team wins all five points. Hermie is the top scorer with a 675 series, followed by Charlie with 640, then Julio with 630, and Scott with a 620. On the other hand, the "Coach's Team" didn't fare so well. Their top bowler shot a disappointing 610, followed by a 570, 540, and 500.

Hermie is not impressed with these guys. He is convinced they are lucky because they are related to the coach, because if they would have bowled the qualifier, none would have made the cut. The coach comes up to Hermie and his team and congratulates them on some good bowling. He mentions that two members of the other team were just getting over a cold, thus the low scores. Hermie ignores him.

Hermie tells his team, "Did you hear that? The coach is already making excuses for his team. He said a few of the guys were getting over a cold."

"A cold? Whatever," Scott asks. "Why didn't he use subs? He's got 2 of them. Why can't he admit these fools can't make a spare?"

"He's too ashamed that we whipped their asses. It felt great!" says Charlie.

That Saturday morning before their bowling begins, Charlie notices a new team that just joined their league. It's Lou's team. This surprises all of them and makes them laugh. They are all thinking the same thing as to why Lou's team is there.

Charlie says, "I bet the coach made 'em join because they needed some practice after the shellacking we gave 'em. Buncha posers."

"Let's see how they do at the end of the season," says Hermie.

"Better yet; let's see how they do when we take them on," says Scott.

"I'm already waitin for that day," says Charlie as he starts to salivate.

On Monday Hermie sees his friends and Laurie at school. Then he notices Lou and Lou's teammates also in the hallways.

He knows they have been there all year, but this is the first time he has seen them at school. Perhaps it's because he already sees them on Thursdays and Saturdays.

That Thursday, the boys travel to Austin for their second week of school competition. They face a team that looks pretty tough. They find out that this team has been to the state semifinals the last three out of four years. This could be a challenge.

After a fierce battle and three close games, Hermie's team takes two points from their opposition. They feel fortunate because two of the guys shot over 700. Julio was the top scorer for his team with a 680 series, followed by Scott with a 660, then Hermie with a 650. Now they know the competition is tough and they know who to watch out for.

It's finally Saturday morning and Hermie wakes up excited. Tonight is the night for a window visit at Laurie's house. He goes to work thinking about what the evening has in store for him. He thinks of all the great times they've had and hopes for another memorable night. He knows it's been a long time since their last visit and both are due.

That evening he drives his car to Laurie's house, parking at the end of the block. He arrives at 9 o'clock, carefully walks to her house, and gently taps on her window.

Seconds later she opens the window and gives him a hug and a small kiss. He smells booze on her breath and remembers what happened the last time they drank that junk. He is cautious and the first thought in his head is, "Oh no, here we go again. I wonder what'll happen this time."

She invites him inside and he casually climbs in through the window. She is wearing some blue denim shorts and a small white button-up blouse. She has no shoes on, just socks, and her room is dim, as usual. Hermie smells her soft powdery perfume in the air.

She is not talking very much and has him sit on the bed as she goes to her dresser and pours two whiskey shots. She hands him one. Hermie refuses the drink at first, but she strongly recommends that he take the drink with a nervous smile on her face.

Hermie almost chokes on the booze, remembering that he is not very fond of this sour mash. Luckily she has some soda to wash it down. He is sitting on her bed and she sits beside him. She asks him if he wants another shot and he politely refuses; she refuses too. Hermie senses that she's already had her share of this stuff.

Laurie begins the conversation by asking him, "So, how's it going? How is your job coming along?"

"I'm cool, and the job is still there," Hermie says in between coughs. "So far nobody has busted me for leaving early sometimes, so I guess I'm lucky. So, what's new with you?"

After a short silence she tells him, "Hermie, I have been doing some thinking. Ever since we started dating, I think we've been moving kinda fast. And our window visits are getting crazier and crazier each time. I don't know what's going to happen next. I'm scared we're going to get caught or get in trouble one day. And if we get caught, my parents won't ever let us date again."

Hermie looks confused and asks, "What?" knowing more ranting is on the way.

Laurie responds, "I really like you a lot and I still want to date you, but I think we need to slow down a little. I think my parents know about this window stuff. Maybe we can go out every other week and slow down on the window visits until this cools off."

"Slow down? You wanna slow down? We're barely moving already," interjects an excited Hermie. "Every date it's the same old thing and now you just joined the book club. Then I bowl on Thursdays. We hardly see each other. How can we be going too fast?"

Hermie and Laurie do not know it, but Laurie suffers from an acute case of Attention Deficiency Disorder. She gets easily overwhelmed and confused if she has to multitask or process lots of information at once. This makes her seem slower than her classmates. She is also not very good at making big decisions or dealing with confrontations.

Laurie adds, "I don't know. It's like everything's happening real fast and I'm getting confused. I can't keep up anymore. I'm watching my sister suffer and she hates her life and complains about Javier all the time. They're always mad at each other. She thinks they moved too fast and I'm scared that we might be moving too fast too."

Hermie is starting to fume and interrupts, "How can you compare us and them? How? They're 22 years old, they're out of college, and they have good jobs. They also have their own place and have pretty hair. We're different. Got it? Geez." He takes a deep breath, walks to her dresser, and pours a shot for himself.

Laurie says, "We can slow down a little until things cool off. You know, until my head isn't so dizzy anymore and until I can start figuring things out again. We can still date, but we have to slow down these visits. Then we can be back to normal. I promise."

Hermie is still steamed and blurts, "You're dizzy cause you're drunk again. All this time, I thought I was having a blast with my chick. At least I thought she was my chick. We had lots of good times like the arcade and the movies and these window visits. Now you're gonna kill 'em all cause you're scared? What are you scared of? Moving fast? It's not like we're gonna get hitched next week! Gimme a break!"

Laurie's eyes start to water, "I am so sorry and I don't mean to hurt you. I'm just afraid we're gonna get caught. And I don't want that to happen because I like you a lot and I am afraid of not seeing you anymore. I don't know what else to do."

Hermie is trying to calm down but he is still frustrated as he speaks. He looks down, shakes his head, then says, "You should have left this alone. So what if we get caught? Wasn't it fun getting here? If we get caught, we get caught. It happens to everybody! It's not like your parents are gonna take you out of school and move to the Artic Circle. Did your sister make you do this, cause you ain't talking right?"

Laurie looks like she is about to cry as she pours herself another shot and pours one for Hermie with her trembling hands. What she just said is life changing. She slams the shot down without even flinching. Hermie is about to throw the glass.

Hermie retaliates with a disgusted voice, "I don't believe this crap. We're not even heavies but we're moving too fast. I don't get it. I gotta split. You're trippin' and I'm about to break stuff. See ya." Hermie is visibly upset and climbs out the window.

Laurie is sobbing and pleads, "Wait! Please don't be mad at me. I don't want to break up, I just wanna slow down. Did you hear me? I still want to date you!"

As Hermie walks into the dark horizon, he has a walk that represents fatigue, pain, and confusion. He is so upset about the "slowing down" comment that he completely ignored the comment about "not breaking up." Laurie rushes to the window sill and apologizes over and over again, but Hermie cannot hear her anymore. He doesn't want to.

She stands there in a daze, not realizing what she just did. He gets into his car and drives home. He doesn't even look in her direction. She starts to cry again knowing it's probably over between them. She falls to the floor crying.

Hermie drives home and is replaying tonight's events in his head. The short drive home feels like forever. He tells himself, "That chick just fried my night. Where does she get off saying that crap? Moving too fast? What gives? Maybe she's got bad brains."

What Hermie doesn't realize is that Laurie didn't want to break up. She wanted to slow down the window visits because she thinks her parents know about them and are waiting to catch Hermie in the act. Unfortunately, Laurie is not good with words and her verbiage came out all wrong. Hermie interpreted it as a breakup.

Hermie goes to bed and cannot sleep. He tosses and turns all night because he cannot believe that it's over between him and Laurie. All the great times are gone as he replays them in his head all night. What happened? Could he have done anything to prevent this? What will he do now? Is there any way to make up after

165

this crazy event? What will happen when the boys find out? Maybe the whiskey made her talk silly.

Sunday morning arrives too early for Hermie, and he is startled by the ringing of the telephone. He figures it's either Scott wanting to play basketball or Laurie wanting to torture him some more. He does not answer it and goes back to sleep. The phone rings a few more times and somebody finally leaves a message. He does not care and refuses to listen to the message. He is still angry, sad, and confused all at once. He is still thinking about Laurie and what happened last night.

On Monday, he goes to school but is not in the mood to see anybody. He sees Laurie and avoids her before she sees him. He sees his friends before they see him and he hides. He brings his lunch from home and eats in his car just to avoid socializing in the cafeteria. He plans on doing this all week until he figures out a plan.

On Wednesday, Scott surprises him in the hallway and asks how he has been doing because he hasn't seen him since Saturday. Hermie mentions that he has not been feeling well the last few days. He thinks he might be catching a cold. He is not sure if he will bowl on Thursday, but he will show up and see how he feels.

On Thursday, Hermie rides with the boys to Austin again for the third week of their school bowling competition. Hermie's mind is on the breakup, not on the lanes. The guys have no idea about the breakup, but Hermie is anticipating their questions all day.

At the end of the day, Hermie's team struggled and had a horrific day on the lanes against the defending city champs. Hermie was still the 2nd highest shooter on his team with a 580. Julio was the top dog with a 615. They win only one point out of five and drop to about halfway down in the standings, but they are still a few games in front of the coach's team. Hermie didn't realize that it was going to be this tough to win points, but then again, his mind was distracted.

That Saturday, Hermie forces himself to bowl in the morning and forces himself to go to work at the store. He doesn't have any plans for the weekend and doesn't want any. He is thinking about isolating himself from the whole world to ease the pain of the breakup and to forget Laurie and everything else for a while. He just wants to be alone to clear his mind. He will not answer the phone or the front door.

As soon as he gets home from working at the store, he gets a phone call. It's Charlie and he wants to vent. Hermie is not amused and is acting secretive and bothered. Hesitantly and eventually, Hermie gives in and invites Charlie to come over and visit. Charlie hints at soaking in the hot tub and Hermie likes the idea.

Charlie shows up about 30 minutes later. And in fine tradition, Charlie brings some beer and a bottle of booze, and the two boys decide to have their own party. It looks like Charlie already had a couple before showing up. Hermie is now in the mood for a drink.

Charlie begins by mentioning, "Damn, dude, my old man's constant complaining is driving me nuts. I can't take it no more. He whines about nothing. Shoot, I had to leave the house tonight before things got ugly. And I took his last 12-pack."

"Geez, that's no good," says Hermie.

"How are you and the chick doin? I haven't seen y'all in the hallway all week," asks Charlie as they have a shot of rum.

Hermie is starting to feel pretty good and is not scared to talk about his breakup. He says, "Check it out, man. Me and the chick broke up. She dumped me. Can you believe it? She said we're moving too fast."

Charlie almost spits out his beer in shock and replies, "Moving too fast? What's her deal? Y'all barely saw each other. Is she trippin or was she high on some cheap crap? That's not cool."

"I think she was drunk again. She said her oldest sister hates being married and now it's bugging Laurie," Hermie says. "Big sis thinks they were moving too fast, so now Laurie thinks we're moving too fast. Them two girls are real close; whatever big sister does, little sister has to do. Laurie thinks that we're like her sister and her husband. But we're real different."

"Yeah, you cats are real different. They have college degrees and real jobs and don't live at home anymore. That's different," Charlie admits.

Hermie retorts, "She said we were going Speed Racer but we weren't even heavies. She blew a fuse and closed shop. I can't believe it. All those good times are gone. She was cute and kinda hot and didn't care about my bad haircut."

"I noticed she changed her name to Laurie. What's that all about?" asks Charlie.

"She said some mumbo-jumbo about using a serious name so people can take her serious. I think her first name is Laurie and her middle name is Jane. It's all psycho to me," mentions Hermie.

Charlie gives his advice, "Forget about her. There are lots of other hot chicks at school that you could check out. They all know you're a cool dude and you're a real nice guy. And this big pad shows your old man's got bread. They might think you got bread too."

Sulking and looking down, Hermie asks, "Oh yeah, what chicks?"

Charlie answers, "Aw, wake up, man. Maria is smokin' and you know she's got some killer legs. Carol dresses hot and smells great. And Loretta is a brain and cute and I bet she's packing under that shirt. Then there's Angie and she's got all the right curves. All them chicks are delicious and they all know ya. And you know them broads have buddies that are probably hot too. See, you got choices. Maybe it's time you dump the baggage and move on. They're just chicks and that's it. Have a drink; it works for me."

Hermie thinks about the words of wisdom for a minute and replies, "Wow, I never thought of it that way. All them chicks kinda know me but maybe you're right. Maybe I should start checking them out."

"I know it's tough to get over your first girlfriend. It happened to me a long time ago and it hurt real bad. I hated the world and wanted to kick its ass. But I got over it and moved on. You should too. Don't waste yourself trying to go back. It won't be the same," says a philosophical Charlie.

Charlie has a little-known secret. He has no respect for females at all. He is still very angry at his mother, who divorced his father a few years ago, moved away, and took his little brother with her. This event caused money to be real tight at home and made Charlie drop out of school for almost two years and get a job, just to help his father pay the rent and eat. His attitude toward girls is bitter and his philosophy is to "use them and lose them," which makes him treat girls like property.

Hermie and Charlie "drink and drown" into the late hours. Charlie ends up spending the night because he is too drunk to drive. They bond by talking about some private things and about girls. Hermie is so drunk that he almost tells Charlie about his most hidden secret, but catches himself before spilling the beans. They fall asleep on the couches once they enter the house.

Sunday morning arrives a bit too early. Hermie and Charlie wake up to the sound of the telephone ringing and it hurts their heads. Nobody wants to get up to answer it, but they are curious. They let it ring to see if the caller leaves a message. It's Laurie, she wants to know how Hermie is doing because she has not seen him all week. She wants to know if he is okay.

Hermie throws a shoe at the machine yelling, "Bullshit!" and goes back to sleep.

Charlie laughs at Hermie's obnoxious behavior because Hermie is usually calm and controlled. Charlie rolls around and goes back to sleep too.

They wake up around noon and have a serious case of the munchies. Hermie has an idea where they could go for some good grease. He suggests Al's Chicken Shack. It's been a while since they went over there and both are licking their chops.

They arrive and Hermie stands frozen just staring at the building. Every time Hermie visits this restaurant, he thinks of his parents because they both worked here when they were teenagers right out of high school. This is also the place where their relationship blossomed and grew.

Charlie catches Hermie staring and asks, "Hey man, are you feelin alright? You're kinda zoning out. What's up?"

Hermie replies, "I'm cool. It's just been a while since I got some good bird. And this is the right place to get it. We gotta get the family box and the fries. I bet we can slam it down, no problem."

They enter the establishment and order the family box. After devouring a 20-piece order of chicken strips with gravy and crinkle fries, they walk out ready to sleep again. They go back to Hermie's house and just lounge around watching TV. Hermie notices there are two new messages on the machine. He bets Charlie that one of them is Laurie. Charlie does not take the bet.

They listen to the messages; one is from his grandparents and the other is from the store where Hermie bought the tub. Hermie takes some notes and both boys sleep all afternoon. In the evening, Charlie goes home. Both had a great time and want to do this again real soon. Hermie has a feeling it might happen sooner than he thinks.

That night he thinks about how different it would have been if he was by himself all weekend and how boring it would have been. He is sort of glad that Charlie came by and shared his problems with him. Now Hermie knows that he's not the only one with problems. It seems that everybody has problems too.

He starts thinking about how next week will play out. He is almost certain he will see Laurie in the hallway and wonders what she will say to him. He wonders how differently he will treat her. Hopefully she will not hurt him again. He has never broken up with a girl before. Is it supposed to be like this? Is he supposed to be nice or mean or just ignore her? He is also thinking of what to say when the rest of his friends find out about the breakup.

Once again, his mind almost spins out of control as he tosses in bed. He finally falls asleep around 2 o'clock, not realizing that he has to go to school in the morning.

Chapter 13

Grammar of Despair (The Makeup: Part 1)

The following week Hermie changes his attitude and decides not to hide from his friends but is still thinking about avoiding Laurie. He is not sure if he is ready to deal with her. He is not sure what the next step is supposed to be. He thinks the talk with Charlie did him some good. Maybe he should drop Laurie and move on.

There are other girls at his school, but would they really go out with him? Hermie isn't that perfect. He has a bad haircut, has many bowling balls in his room and he has to constantly decide whether to eat fried rice or brisket sandwiches. The way Charlie said it; there are some possibilities with all of those girls.

On Tuesday, he goes to his locker and finds a note. It's a piece of white notebook paper folded up several times to the size of a silver dollar. The only writing he can identify is his name, and it looks like a girl's writing, possibly Laurie's. Hermie unfolds the paper until there is one fold left. He chickens out and folds it back into a small square and stuffs it into his jeans pocket. He will look at it later.

That night, Hermie is at home having a TV dinner and watching "The Bowlers Challenge" on TV. Next to his dinner are the contents from his pants pockets. He has the usual assortment of coins, rubber bands, and candy, but today he stares at the mysterious note that he found in his locker. He is not sure whether to finish his meal first, in case the letter upsets his stomach. He was really enjoying his cardboard Salisbury Steak dinner with plastic mashed potatoes. Yum, yum.

He opens the note and quickly reads the name at the bottom; it's from Laurie. He can tell it's from her because of the misspelled words and her grammar of despair. He shakes his head, takes a deep breath, tells himself, "Oh God, here we go," and reads it. It says:

"Dear Hermie,

I hope you are reading this becaus it took me a long time to write it. I made a big mistake. I never tryed to break up with you and I am so sorry if I said it wrong and hurt you. I just wanted to slow down a little becaus I think my parents know about our windowe visits and I didn't want them to catch us and make us stop seeing each other and beacaus I like the window visits too much to make me stop doing them and I don't want to stop.

I miss you so much and I can't stop thinking about you. I should not have said what I said and it was wrong. I cryed for 3 days straite. I wanted to say sorry but I didn't see you in school last week. I feel so bad for hurting you and I promis I will never hurt you again. You are so special to me and I feel good when we are together. Please give me a second chance and let me make it up to you. I promis you won't be sorry.

I want to come over Friday night so we can talk. Your a sweat friend.

Laurie"

Hermie has a small laugh at the poorly written note. "I'm a sweat friend? I think she means sweet. What a chick," he tells himself.

He puts the note down and looks at it. Now he has a choice to make. Does he give her a second chance or does he get tough and move on, like Charlie said? He really does miss her and she could hurt him again, but making up could change things. He will have to really think about this. It could be a life-changing decision. At least now he knows that she didn't want to break up, so that's a relief. But now he feels bad because he treated her like dirt and ignored her all week. This will be a tough decision.

During the week, Hermie thinks about that note and about the decision he has to make. He purposely avoids Laurie and sometimes he can sense that she is watching him when he is at his locker. He sees her a few times in the hallways but ducks out before she can see him or greet him. He is not ready to talk to her just yet.

On Thursday, Hermie and his team travel back to the small town of Antler, without Hank. They are feeling pretty hungry to win, since they got whooped last week by the city champs. The team they face does not look very strong, but they are leading their district. Hermie reviews the stats for this team and discovers that their opponent's district is pretty weak. During practice he is not impressed and thinks it should be an easy victory.

Hermie's mind is really not on bowling, but he is going through the motions. His mind is really on what he plans on doing about Laurie and Friday night. He does his best not to make his emotions obvious, but sometimes it's tough.

The lanes are not very well maintained and the scores are low even for that center. In the end, Hermie is the top shooter for his pair with a 630 and Julio is a close second with 615. Nobody else's scores are worth mentioning, but Hermie's team won all five points and improves their record. This should move them up to 2nd or 3rd place in their district.

Out of curiosity, Hermie looks for the results of Lou's team and finds out that they got swept again. He guesses their record is about 7-13 or less, which keeps them in last place in their district. This makes him feel good because hopefully they are showing the coach they are for real. He and the team leave the building and look for some chow.

After dinner Hermie goes home and is pretty fidgety all night. Tomorrow is the decision day. He does not know what to tell Laurie. He writes down a list of positives and negatives about getting back together; unfortunately the list is even.

He is still a little upset at what she said, but he does miss her. He also misses all the fun and crazy things they did. He misses her pretty eyes and soft skin. He believes that her letter was honest and she was telling the truth. He tosses and turns all night.

On Friday Hermie contemplates going to school and wonders what will happen. He is a little tired from being up all night thinking about what he will say to Laurie about her note. He has thought of two plans of attack.

Plan A is the "nice guy" plan. This involves telling Laurie that she can come over tonight and talk about their friendship or whatever. This plan also allows the possibility of a makeup and maybe more. Both end up happy and continue seeing each other.

Plan B is the "mean guy" plan. This involves telling Laurie that she can stay home because there is no chance for a makeup. He also plans on telling her that he does not want to see her anymore. This plan allows both kids to see other people and move on with their lives. There may not be much happiness in the beginning.

He decides to go with Plan A unless the situation gets ugly from the start. He rehearses what he will say and thinks about questions she may ask. He also decides how he will transition from one plan to the other. He does miss Laurie and hopes they can get back together. He also hopes that she does not flip out again. He can't handle this kind of pressure and stress. Soon, this whole ordeal should be over.

Hermie arrives at his locker in between classes. Laurie finally finds him and gives him a huge hug from behind and is so happy to see him.

She sounds so excited and asks him, "Hi Hermie, how's it going?"

He tells her, "Hi Laurie, I read your note…"

She is in suspense and asks, "And? What did you decide?" as she looks up at him with her big innocent eyes and eager smile.

"Okay, you can swing by the pad tonight. How does 7 o'clock sound?" asks Hermie.

Laurie is ecstatic as her face lights up and she jumps up and down. She hugs him and tells him, "Thank you, thank you so much. You won't be sorry," as she is about to cry from excitement.

She pulls him lower and gives him a big kiss, which excites both of them. She squeezes him tight and leaves to go to her next class with a big grin and a hoppy walk.

She tells him, "See you at seven!"

Hermie tells himself, "Have I lost my marbles? I hope I don't regret this," as he quickly remembers her powdery smell and how soft she felt.

After school, Hermie goes to work for a couple of hours, mainly to avoid going stir crazy at home waiting for Laurie. He works until 6 o'clock, even though the store closes at 8:30 tonight. He goes home, takes a shower, and has a quick meal. He thought of making dinner for the both of them but reminds himself that it's not a dinner date. It's just a discussion about their relationship … he hopes.

After dinner, Hermie is waiting for Laurie to show up. What will he say? What will he do? Will he let her talk all night? What if Plan A begins to crumble and it's too late to use Plan B? What is the expected outcome? All of this over-analyzing is making him batty and fidgety. He decides to play a video game on his computer to mellow out.

At exactly 7 o'clock there is a knock on his front door. Hermie knows exactly who it is as he rolls his eyes, stands up, and steps away from his computer. He slowly walks downstairs telling himself, "Turn me on, dead man."

He opens the front door and it's Laurie. She is bright eyed and greets him with a very joyous "hello." He lets her inside and both sit on the couch. She practically eyeballs him the entire time while having a happy and satisfied smile on her face. She is giving him her total undivided attention. It does not bother Hermie too much.

So what did you wanna talk about?" asks Hermie to start the conversation.

She comes out and says, "This breakup thing was wrong and I want to redo it."

Puzzled, Hermie says, "You want to break up again?"

Laurie responds "No, I want to undo it. You know, make up. I never wanted to break up with you; I just wanted to slow down a little. But when I said it, you thought we were breaking up for real and that's not it. I just said it all wrong. I should have just shut up. I am so sorry for putting you through all this. It's all my fault. You're probably hurt and mad at me and I deserve it."

"Okay, that's cool. I guess I just heard it wrong," Hermie quietly says. "You were acting weird all week and then when you wanted to break up, that was the final blow. I mean, I don't know what I did. I just got mad and didn't care anymore after that. Now it's cool and I'm not mad at you."

Laurie responds, "I know that we're not going fast, but my sister gave me hints to slow down because she feels she was going too fast. I don't know why I listened to her this time. I guess I take her advice a lot because she and I are real close."

"Well, I don't think we were going too fast. That was our first window visit in weeks. I don't get it," retorts Hermie.

She looks at Hermie and he is sitting on the couch shaking his head. He is waiting for more of her story.

"When you left my room, I tried to call you back and you kept walking. I don't know if you heard me or if you were just mad at me," Laurie adds. "I felt really bad and I wanted to make it right. I cried all night. I cried for three days straight. My friends thought we had a huge fight. I didn't know what to tell them."

"Well, I was kinda torqued, but I don't remember hearing you," he replies.

Laurie sits closer to Hermie and tells him, "I've missed you so much. I've missed being around you and talking and doing stuff. It was great. You are so sweet."

Hermie gets a chance to speak and tells her, "When you said you wanted to slow down, I thought I did something that bugged you. I freaked. I thought about it some more and I knew I didn't do anything wrong."

He pauses then adds, "I was trippin 'cause you put me in the wringer for being me. We were just having fun and that's it. I don't want us to stop either. You're real cool. Your sister might be right about some stuff, but not about our stuff. We're us."

"You didn't do anything wrong. It was me. I made a mistake and I wish I never said those things to you. You are so nice and I'm sorry I hurt you. Maybe I had too much to drink and didn't say things the right way," she says.

"I think you had too much that night. It made you crazy," Hermie says as he circles his finger around his head.

The two kids discuss their friendship for the next two hours and Laurie is doing most of the talking. She mentions how she misses him so much and how she really enjoyed their times together. She wants to go back to the way they were, but knows it will be difficult because of her book club membership and his spot on the bowling team. She also promises to visit him at the lanes more often and wants to be a better friend.

Both kids admit they like the window visits and want to keep them going, but Laurie warns Hermie about those visits. She thinks her parents are watching her real close, and she thinks she hears noises in the hallway every time Hermie is in the house. She is afraid of getting caught and being restricted from seeing him. Hermie recommends going to his house on date nights and just hanging out, and Laurie likes it.

By the end of the night, the two kids seem to have worked out their problems. One sign is that she is leaning on him with her head on his shoulder and his arm is around her. Hermie says that he is not upset with her anymore and will not ignore her like he did last week. Laurie considers this to be an official makeup and promises never to flip out. Hermie also wants her to drink less because that juice makes her do strange things and she hates the awful headache she gets the next day.

Laurie leans over to kiss him and both begin to kiss. She is in the mood to make out and she moves fast, but Hermie is not moving as fast, but keeps playing the game. The two kids continue making out for a while and hold each other tightly several times. They roll around, remove some clothing, and both end up having a great time.

After they finish playing around, Hermie looks a bit distant and tired, but tries to play it off. He is rather silent and gets dressed on the other couch.

Laurie notices his behavior and asks, "Is something wrong? You're being real quiet."

"I'm cool, but I don't know if this was the right thing to do, you know. I mean, I missed you a lot and just now it felt great, but it didn't feel right to me. Not right now. I played along because I didn't want to hurt your feelings. Isn't that crazy?" he says.

She gets the hint on how he feels and tells him, "It's not crazy. I can understand if you're not ready right now. I'll wait until you're ready."

"That's cool. Maybe I need some time or something. Kinda like time to figure things out. I don't know if its gonna be the same anymore," he replies.

She walks to the front door and tells him goodnight. Hermie asks how she is getting home and she says she will walk home. Hermie offers her a ride in his car, but she declines the offer saying that walking home is her punishment for being mean to him. He watches her leave the house.

He tells himself, "What was I thinking? I had my cake on a plate and I dropped the fork. Talk about a bonehead move." Hermie thinks he blew his chances as he sits on the couch looking down. He tells himself, "I bet if I call her back now, she'd come runnin'. She was on me like white on rice. It's gone now."

As Laurie walks home, she knows that Hermie is very special to her. He may not be the biggest or be the most handsome guy at school or have the biggest car, but he is smart, witty, and very polite. She likes his odd sense of humor and likes being around him. She also suspects that he has more money than he leads people to believe and that his parents are rich considering the big house and nice neighborhood they live in.

Laurie got many of these facts from her sisters, when they first met Hermie. She believes that if another girl at school got to know him and how nice he was, they will like Hermie too and might take him away. She also knows that Hermie checks out other girls and she can't stop that. She just hopes that they can get back together to the way it used to be because she doesn't want to lose him.

Hermie goes to bed thinking, "I have no idea what the hell just happened tonight. I guess we made up, but I don't think it's the same anymore. It didn't feel right. It's like something was missing. But at least we're friends again."

He lies in bed wondering if he made the right decision by letting her make out with him. He knows she wanted more, but so did he and he almost gave in. He thinks that by making out, Laurie believes that everything is back to normal. Hermie does not think everything is back to normal and knows it will never be. All he can hope for is to be friends with her again; but this will take some time.

On Saturday morning, Hermie and his teammates are at their local bowling center ready for another week of league competition.

Hermie begins with eight strikes before leaving a single pin spare in the 9th frame. Then he spares again in the 10th frame for a very nice 268 game. He was only two frames away from his first 300 game and is very excited.

As the second game begins, Scott tells Hermie that Laurie and some of her buddies just walked in. Hermie looks excited and waves at her. She waves back. Laurie has a few friends that bowl in this league and she is hanging out with them. Charlie sees Belinda in that crowd and decides to walk that way. Hank is thinking about joining Charlie. Scott sees Suzi over there and his eyes almost pop out of their sockets.

During the second game Hermie is stringing strikes again. He is trying to show off for Laurie and her friends, but nobody is watching because they are too far away. Charlie comes back with a happy look on his face and tells Hermie that Laurie says hello. Hermie tells Charlie that he will be over there real soon.

He walks to the other side of the bowling alley and sees Laurie, Belinda, and Suzi sitting with an all-girl team. The only girl on the team that looks familiar is Angie. He didn't know she bowled, but he might have to start paying attention from now on.

Laurie finally sees Hermie and her entire face lights up. She quickly jumps out of her seat and gives Hermie a hug and holds him like a big teddy bear, putting her head on his chest. He tells her about his first game and she congratulates him. It's Hermie's turn to bowl, so he goes back to his lanes.

Hermie gets a couple of spares in the middle of the game, then gets five strikes in a row to finish with a 257 game. He is showing some attitude and some controlled aggression, plus his new equipment is rolling well. He is loose and happy and nothing seems to be bothering him. Charlie can tell there is something different about him.

Laurie shows up for the end of the game, and she is very impressed as she gives him a high-five. His team also won the second game. Scott is telling the team that Hermie may break his personal high series of 750 at the rate he is going, but won't tell Hermie that because he probably already knows.

The third game begins, and Belinda and Suzi join Laurie in watching Hermie's team. The boys see this and begin to ham it up acting like the pro bowlers they watch on TV. Hermie starts off with a couple of spares, but Charlie and Scott start with four strikes in a row. The girls begin to clap and act like a cheering section. Hermie's team doesn't even realize how they are bowling because they are busy showing off for the girls.

In the end, Hermie shoots a 235 game for a super 760 series and their team wins all five points again. Their team is climbing in the standings early in the season. They are currently in 2nd place, up from 3rd. Hermie is very excited that he beat his personal high series from week 1. He struck less in the third game but is still really happy with his scores because he got no splits and no missed spares today.

Hermie is in a great mood and invites the whole gang to have some barbecue at a little restaurant on the edge of town because he is craving brisket and sausage. He says it's his treat because his parents sent him a pretty big check for his birthday. Everybody plans on going, even the girls. Hank cannot make it because he has other plans. Everybody piles up in their cars and makes the drive.

At the restaurant, the kids order their food and sit outside because the weather is nice. Hermie gets his trough of brisket, sausage, and fries, and licks his chops. Everybody else got a meat plate too, but Hermie's is the biggest in the crowd.

Scott tells Hermie, "Hey check this out. When I was in Houston a while back, I went to an alley and got some practice. When I left, I found this flyer for an upcoming doubles tournament in Houston near Christmas time. I got permission to bowl it. Hermie, do you want to bowl it together?" He slides the flyer to Hermie.

Hermie reads through the flyer while Scott is waiting in suspense. About halfway down the page, Hermie says, "Sure, we can shoot it together. I think that would be cool."

Scott almost faints from excitement and says, "Yes!! This is gonna be great! Hey Charlie, when you see Hank, ask him if he wants to go too."

Hermie notices that Laurie is sitting very close to him, almost like she is hovering over him. He really does not mind because he likes that soft powdery smell she has, but he likes to have some room when he eats. He feels a little cramped, but will not worry about it. He is also not sure if she will try to steal some of his fries.

She puts her arm on his back and tries to spoon feed him some green beans like a baby. She tells him to try them because they are really good. He thinks it is odd behavior but plays along with this game. The guys get a small laugh at this charade.

After the kids finish their meal, they just sit around and talk. They are all pretty stuffed. Laurie looks at Hermie as if she is waiting for him to ask her something, but he does not get the hint. But she sits there content anyway.

Although he is glad they are still friends and she seems happy to see him, he is not sure how to handle this whole "make up" thing. Are they supposed to continue as if nothing ever happened? For some reason, he still replays that fateful night of their breakup in his head. He knows he has to stop thinking that way and think of the great times, otherwise it will eat away at him and really mess him up.

Hermie looks at Laurie's pretty eyes and innocent face and knows they are buddies again. That makes him feel good. He knows the breakup was not his fault. He also knows she is waiting for him, but is not sure if he is ready to get that close to her right now. It did feel good the other night and he does miss her.

The guys ask Hermie what his plans are for the rest of the day, and Hermie tells them he will be spending the weekend at his grandparents since he has not seen them in a while. The kids get in their cars and go their separate ways. The rest of the team congratulates Hermie on his high scores, then leave.

Hermie walks Laurie to her friend's car and thanks her for showing up and cheering him on. He gives her a hug and they have a small kiss, then two, then three. She smells like barbecue and he likes it. She thanks him for lunch and tells him to call her anytime. She holds him a little longer then gets into the car and leaves.

Hermie drives to the lake by himself and watches the water flow. He stares at the water for about an hour or two and does a lot of thinking and dreaming. He thinks of his parents, his great bowling year, school, getting back with Laurie, and the lawsuit. He begins to play with the water and suddenly all those thoughts disappear. He relaxes, clears his head, and enjoys the great weather during the afternoon. Eventually he leaves the lake and visits his grandparents.

Chapter 14

A Nice Pair from Any Angle

School is out for the Thanksgiving break. The kids get an entire week off even though turkey day is on a Thursday. Hermie makes the same plans as always to go to his grandparents' house and does not mind because he knows they cook the best turkey ever.

Scott and Hank are going out of town with their families. Hermie invites Charlie because Charlie is going to be stuck by himself at home. His father has to work all weekend and he doesn't feel like being all alone. Charlie accepts the invite.

The Thanksgiving Day event is a success and everybody gets their fill from the tasty homemade meal. Charlie is in the mood for a drink and excuses himself as he goes outside to his car. Hermie's grandfather knows where he is going and mentions that he should not be drinking, but if he has a drink then he cannot drive home.

Charlie goes to his car and comes back with a large brown bag of beer and a bottle of whiskey. Grandpa confiscates Charlie's and Hermie's keys just in case. Charlie takes the beer to the fridge then pours himself a shot, much to the surprise of Hermie. They end up sipping and watching football all afternoon. It's a good day.

November was a very successful month for Hermie's school team, winning 14 out of 15 points. They are finally in 1st place in their district by only two games and have two more bowling weeks in December before the Christmas break.

Hermie and Laurie are back to hugs in the hallway and an occasional kiss. He still thinks about her a lot and remembers the great times they had. Part of him wants to get intimate with her again, but part of him wants to start seeing other girls. He is also not sure if he can trust her 100 percent anymore. In his mind he thinks that if she flipped out once, she could do it again. But they are getting closer again and that's good for now.

In early December, after their Saturday bowling, Scott and Hermie talk about the tournament in Houston later this month. Scott is excited because now he has a doubles partner. Hank cannot make it due to an injury from football practice. He is bummed out because this injury will keep him from playing football and bowling for a couple of weeks. Charlie says he will still join Hermie and Scott up in Houston to root them on to victory.

That week, Hermie begins a serious practice regimen for him and Scott. He wants to learn to throw the ball from different parts of the lane and work on his spares. He also wants to make adjustments faster when the lanes change. Even though the tournament is two weeks away, Hermie wants to practice every other day. Scott has no problem with Hermie's wishes because he is ecstatic just to bowl with him.

That Thursday, the school bowling league ends up in Pibb. This is the home turf for Hermie's team. The boys are already feeling confident, plus their emotions are elevated even higher when they discover they are taking on "the Coach's Team" again. They are practically celebrating a victory before throwing their first ball.

They look at Lou's team and try to greet them, but get ignored. Charlie suddenly gets in one of his "If he won't say hi, then forget 'em" attitudes. Hermie is just full of animosity against this team and their coach.

Both Hermie and Charlie start off with six strikes. Charlie ends up shooting a 248 game and Hermie finishes with a 268. Hermie and Charlie are fired up, slapping hands and getting Scott and Hank excited too. The way they are carrying on, they sound like they are very angry, but they are having a great time and scoring well.

That whooping seemed to subdue the usually loud "Coach's Team" because their next two games result in lower scores. At the end of the day, Hermie shoots a 690 series and Charlie a 660, while Julio and Scott barely break 610. Hermie's team wins all five points again, and the coach and his team congratulate them for their win.

After bowling, Hermie and his team find their favorite local barbecue joint and have dinner there. Hermie asks them, "Why do we call him coach? He doesn't coach us and he barely talks to us. I think it's because he is too busy pampering his favorite team, the same team that probably won't be in the playoffs this year."

Hank says, "I saw the standings and it's too late for them to make a charge."

"As if them sissies had a chance," says Charlie.

"I know they're watching us, especially after beating them a second time," replies Scott. "I'm sure they'll win a few more games, but it won't be many."

After dinner Hermie goes home and sees the answering machine blinking with a "1" next to it. He is guessing it's Laurie. He listens to the recording and he's right. She wants to know how he bowled today and wants him to call her back. Hermie sits on the couch and contemplates calling her. He begins to weigh the pros and cons of this conversation. He continually tells himself, "It's only talking on the phone, that's all."

Hermie calls Laurie and she sounds very excited to speak to him, just like old times. He tells her that they beat up on the coach's team again and it felt great. She knows that Hermie can't stand that coach and congratulates him on their victory.

The two kids talk for about an hour, which is 50 minutes longer than he anticipated. In the end, Hermie feels better for talking to her and feels like a weight has been lifted off his shoulders. He is starting to feel better about her.

It's now Friday, the middle of December and the last day of school for the year. Hermie gets a note in his locker. He guesses it's from Laurie so he opens it and reads it. Again he is right; she says it's been so nice seeing him again and hearing his voice too. She wants to wish him well on his Houston tournament and would like to give him a good luck kiss, if that's okay with him.

Just as he turns around, there she is, waiting, with her bright eyes and a big smile. She hugs him and tells him to lean down a little. They have a small kiss, which turns into a longer kiss, and then she holds him like she hasn't seen him in years.

She tells him, "Good luck in the tournament and maybe we can go out and do something when you come back. Call me when you get back."

Hermie was not expecting her to say that but knew the subject was going to flare up sooner or later. He replies, "Uh; yeah maybe. I'll call you when I come back."

"Maybe we can see each other during the Christmas break," she says.

"Okay," says Hermie.

Both kids go their separate ways. He is feeling pretty good right now; it almost feels like old times with Laurie. He also didn't realize that today is the last day of school. Where has his mind been lately? He forgot to get Laurie a Christmas gift. He can always buy her one next week and deliver it to her house, since he knows where she lives.

That evening, Hermie and his buddies go through their usual tournament ritual; they spend the night at Hermie's house before the big day. Charlie is also bringing his equipment in case somebody needs a sub. The three friends stay up until about midnight, watching TV and playing video games. Charlie doesn't even have a drink, which surprises everybody. His excuse is that he was broke this week, but he did bring a small stash of juice just in case they need a celebratory drink.

The next morning, all four friends get up at 7 o'clock, shower, eat, and pack Hermie's car. They finally start driving at 8:30 and estimate it's about a three-and-half-hour drive. That would put them at the center around noon and the event starts an hour later.

On the road they talk about bowling, but they talk more about girls. Charlie mentions, "Man, I'm diggin that Belinda chick; she's hot! When I first asked her out, she used to tell me she was seeing someone. But I started noticing she'd show up stag to our parties. Then she and I started rappin and we finally hooked up. I figured her story was bull or that her dude was as boring as a Joe 'cause we never saw his mug."

Hermie jumps in and says, "Yeah, I did some investigator work and asked Laurie about her. She said that Belinda used that excuse so guys would leave her alone. I guess that worked for a while. Then she waited for Charlie to ask her out."

"Wow, I didn't know that. I guess I can't keep her waitin," responds Charlie.

Scott asks Hermie, "Hey, speaking of Laurie, it looks like you guys are together again. Is that true? Are you guys cool?"

"Yeah, kind of," says Hermie. "We made up but we're starting off as friends again. In a way we never broke up, but it sounded like that to me, you know? I had a bad day at work then I went to see her and she was boozed up and rambled on about some junk. She told me that her parents were watching us under a microscope so we had to be cool and slow down."

"Slow down? From what?" Scott asks.

"I don't know. She said stuff about seeing her too much at her window at night. She either said it wrong or I heard it wrong and I thought she wanted to end it. I flipped my lid and had to split so I could figure things out. But now we're cool again and that's okay," replies Hermie.

"Wow! You went to see her at night by her window? You are a wild man," exclaims Scott. "I don't have the guts to do that."

Charlie says, "That's decent y'all are going around again. I remember you both were so happy together and you were a different dude. You were in a great mood and positive and all that stuff. You also bowled better. And she's a nice girl too."

After a stop for food, the boys make it to the center early, around 12:15, and go inside with their equipment. It's very fancy and slightly modernized. They think the President of the United States bowls here because of the beautiful interior and the sound architecture. Scott notices the smell of the new carpet, and Hermie notices the redecorated snack bar. Nobody knows it but the bowling lanes themselves got a facelift. The owner replaced the obsolete and distressed wooden lanes with more modern ones that have a tougher synthetic surface.

Hermie and Scott sign up and pay the entry fee. Charlie puts his name on the substitute list and is second on the list. The two bowlers find a seat and wait for their lane assignments to be called. While they sit, they watch many of the competitors enter the building. They start to see other people walk in; many of them are unknown but they expected that.

They finally see Sam, whom they expected, walk in with his partner, some other guy that Hermie has beaten before. A few minutes later, Lou walks in followed by Earl, the coach's other nephew. Lastly, the coach walks inside, in a pretentious and conceited manner. Hermie cannot believe his strut and starts to laugh.

At 1 o'clock, the tournament director speaks over the P.A. system. He goes over the rules and discusses how the double elimination system works. Each person bowls two scratch games for their team, and the team with the highest total pin fall wins and advances. The losers go into a losers' bracket where one more loss ends their day. Ties will be decided by a two-frame rolloff. Both team members will participate in the rolloff.

The director mentions that the age limit is 23 as long as you are in college. There are no professionals allowed. There are 32 teams and he calls out lane assignments. Hermie and Scott are on lanes 3 and 4, and they get to bowl against Sam and his partner. Hermie is smiling from ear to ear and thinking this match is a gift from the gods.

The practice lights come on, and for the first time in his short career, Hermie is throwing the ball really well. He cannot believe this and tells Scott, "Check this out, for once I am throwing more strikes than splits in practice … this could be a sign. Not just that, but we're bowling on those 'table top' lanes, you know, the synthetic ones. Maybe this is helping the pins fall down. Either way, I'm gonna ride it out." Scott nods his head in agreement. Practice finishes up and they get ready.

The first match begins and Hermie is already heckling his on-lane nemesis. He tells Sam, "This time, lift the ball." Sam starts out his game with two splits and gets angry while Hermie and Scott stay clean for most of the game. Hermie strikes out in the 10th frame to start with a 225, while Scott finishes for a 208. They win the first match 433–401. Sam is already a little upset due to his 206 game.

The second game begins a little differently. Sam begins with four strikes, but Scott is matching him. Hermie is alternating strikes and spares each frame. Sam's partner, Barry, seems to be lost but is having lots of luck carrying off hits to keep their team close. This is starting to frustrate Scott, who usually doesn't worry about these kinds of things. Hermie tells Scott not to worry about that stuff because it's out of his control. He tells Scott to bowl his own game.

Sam looks at the scoreboard and notices that their team is ahead by 20 pins, but they must win by 33 to advance to the next round, because they lost their first game by 32. Sam strikes out for a 242 and gets loud, letting people know about it. Scott gets a split in the 10th frame for a 224 game and looks like he is ready to launch a bowling ball through the window. Hermie tells him to cool off because the match is not over just yet.

In the 7th frame, Hermie is losing to Barry by 15 pins. If Barry strikes out, it could mean a loss for Hermie's team. He does not want to ruin his perfect record against Sam. Winning is very important to Hermie, and beating Sam is getting to be fun so he gets vocal and tells Barry, "What are you going to carry this time?"

In the 9th frame, Barry gets a split and in the 10th frame, he gets a five-count washout and is visibly upset, practically kicking a ball return. He is so angry that he throws his second ball in the gutter, finishing with a 158 and guaranteeing them their first team loss. Scott breathes a big sigh of relief, but Sam is pretty upset at Barry.

Hermie casually finishes out his 10th frame knowing he just has to mark. He gets a spare and strike and a 191 to win the second match 415–410. Sam and Barry hastily leave their lanes and walk to the table so they can check in for their first round in the Loser's Bracket. Scott points to the table with a smirk on his face.

Hermie laughs and tells Scott, "I didn't know Barry was that weak. I guess that's why they're teammates. I just said a few words to him and he let it get to him. And Sam still can't beat me."

Charlie comes up to Hermie and Scott and tells them, "Congrats on whipping their sorry asses. I bet that win felt as good for you as it did for me. I can't stand them punks. Alright guys, keep the fire burning. These next guys ain't pushovers."

Hermie and Scott move to lanes 5-6 for their second match. They face two guys from the Houston area. Hermie is impressed at their game and notices one player has a very volatile back-end reaction that looks nice and blasts apart the pins.

The match begins and Scott is fishing all over the lanes while Hermie is going at a good pace. The scores are about the same and Hermie finishes out with a 217 and Scott struggles for a 179 game. This falls a bit short and they lose 420-396. This is their first team loss; but they know they can't lose the next one.

In the second game, Hermie watches the cranker get himself into trouble on the right lane three times in a row, resulting in costly open frames. Hermie and Scott are on a 200 pace and are ahead by 40 pins and it's only the 5th frame. The cranker never gets on track and shoots a 174, while Hermie and Scott keep the ball in play, avoid splits, and shoot in the low 200s to win the second game 411–370 and win the match by 17 pins.

Hermie and Scott are astonished and move on to their third match. Hermie tells Scott, "We are 2-0 and with a 32-team field plus the Loser's Bracket; if we end up 6-0 we win the whole thing."

Scott is excited and says, "That sounds good to me but we still have some work to do. I feel like I am finally getting loose. Maybe I will start scoring better."

Charlie shows up and says, "You guys are doin a great job. Keep rolling like you are and you will go far. This tournament has a lot of good and lucky players. Just keep your heads and play your game."

In the third round they face a team of brothers. They are both stout and look like bodybuilders. Both have lots of revolutions on the ball, throw a big hook, and are very exciting to watch. When they throw the ball, their arms and wrists bend and flail as if made of rubber, so Hermie calls them the "Behemoth Brothers."

The match starts out pretty even, but then the brothers go into overdrive and shoot 248 and 254. Hermie and Scott shoot 244 and 216, which is their best series so far today, but still get buried 502–460. Hermie knows these boys are tough but they are human, so he thinks. It's another loss for his team, but they have come back once before.

The second game starts the way the first game ended. These brothers are throwing atom bombs at the pins while Hermie and Scott watch the match fly away. They are no match for the intensity of these power players who shoot 248 and 227, while Hermie and Scott shoot 223 and 229 to lose the second game 475–452. Hermie and Scott are shell shocked and can't believe they lost a match.

They go to the Loser's Bracket in a subdued manner and Hermie says, "Wow, dude, we got smoked. That was our best series so far and we still got beat. Those guys were real good and I won't be surprised if they win it all."

Scott replies, "Yeah, they were tough. I just hope that the next match is lucky for us this time. Geez, if we lose one more match, we are done for the day. We didn't drive all the way out here to get knocked out early. I ain't ready to go home yet."

"My ball feels really good coming off my hand, and everything is there except the pins falling. I need to find something to get to the next level. It feels like I'm just half an inch away from carrying the world. Man, we just need some luck," says Hermie.

"You're throwing the ball really good," says Scott. "You're just getting some bad breaks. That's all. Them guys that beat us are probably from this area and bowl on these lanes all the time. Forget 'em. Let's pound out the rest of the day."

Charlie adds his two cents, "Those twisty brothers are gonna get themselves in trouble sooner or later. With so many revs on the ball, they're gonna dry out the lanes real quick and leave garbage they can't pick up."

Their first match in the Loser's Bracket pairs them up against Lou and Earl, the coach's nephews. Hermie and Scott look at each other as if they won the lottery. They are already smelling victory as they begin the match.

The first game starts off very close and they trade strike for strike. In the 7th frame, Scott gets a flurry of precise strikes and finishes with a 237 score to help them win 452–430. Lou shoots a 232, but it's not enough and Hermie's team has a 22-pin lead going into the second game. The loser of this match goes home.

The next game is just as close as the first one. Lou begins with a string of strikes and his team builds up a 30-pin lead. Suddenly the coach gets vocal. This really chafes Hermie because it's eminently obvious who the coach is rooting for even though he "coaches" all four of these guys. Hermie begins to focus more and starts to taste victory. He is acting like a different person: hungry and serious.

Lou gets a split in the 9th frame and chops a spare in the 10th frame to shoot 213. This changes the outcome of the match. Hermie and Scott just have to avoid disaster to advance. Scott shoots a 198 and Hermie shoots a 195. Their team loses 402–393. But since Hermie and Scott won their first game by 22, they win the overall match by 13 pins. Lou, Earl, and the coach congratulate Hermie and Scott and wish them well on their next set.

An excited Charlie rushes up to his two buddies and says, "Yes! You beat them fools again. Won't they ever learn?"

Hermie tells his friends, "What's up with that crap? Them laimo punks almost beat us. That woulda sucked royal. I'm just glad that Lou opened up the last two frames to help us out. I don't know how his turtle ball does it, but he makes it work."

Scott says, "I'm just glad we won, cause I would have been pissed and you know the coach would've rubbed our faces in it. This junk ain't easy, man."

"Check this out; the coach complimented me on my timing and release. He said it was super. Maybe he is starting to change," says Hermie.

"That's cool," says Scott.

"I think he's starting to realize that we're the real deal," confidently says Charlie.

In the next round, Hermie and Scott face a team from Dallas. One of the guys looks like a pro he has seen before, while the other one looks like a poser, having all the equipment, shirts, bags, and attitude like a pro with a problem. What a dork.

The lane conditions have gotten worse as the day drags on. If the ball hits the "track" area, it hooks early. But if the ball goes around the track area, it hits the oil and just skids, never going into a full roll. Throwing the ball harder might be a solution, but the increased speed can result in an inefficient ball and weaker pin carry.

Everybody is struggling and the scores have gotten lower. Hermie and Scott are no exception. Hermie finally changes to an older ball that's shinier, hooks less, and helps him avoid splits. He tells Scott to do the same. They end up shooting lots of spares and Scott survives with a 177 and Hermie shoots a 194. The opposition had their share of problems, as the poser shoots a 138 and allows Hermie's team to win the game 371–346.

In the second game, the poser starts off with three out of four splits. Hermie and Scott have one open frame when Scott throws a double in the 5th frame to take a 50-pin lead halfway in the game. The poser bowler throws a gutter ball, gets frustrated, and quits. As he walks out, his partner persuades him to stay, but it's no use; the poser has left the building. Hermie and Scott cannot believe they just received a gift from the gods and want to take advantage of it. They finish their game and muddle along in the 180 range.

Hermie looks at the Loser's Bracket and tells Scott, "That's cool. We have to win two more matches to reach the finals. I think there's only 8 teams left in this bracket."

Scott says, "That doesn't sound too bad. Let's get some chow since we have about 15 minutes thanks to the forfeit."

Both boys look tired and hungry as they run to the snack bar for some food. It looks like Charlie read their mind because he is sitting next to a small hill of food. They see some hamburgers, corn dogs and tater tots neatly stacked on a large plate. Hermie and Scott salivate as they sit down and enjoy their vittles. In the distance they can still see their last opponents arguing about the match they gave away.

In the 6th round, they are paired up against the "Behemoth Brothers" again. Hermie shakes his head and tells Scott, "Oh great, here we go again, the rubber band brothers."

Hermie and Scott feel recharged after eating and show it by starting the match at a grueling pace. Scott shoots a few spares and ends with a 219 game, while Hermie finishes with a 256 game to win 475–460 over the powerful brothers. Hermie is so pumped up that he is sweating like a rabid dog. He looks like he just tasted blood.

Hermie tells Scott, "These guys are still shooting good, but not as good as last time. We just have to keep trashing the rack. These guys can be beat! Some team already beat them. Let's get it on!" He gives Scott a high-five to get him fired up too.

In the second game Hermie and Scott each start with four strikes. Scott leaves a single pin in the 5th frame, while Hermie keeps striking. The Behemoths are striking too but they are starting to leave single-pin spares due to over-hook. Hermie knows the brothers will not shoot big games like last time, but knows he has to keep striking.

In the 9th frame Hermie leaves a solid 7 pin and converts the spare. He strikes out in the 10th frame and shoots a 279. He slaps his hands together with authority, showing everybody that he came to play. Scott shoots a 233 and nobody even notices. The muscle-bound brothers shoot 231 and 222 respectively, but still lose the second game 512–453. Their day is over. Hermie and Scott are in shock that they beat these guys.

The brothers congratulate Hermie and Scott and commend them on their win. Hermie and Scott sit down as if they just ran a marathon and feel exhausted. They have one more match before they reach the finals. They are excited and their hearts are pumping at 100 miles an hour.

Charlie shows up and says, "Holy Mackerel! I think you just beat last year's semi-finalists! Those guys were good but you guys were better. Nice shootin Herm!"

Scott says, "Wow, I'm so tired. That match just drained me. I need a breather."

Hermie says, "I hear ya, man. Those dudes weren't easy, but I'm glad that's over. I don't know how much more I can take."

"According to my calculations, you guys just made the finals in the Loser's bracket. You win this and you get to take on the winner of the Winner's bracket," says Charlie.

In the semifinal match they are paired up with last year's winners. These guys look good. The right hander throws the ball pretty straight and plays a "down and in" shot. The left hander twists the ball and hooks it across the lane in a very convincing manner, destroying everything in its path with a very sharp and powerful hook. These guys are smooth and look old enough to be college players.

Scott reminds Hermie, "Don't pay attention to his game, pay attention to yours." Hermie nods his head in agreement as they prepare for the match.

The teams start out even, but the opposing left hander starts with a six bagger before leaving two single-pin spares. Hermie and

Scott are throwing a few strikes of their own, but it's not enough. Scott strikes out for a 224, but their 440 is not enough to beat the 481 shot by the ex-champs. Hermie and Scott know that it's now or never and must win the next game.

The next game begins as a strike-fest. Hermie is keeping up with the lefty with six strikes apiece, while Scott has a ten-pin edge over his opponent. Both Hermie and Scott know they must win this game by at least 31 pins or their day is done. Hermie has slowly been moving to the leftmost part of the lane and throwing his sanded ball very close to the gutter. He is not scared of throwing a gutter ball, because he is feeling real good right now and his pin carry has been phenomenal from there.

In the 7th and 9th frames, the lefty leaves single pins and converts them. The lefty is getting frustrated while Hermie continues to strike. Scott is up first in the 10th frame and throws a strike followed by a "stone 8" and a spare. He winds up with a 236. Scott's opponent matches Scott's pins in the 10th frame and ends up with a 225. Scott has gained 11 pins for their team, but now it depends on how the lefties perform in the final frame.

Hermie looks at the score and his team is down by 30 pins total. If his opponent strikes out, he will shoot a 259 and force Hermie to get the first strike and put his score in the 280s. He also discovers that he is three strikes away from his first ever 300 game.

Scott catches Hermie staring at the scoreboard and tells him, "Forget the 300, get the first strike and a good count and we win, no matter what he gets." He pats Hermie on the back.

The lefty is slow playing Hermie and is trying to "ice" him, because if Hermie gets the first strike, then Hermie's team advances. Hermie senses that and decides to post his score first and put the pressure on the other team. He likes it that way. He is not scared and gets up on the approach thinking only of throwing a good, quality shot.

He gets up and throws his ball near the gutter. The ball starts to hook early then rolls out and packs the pocket for a strike. Hermie looks at the pins and yells, "OH YEAH!!!!" nearly popping a vein in his neck. That's one down and two to go.

Scott, Charlie, and some other people clap their hands. Hermie looks at the scoreboard again. He is so nervous that he forgets what he needs to win. Scott and Charlie tell each other that Hermie needs at least seven pins for the win as they cross their fingers. Scott is trembling.

Hermie gets up, takes a little extra time, and throws his second shot a little faster than the first one. The ball hooks a little bit and it too "packs the rack." All ten pins are in the pit as Hermie clenches his fists and shouts, "GOING FOR IT ALL!!"

More people cheer and Hermie does not know that they already won the game and the match. Scott knows who won and is about to pass out from the anticipation. The other team just sits there stunned as they just become spectators. Now Hermie is really thinking of that elusive perfect game. It is one shot away and he can smell it.

Hermie gets up for his final shot. The entire building is very quiet. Even the air conditioner sounds loud. Hermie is shaking in his shoes. He forgot where his mark is and a few beads of sweat are coming from his forehead and brow. He remembers to take a deep breath and delivers his shot. His speed is good and his release is near perfect.

The ball rolls down the lane and hits the headpin very lightly. It bounces off the wall and knocks down some other pins for the 12th and final strike. It was a little sloppy, but it worked. Hermie just bowled his first perfect game! He just stands by the foul line with his arms up in the air shouting, "Yes! Yes! Yes!" He never thought he could shoot 300! People are clapping and cheering loudly.

As he walks off the approach, Scott and Charlie give him a high-five and a hug. Others in the crowd shake his hand and pat him on the back as he walks by. Even the coach and his boys congratulate him. Hermie sits down and looks like he can't decide whether he will cry or faint. He is trembling really badly. He sits and tries to breathe.

Then, unexpectedly, Sam congratulates him and says, "Awesome."

Hermie's head is spinning at 1,000 miles per hour as he is still sweating and shaking from all the action. Charlie hands him a large glass of water and tells him to slam it down to calm his nerves because he has one more team to beat.

The tournament director announces the honor score and Hermie gets a round of applause. Then the director announces the final match and the pair. Charlie carries Hermie's equipment to the lane while Scott and Hermie are smiling from ear to ear. They see their opposition; they are from the Dallas area.

Hermie and Scott know that they have to beat this team twice because they are the last unbeaten team in the tournament, whereas Hermie's team is the winner of the Loser's Bracket. So they have to win two sets, while the opposition has to win just one match. If the Dallas team wins this match, it's all over.

Hermie slowly calms down from the 300 jitters and begins the tournament finals. He and Scott begin with four strikes in a row and are feeling pretty good. The opposition starts off striking too, but loses their ball reaction later in the game and becomes frustrated. Scott stops striking and ends with a 218, while Hermie strikes out for a 227 game to help the team win the first game 445–406.

Hermie says, "Wow, I thought I was gonna shoot a bad game because of my 300 jitters, but I guess they went away."

Charlie reassures him and says, "You've been throwing the ball great all day. Keep it there and keep it goin."

The second game is a different story. Both boys are "nailing the hole" but leaving single pins. They make a ball adjustment and are leaving fewer single pins. Scott finishes with a 202 while Hermie gets a 209. Scott's opponent gets a few late strikes and shoots 222 to make the game very interesting. Here comes the suspense.

The anchorman needs three strikes to win the game, match, and tournament. He knows it and so do Hermie and Scott. Scott cannot look. The anchorman throws his ball and gets the first strike as he claps his hands. Hermie looks down and shakes his head, knowing that this guy will get the second strike and end their day.

On the second shot, the anchorman leaves a single pin, which wins the game 440–411 but gives them their first loss of the day by only ten pins: 856–846. The anchor bowler is very upset because now his team has to bowl another match.

Hermie and Scott are excited that they get to bowl another match. This is the final match of the day. Hermie and Scott breathe a heavy sigh of relief as Hermie tells Scott, "Wow! That shot could have ended our day. We got a major sprout and we got one more chance to take this tournament. We are this close."

Scott replies, "I still can't believe we're still alive. This is so awesome!" Scott sounds real nervous but also really excited.

Hermie says, "Well, this is a new match; let's just stick to basics, nothing fancy."

Hermie begins the final match with a split followed by two spares that he almost missed. He is showing signs of fatigue. The opposition starts with three strikes in a row then a few spares afterwards. Scott begins with three spares and a split, but starts tossing strikes again. Hermie and Scott don't realize it, but they are eyeballing the scoreboard more than they think.

The rest of the game is a dogfight. Scott is scoring well while Hermie is struggling. The Dallas duo has evened the match with strikes in the 8th and 9th frames, but Scott spares in the 10th frame for a 206. Hermie gets a spare in the final frame to shoot a 194 and helps his team win this game 400–385.

Hermie tells Scott, "Well, this is the final game of the day. Somebody's gonna win and somebody's gonna lose. Let's hope we win it."

Charlie gives his two friends a high-five and tells them, "That's cool. You guys have a 15-pin lead going into the last game. Just lose by ten and it's all yours."

Their plan is to keep up with their opposition, because striking has become difficult. Hermie has decided to change to a harder-shelled ball so it slides further down the lane. He is too tired to throw the ball hard. He will just throw less of a hook and play a straighter line. He convinces Scott to do the same.

Hermie starts off better than the last game and is on a 210-220 pace. Scott decides to throw the ball near the gutter, and his pin carry improves. He is also shooting at a 220 clip. Both know they are just half an inch away from carrying all their shots.

The opposition almost seems to have run out of steam as they begin with three out of six open frames. Hermie keeps the ball in play on the left lane and shoots simple spares. The right lane is being very generous to him and letting him strike with almost every shot. Scott is a little nervous throwing his ball near the gutter but is staying out of trouble.

During the game, the opponents begin to string strikes while Hermie and Scott shoot mostly spares. In the 9th frame Scott looks at the score and it's almost even. All he and Hermie have to do is match the opposition and they win. Scott's opponent throws two strikes and a 9 count to finish with a 212. Scott throws a strike and a 9 spare for a 191. Scott is a little upset and hopes that the 9 count doesn't come back to haunt him.

Scott tells Hermie, "Sorry dude, I was hoping to shoot better, but I left a bunch of 9 counts at the end. Our 15-pin lead has turned into a seven-pin deficit. You just have to match him in the 10th frame and you're cool."

Hermie says, "I got a small lead against my dude, so we might be okay as long as I stay out of trouble. But if he strikes out in the

10th, I'll flip my lid and quit. He can have the tournament. I can't strike on this garbage."

Hermie takes a few slow deep breaths and tries to calm down from his motivational pep talk. Now he is trying to ice down his opponent. Both guys are slow to get to the approach. Neither of them wants to go first. Hermie steps back to tie his shoe.

Hermie's opponent gets up and throws his first shot. The ball looks good and gets nine pins. Hermie's opponent is pretty ticked off and yells, "Come on, man!" Now he waits for Hermie to throw his first shot. Hermie knows that a strike will practically win it for his team. Hermie takes his time and looks around. Now it's his turn.

Hermie stands on the approach as most of the bowling center is watching. He is very nervous. He throws his shot a little fast and he also gets nine pins. Hermie exhales and tells himself, "Whoa; that was close. Good shot; that was a good shot." He looks at Scott with a shocked expression while waiting for his ball. That corner pin looks so far away.

The anchorman gets up to shoot his spare and tries to slow play Hermie. Hermie plays the game again and decides to tie his other shoe. The center is super quiet. The anchorman looks at the scoreboard and knows he must make the spare and get a strike to shoot 200 and force Hermie to make his spare and get at least five pins.

He throws his ball a little fast and wide. Just before the ball touches the pin, it falls into the gutter for no score. The crowd lets out a surprised "oooooohhhh." The anchorman shouts and stomps his feet in anger. Hermie and Scott just won the tournament! They look at each other in disbelief over the 7 pin victory.

Hermie misses his spare and just stands on the approach in a frozen state with his mouth open. He turns around and looks at Scott who is in tears because this is his first tournament win. The crowd starts to clap and cheer for the new champions.

Scott jumps up as if poked with a needle, walks around, then sits back down with his head in his hands and starts to bawl. Charlie pats him on the back saying, "Holy cow! You did it, man! You did it! You won it all! Not bad for a kid with crooked hair!"

Hermie is lying on his back right there on the approach with his hands covering his face. This is his third tournament win, all in the same year! What a tremendous run!

The director announces Scott's and Hermie's names, and they get a round of applause. They each receive a trophy and a scholarship worth $2,500 apiece. Hermie and Scott are smiling but trembling while many people come by to congratulate them. Scott calls his parents. He can barely speak because he is so nervous.

Eventually the place settles down. Most of the crowd has already left the building. Hermie and Scott have finally mellowed out and they do not have the nervous jitters anymore. They gather their equipment and leave the building. They load up Hermie's car and leave the center, giving the building one last look with a smile.

Hermie says, "Wow, it's 8 o'clock and I've got the serious munchies. Let's eat."

Charlie is driving and tells them, "Help me look for an expensive place to eat. It's my treat tonight. You guys kicked ass all day long and y'all deserve a good meal." A few minutes later they find a nice seafood restaurant and step inside.

At the table, they talk about how they bowled today. Hermie is a little quiet because he is still in shock, but Scott is talking a mile a minute. This is Scott's first tournament win ever. Charlie really wanted to bowl, but at least he got to see his buddies win the whole thing. Dinner is served, and Hermie gets busy chowing down his grilled salmon while Charlie and Scott gobble up their flounder.

After dinner they get back in the car and drive home. All three friends are in a great mood and talk about "the 5 B's." Charlie pulls out his flask and offers a celebration swig. He says, "Here's to my good buddies who won the whole damn thing. Cheers!"

Hermie takes a swig of this whiskey and chases it down with a soda. Scott also takes a swig and sips on his soda too. Charlie congratulates the new champs and takes a tilt. They pass the flask around a few times and celebrate a spectacular day on the lanes.

Around midnight they arrive at Hermie's house. Charlie wakes up Hermie and Scott, and all three all go inside forgetting to unload the car. They will do it tomorrow. Charlie and Scott are too tired to drive home, so they make arrangements to spend the night at Hermie's place, and each boy takes a couch and promptly passes out.

Hermie goes upstairs and falls into his bed, not even changing his clothes. As the Sandman enters his room, Hermie thinks about the great accomplishments he's had over the year with his job, school, bowling, and Laurie. It almost feels like a dream and it makes him feel good as he goes into a deep sleep.

Even though his bowling career is in its infancy, he knows a new phase has begun and he loves it. He wonders what's in store for him next year and cannot wait to find out. The origin of Dreamer has begun.

What's Next?

Hermie has just bowled a perfect 300 game. Does he have enough
to do it again?
When will Hermie win another tournament?
Will he and Laurie ever make up and start dating again?
Is this the end of the window visits?
Will Hermie ever ask Maria out on a date?
What's in store for Hermie's high school bowling team?
What's the next thrilling event in the Acme Chemical case?
What does Hermie like better; pork rinds or beef jerky?

Find the answers to these questions and more in the second book
of the series "Growing up as Dreamer."

What are people saying about Hermie?

"He's a real sweet guy. He lives in a big house and bowls really good. He's cute too." - Laurie, Hermie's girlfriend

"He's a great friend. He may have a higher bowling average than me and he may have bowled a 300 before I did, but I'm still a better bowler than him. He just doesn't know it yet. He's just better at talking to girls than I am." - Scott, a friend

"I think he's a little wet behind the ears, but he's a good kid. He'll pick it up real soon. He's one hell of a bowler too." - Charlie, a friend

"I don't know him that well but Charlie says lots of nice things about him. He lives in a nice house and his parents are very cool to let him throw parties." - Belinda, Charlie's girlfriend

"I wish I was as cool and controlled as he is. I would love to be as good as him." - Hank, a friend

"Not a bad kid; pretty clean too. He wasn't interested in basketball even though he shot pretty well and can't dribble. He needs to pick up the pace if he'll ever be a runner." - Hermie's Physical Education coach

"He was very impressive with basic kitchen and household knowledge. He actually taught some of the girls how to do things around the house and kitchen." - Hermie's Home Economics teacher

"What's all the fuss about fried rice? It's just rice for Pete's sake. Anybody can make it." - Hermie's grandfather

[no comment] - Sam, Hermie's bowling nemesis

"He works pretty hard when he wants to. He doesn't always show up on time but he can hustle when he has to. He's snuck out early before and thinks that I don't see him, but I do. It's ok, he's a good guy." - Grocery store manager, Hermie's boss

"He always checks out books about sports, bowling and comic books. And sometimes he brings girls in and they make strange noises. But he isn't very loud." - Librarian at Hermie's school

"He and his friends love my fried rice. When they arrive, I make an extra batch because they eat it all. We have noodles too but they don't eat that." – Owner of the local Chinese restaurant

"He always comes in for either a brisket sandwich or a burger with bacon, cheese and onion rings. That's his usual order; nothing else." – Owner of local BBQ restaurant

Addendum 1: Chronological timeline

Chapter 1 — A Night in the Point of Time

Dec 15 - Hermie and Jane have their second window visit and first kiss. Hermie goes home feeling great and excited. In bed he thinks about how they met and how cool she is.

Dec 16 - Hermie has dinner with grandparents, Grandpa says he got letter from their lawyer about the Acme lawsuit. Letter states that Acme acknowledges the letter and the lawsuit.

Dec 17 - Jane tells Hermie she thought about him and the kiss all weekend. Jane wants more and they begin to kiss in the hall in between classes.

Dec 21 - Hermie gives Jane a Talking Heads cassette, she gives him Pink Floyd.

Dec 31 - Hermie and Scott have New Year's Eve at grandparents' house. They play board games and drink apple cider. At midnight they have champagne, get dizzy, grandparents laugh. Hermie's resolution is to bowl more tournaments and get better. Scott wants to talk to Suzi more often.

Chapter 2 — Saturday Night Scoring

Jan 14 - School starts up again. Hermie sees Jane at school and they talk and play catch up. They start becoming good friends and are seen together a lot at school.

Feb 1 - Scott is 15 years old and has his party at the arcade. They eat and play video games.

Feb 21 - Hermie has window visit at Jane's, it's cold outside and Hermie won't come in. Jane is wearing shorts and tank top and convinces him to enter. They begin kissing and she throws him on her bed and they make out.

Mar 1 - Charlie is 17 years old and has party at the theater with older friends and flasks. Hermie takes swigs of flasks and gets a buzz; he likes rum but hates vodka.

Chapter 3 — The Origin of Dreamer

Mar 14 - Hermie sees Jane at theater. They get private seat, hug and kiss. He walks her home, she invites him inside, she spikes his soda, he passes out.

Mar 15 - He wakes up in the morning in her bed and is late for bowling. Both are in a hurry leave the house. Hermie is panicking and both run to theater to get his car. He bowls lousy in practice but shoots 246-211-268 for a 725 series, his best ever. The gang goes to lunch and Jane calls him Dreamer because of his pro dreams. Hermie and Jane go back to her house and take a nap on the couch.

Chapter 4 — A Weekend with a Girl

Mar 15 - Hermie and Jane wake up an hour later with a phone call. Jane's sister is spending the night at a friend's house so they are all alone. They go to the mall in the big city. Hermie buys a new computer game, he buys Jane a nice blouse. She sees roll of cash in his pocket and is impressed. Kids eat at food court, play mini-golf, eat at a nice steakhouse, and drive home. The house is trashed, kids play Monopoly and drink, Hermie spends the night.

Mar 16 - Hermie and Jane wake up and clean the house before her parents come home.

Chapter 5 — Front Row Window Seat

Mar 21 - Boys play basketball and talk about Spring Break plans. Scott will be in Houston with family, Hermie tells him to bring tools to practice. Hank is upset because he is a benchwarmer, but coach still wants him to practice. Charlie is broke, so he will not go to coast but will find a party or two.

Mar 26 - Spring Break week: Hermie and Jane have a window visit. Jane is wearing robe, pulls Hermie through window, and he hurts his back. Jane disrobes and is naked, Hermie discovers that Jane is drunk. Hermie has shots and spends the night.

Mar 27 - Hermie leaves work, goes to Jane's house to talk. He meets Jane's sister Kelly and boyfriend Kerry, has spaghetti dinner, wine, talk.

Chapter 6 — Summer Slam

April 10 - Hermie and Jane have a window visit and nearly get busted. Hermie loves the visits but thinks that Jane's parents know what's happening.

May 7 - Boys minus Hank go to Austin and bowl a tournament; all qualify. Hermie meets Sam, Hermie beats Sam, Hermie wins his first tournament.

May 14 - Hermie and boys win their Saturday morning league; first time for all the boys. Hermie also wins high average for the league with a 202.

May 16 - Boys begin to play basketball and practice bowling.

May 21 - Boys go to big city and go to mall, see Jacuzzi, fall in love with it.

May 28 - Hermie gets letter from Acme that a preliminary hearing will occur sometime in September.

Jun 1 - Boys minus Scott bowl local tourney at home lanes, low turnout. All boys qualify, Hermie beats Charlie for title; Charlie upset he lost but is okay.

Chapter 7 — Rate the Date

Jun 4 - Jane calls Hermie to invite him and the boys to her birthday party.

Jun 7 - Jane is 16, has birthday party, Hermie and boys show up, meet parents. Hermie tells boys about buying the Jacuzzi, announce July 4th party, invite all.

Jun 8 - Charlie has fight with his dad, hangs out with Hermie for the day. Jane tells Hermie that his dad must call her dad before dating approval is given. Charlie calls Jane's dad, impersonates Hermie's dad; Hermie gets nod to date.

Jun 9 - Hermie and Jane have first date; go bowling, go to the library.

Jun 14 - Hermie and Jane have first evening date and parents tag along as a surprise. They have dinner at a nasty Mexican restaurant and go to church for a retreat. Jane's dad pushes religion on Hermie, ruins Hermie's night; Jane apologizes.

Chapter 8 — Wet Days and Buzzed Nights

Jun 15 - Jane calls Hermie to apologize about parents and promises no more parents.

Jun 18 - Hermie goes to grandparents' house, they drive to big city and buy the Jacuzzi.

Jun 21 - Hermie has Jacuzzi installed, invites boys and Jane to check it out.

Jul 4 - Hermie has party at his house, lots of food, booze, and people; great party.

Jul 7 - Hermie and Jane have an evening date without her parents. They play mini-golf, watch a movie, and visit the arcade; both have a great time.

Jul 21 - Hermie and Jane have a date. This one is not mentioned in the book.

Chapter 9 — Not So Green 17

Aug 15 - Hermie is 17 and has a surprise party at grandparents' house. He gets two new bowling balls, computer game, and a watch. Party moves to the lanes to watch Hermie throw the new tools. Party moves to Hermie's house; he shows Jane the secret bench by the stream. Jane gives him another gift.

Chapter 10 — Junior Daze

Aug 19 - Hermie and Jane have a date; he notices it's getting boring doing the same stuff.

Aug 21 - School starts: Hermie and Hank are juniors. Scott and Jane are sophomores; Charlie fails and is still a freshman.

Sep 1 - Hermie uses new equipment for first week in league, shoots 750.

Sep 7 - Hermie and Charlie meet Vinny; attend his party; crazy experiences.

Sep 14 - Hermie invited to wedding of Jane's oldest sister Sheryl to Javier. He goes to reception; he and Jane drink, get drunk, and make out in car.

Sep 21 - Hermie and grandparents attend preliminary hearing on Acme case. Acme is unorganized and tries stalling; judge is angry and gives a warning.

Sep 27 - Hermie and the boys have slumber party and play video games. Boys attack two robbers; they were paid to find evidence in Hermie's house. Scott finds $2,000 in crooks' car and the boys decide to split the money. Hermie tells boys about Acme case and shows them basement/electronic lock.

Chapter 11 — Team This

Oct 3 - Hermie leaves work and officially visits Jane. Jane's mother fixes him dinner; he praises her homemade sauce; mom happy. Hermie and Jane go for a ride and end up at Hermie's house. Jane slams some wine coolers, strips down, and both do naked tubbing.

Oct 5 - Boys try out for school team; all score well but start to lose ground. Hermie leads, all qualify as starters, Hank is a sub, boys meet Julio.

Chapter 12 — An Expected but Rudimentary Alteration to a Blissfully Busy but Predictable Lifestyle

Oct 9 - Hermie sees Jane in hallway, she wants to be called Laurie, not Jane.

Oct 12 - Hermie and Laurie have date, she acts distant, postpones window visits. She tells him about sister's marital problems; when sis is upset, so is she. Hermie recalls that Laurie is strongly influenced by her oldest sister.

Oct 19 - Meeting for school's bowling team, Hermie is captain.

Oct 24 - First week of school bowling; boys win all five points against coach's team.

Oct 26 - Boys see Lou's team in their Saturday league.

Nov 3 - Hermie and Laurie have a window visit; Laurie is already drunk. Laurie says they're moving too fast; wants to take time off, breaks up with him. Hermie is angry, begins drinking, leaves her house; is upset for a few days.

Nov 8 - School bowling — team wins one out of five points; Hermie not focused. Hermie shooting poorly in both leagues; still thinks about what happened with breakup.

Nov 10 - Charlie has fight with dad; kicked out of the house; stays with Hermie. Both drinking in tub, get lit, talk about chicks; Hermie talks about breakup.

Nov 13 - Hermie gets a note in his locker from Laurie; Hermie is already angry. Laurie apologizes for breakup; it was a mistake, wants to talk about it.

Chapter 13 — Grammar of Despair (The Makeup: Part 1)

Nov 16 - Hermie lets Laurie come to his house to talk; she is excited. Laurie comes over; they talk; she apologizes and they make up. They are still friends; she wants to make out but Hermie is not ready.

Nov 17 - Scott asks Hermie to be partner for doubles tournament in Houston; he agrees.

Chapter 14 — A Nice Pair from Any Angle

Nov 24 - Hermie has Thanksgiving at his grandparents' house.

Dec 8 - School bowling — boys whip coach's team 5–0. Hermie makes first phone call to Laurie since breakup.

Dec 16 - School is out until January 15 for Christmas vacation.

Dec 17 - Hermie and Scott go to Houston for doubles tournament. Hermie bowls his first 300 game; boys win tournament.

Addendum 2: Qualifying scores for the school team qualifier tournament

Game 1 results		Game 2 results		2 Game Standings	
1. Hermie	238	Scott	234	Hermie	457
2. Scott	221	Joseph	228	Scott	455
3. Paul	219	Hank	222	Hank	431
4. Miguel	217	Tyler	220	Joseph	429
5. Julio	215	Hermie	219	Julio	422
6. Hank	209	Charlie	216	Miguel	419
7. Eddie	205	Julio	207	Tyler	416
8. Joseph	201	Miguel	202	Paul	408
9. Tyler	196	Eddie	201	Eddie	406
10. Charlie	183	Paul	189	Charlie	399

Game 3 results		3 Game Standings		Game 4 results		Final Standings	
1. Tyler	279	Hermie	725	Julio	245	Hermie	935
2. Hermie	268	Tyler	695	Scott	236	Scott	890
3. Charlie	258	Paul	665	Hank	225	Julio	883
4. Paul	257	Scott	664	Charlie	224	Charlie	881
5. Eddie	230	Charlie	657	Eddie	220	Tyler	880
6. Miguel	221	Hank	646	Miguel	216	Hank	871
7. Julio	216	Miguel	640	Paul	211	Paul	867
8. Hank	215	Julio	638	Hermie	210	Miguel	858
9. Scott	209	Eddie	636	Joseph	190	Eddie	856
10. Joseph	204	Joseph	633	Tyler	185	Joseph	823

Note: Top 4 finishers earn a spot on the team. Places 5 and 6 are substitute players. Place 7 is an alternate position.

Addendum 3: Bowling schedule for Hermie's school team (Oct–Dec)

Week#	Date	Location	Opponent	Day W - L	Cumul. W - L
Week 1	Oct-19	Antler	Pibb #1	5 - 0	5 - 0
Week 2	Oct-26	Austin	Bastrop #1	2 - 3	7 - 3
Week 3	Nov-02	Austin	Lexington	1 - 4	8 - 7
Week 4	Nov-06	Lexington	Antler	5 - 0	13 - 7
Week 5	Nov-13	Bastrop	Smithville	5 - 0	18 - 7
Week 6	Nov-20	Austin	Austin North	2 - 3	20 - 10
	Nov-27	No Bowling—Thanksgiving Break			
Week 7	Dec-04	Austin	Pibb #1	5 - 0	25 - 10
Week 8	Dec-11	Pibb	Giddings	4 - 1	29 - 11
Week 9	Dec-18	Smithville	La Grange	4 - 1	33 - 12
	Dec-25	No Bowling—Christmas Break			
	Dec-31	No Bowling—New Year's Break			

Current standings for Quad City district after 12 weeks

Team Name	W - L
Pibb #2 (Hermie's team)	33 - 12
Lexington	31 - 14
Bastrop #1	30 - 15
La Grange	28 - 17
Giddings	27 - 18
Bastrop #2	24 - 21
Camp Swift	23 - 22
Dimebox	22 - 23
McDade	21 - 24
Pibb #1	17 - 28
Smithville	15 - 30
Antler	13 - 32

Addendum 4: Houston Doubles Tournament recap
(From Chapter 14)

==

Round 1: Start of Tournament

<u>Game 1</u>

Scott	208		Sam	206	
Hermie	225	433 (+32)	Barry	195	401
		----			----

<u>Game 2</u>

Scott	224		Sam	242	
Hermie	191	415 (+5)	Barry	158	410
		----			----
		845 (+37) Winner advances			795 Goes to Loser's Bracket

==

Round 2 (Winner's Bracket)

<u>Game 1</u>

Scott	179		Houston-1	198	
Hermie	217	396	HookBall	222	420 (+24)
		----			----

<u>Game 2</u>

Scott	202		Houston-1	196	
Hermie	209	411 (+41)	HookBall	174	370
		----			----
		807 (+17) Winner advances			790 Goes to Loser's Bracket

==

Round 3 (Winner's Bracket)

<u>Game 1</u>

Scott	216		Behemoth-1	248	
Hermie	244	460	Behemoth-2	254	502 (+42)
		----			----

<u>Game 2</u>

Scott	229		Behemoth-1	248	
Hermie	223	452	Behemoth-2	227	475 (+23)

==

Round 4 (Loser's Bracket)

<u>Game 1</u>

Scott	237		Earl	198	
Hermie	215	452 (+22)	Lou	232	430
		----			----

<u>Game 2</u>

Scott	198		Earl	189	
Hermie	195	393	Lou	213	402 (+9)
		----			----
		845 (+13) Winner advances			832 Loser goes home

==

Round 5 (Loser's Bracket: Semifinals)

<u>Game 1</u>

Scott	177		Dallas Poser	138	
Hermie	194	371 (+25)	Dallas Pro	208	346
		----			----

<u>Game 2</u>

Scott	180		Dallas Poser	Did Not Finish	
Hermie	184	364(+364)	Dallas Pro	Did Not Finish	
		----			----
		735 (+389) Winner advances			346 Loser goes home

==

Round 6 (Loser's Bracket)

<u>Game 1</u>

Scott	219		Behemoth-1	224	
Hermie	256	475 (+15)	Behemoth-2	236	460

<u>Game 2</u>

Scott	233		Behemoth-1	231	
Hermie	279	512(+59)	Behemoth-2	222	453
		----			----
		987 (+74) Winner advances			913 Loser goes home

===

Round 7 (Loser's Bracket — Final two teams in Loser's Bracket)

Game 1
Scott	224		Last Year Winner-1	229	
Hermie	216	440	Last Year Winner-2	252	481 (+41)
		----			----

Game 2
Scott	236		Last Year Winner-1	225	
Hermie	300	536 (+79)	Last Year Winner-2	232	457
		----			----
		976 (+38) Winner advances			938 Loser goes home

===

Tournament Finals (Winner of Winner's Bracket vs. Winner of Loser's Bracket)

Game 1
Hermie	205		Dallas-Area Rookie-1	195	
Scott	218	423 (+27)	Dallas-Area Rookie-2	201	396
		----			----

Game 2
Hermie	217		Dallas-Area Rookie-1	226	
Scott	208	425	Dallas-Area Rookie-2	213	439 (+14)
		----			----
		848 (+13) Winner			835 Loser — 1st loss (forces a tiebreaker)

===

Tournament Finals — Tiebreaker match (each team has one loss)

Game 1
Hermie	194		Dallas-Area Rookie-1	187	
Scott	206	400 (+15)	Dallas-Area Rookie-2	198	385
		----			----

Game 2
Hermie	202		Dallas-Area Rookie-1	212	
Scott	191	393	Dallas-Area Rookie-2	189	401 (+8)
		----			----
		793 (+7) Tournament Winner			786 Runner-Up

Addendum 5: Author's notes

This literary effort began many years ago when I was in high school and learning about people, places, and things. As with any period of time when we grow up, there were some great times and some bad times. And it's just a matter of making the best of them.

One day I decided to capture some of these memories and the memories of other friends, so I began writing down some of the events that happened to me and my friends. I never put my thoughts down into a diary or a journal, but more in the format of a book report. I kept adding pages, never really paying much attention to the content or proper grammar or proper writing techniques.

Over time I had compiled several large notebooks of written pages covering my life and the life of other friends. I knew I had to do something with it. I periodically began to read through these pages to try to make sense of my random thoughts and inspirations. I could sit down for six hours and plow through these pages and never even realize I was up all night. It was fun, but it was a lot of work.

The more I re-read these pages, the more I was able to construct a series of chronological stories. Where there were gaps, I added my own brand of humor and creativity to keep the story alive, but not to get overwhelmed with too much fantasy to make the stories unbelievable.

With more effort and re-reading, I was able to fuse the stories together to form chapters in a book. After I decided on starting and ending points, the book was born. From there, it was a matter of time to complete the book, proofread it, and make sure that all of the events occurred in their proper sequence. For example, I didn't want one paragraph to read that the current month was April, then have the next paragraph say it was January. That would make no sense.

The final phase for me was to ensure that the proper amount of dialogue was occurring. In my opinion, it's very easy to write a chapter with no dialogue or one with all dialogue. I wanted the characters to have conversations, but I didn't want an entire chapter spent on them discussing one or two topics. To me, that could be boring. I had to find a happy medium where events happened and dialogue took place to accompany the event. This was one of the hardest parts of the review process, next to properly sequencing all of the events in the book.

In the end, the book was finished with a beginning and an end. The book also contained characters, each with their own personality and problems. The book also contained enough dialogue to get an idea of what was happening and how the characters felt about it. And finally, the book was finished with a relatively continuous and sequential series of events that corresponded to days and weeks on a calendar to give it a feel of events that really happened some time ago. And some actually did.

Rene Lopez Jr. — January 2009

About the Author

Rene Lopez, Jr. lived in several different parts of the United States while growing up; thanks to his father being enlisted in the United States Air Force. Rene finished high school and attended Saint Mary's University in San Antonio, Texas, where he studied Computer Science. He got married to Sharon Seguin, relocated to Austin for almost 15 years then moved back to San Antonio. Rene and Sharon have 2 children: Larissa and Mateo. When Rene is not busy at the office being a SQL Database Administrator or at home writing his books, he tries to be rock star, likes to spend time with his family and play classic video games in his garage. Rene also bowls in a league in San Antonio where he is averaging a staggering 210.

Made in the USA
Lexington, KY
01 April 2012